Hanging the Stars

"*Hanging the Stars* has all of Rhys Ford's wonderful trademarks: detailed action sequences, robust and well-painted secondary characters, hot love scenes, and that gritty-beautiful and heartbreaking prose."

—The Novel Approach

"I LOVED this book. I've always been a fan of Rhys Ford because she never fails to start a book off with a big BANG that keeps the suspense going and this story was no different."

—The Blogger Girls

Absinthe of Malice

"…as always, Ford really delivers here with the right mix of romance, emotions, and intensity."

—Joyfully Jay

"The writing is smart, the dialogue is quick, and the characters are deep…"

—Crystal's Many Reviewers

Dirty Heart

"If you're a fan of the Cole McGinnis series, this is the book you've been waiting on."

—On Top Down Under Book Reviews

"Hands down, no other qualifications, this is the best thing I've ever read by Rhys Ford. The flow, the characters, the mystery, the love and romance—*everything. was. perfect.*"

—Gay Book Reviews

By RHYS FORD

Clockwork Tangerine
With Poppy Dennison Creature Feature 2
Grand Adventures (Dreamspinner Anthology)
Murder and Mayhem
There's This Guy

COLE MCGINNIS MYSTERIES
Dirty Kiss
Dirty Secret
Dirty Laundry
Dirty Deeds
Down and Dirty
Dirty Heart

HALF MOON BAY
Fish Stick Fridays
Hanging the Stars

HELLSINGER
Fish and Ghosts
Duck Duck Ghost

SINNERS SERIES
Sinner's Gin
Whiskey and Wry
The Devil's Brew
Tequila Mockingbird
Sloe Ride
Absinthe of Malice

Published by DREAMSPINNER PRESS
www.dreamspinnerpress.com

THERE'S THIS GUY

RHYS FORD

REAMSPINNER
PRESS

Published by

DREAMSPINNER PRESS

5032 Capital Circle SW, Suite 2, PMB# 279, Tallahassee, FL 32305-7886 USA
www.dreamspinnerpress.com

There's This Guy
© 2017 Rhys Ford.

Cover Art
© 2017 Reece Notley.
reece@vitaenoir.com
Cover content is for illustrative purposes only and any person depicted on the cover is a model.

ISBN: 978-1-63533-498-2
Digital ISBN: 978-1-63533-499-9
Library of Congress Control Number: 2016958601
Published March 2017
v. 1.0

Printed in the United States of America
∞
This paper meets the requirements of
ANSI/NISO Z39.48-1992 (Permanence of Paper).

This book is for anyone who has stared into the abyss
and wondered if they can or should go on.
You should.
Take that next step forward and go on.
And should you need help finding the strength for that step, reach out.
There are people and places who will help you.
Keep walking until you find the sun on your face
and until you can see the stars again.
You are worth that step. Worth that journey.
The world is a better place with you in it.

ACKNOWLEDGMENTS

MUCH LOVE to the Five, the sisters of my soul; Tamm, Lea, Jenn, and Penn. Also to my other sisters, Ren, Ree, Lisa, and Mary.

A huge heartfelt thank-you to Elizabeth, Lynn, Grace, and everyone at Dreamspinner Press for all of their hard work and faith.

Lastly, thanks to Black Rebel Motorcycle Club, VAST, and Tool for providing me the music I listened to as I wrote this book.

ONE

THE TASTE of metal on the back of his throat tainted the loathing boiling in Jake's belly. His tongue was numb to the acrid bitterness of the gun's muzzle pressed into its spongy flesh, but the roof of his mouth smarted and bled from the barrel scraping along its soft membrane. A bit of powder and oil joined the specks of blood, floating on the spit pooling on his tongue, a peppery sharpness cut with a hint of razor blades and pain.

It was all a welcome taste, muddling the sourness in his belly brought on by cheap whiskey and the lethargic drag left in his body after splattering his bare thighs with come. It dried, stuck to his hair and skin, a pungent, musky smear flaking off when he shifted.

He'd barely moved since he'd pulled his father's gun out from the box he'd tucked onto a bookshelf, then sat down at the battered Formica table he'd scrounged out of a dumpster a few years before. Overcome by the world's heavy boot pressing down on the back of his neck, Jake slid the magazine into the gun and wrapped his mouth around its deadly hole, licking at its rim with the tip of his tongue.

The night was hot and wet, slicking his bare back with sweat, but it was a familiar caress, more familiar to Jake than the touch of his now-dead mother's dry lips to his unshaven cheek. Los Angeles staggered beneath its late summer's oppressive weight, a muggy blanket of tarry skies and still air, and in Jake's carved-out apartment, the dull swish of the industrial fans built into the former warehouse's walls simply pushed the stagnant, damp heat around. Koreatown's flashing lights and come-hither neon pounded through the night, shoving its way into the cordoned-off space.

His hand shook, like it always did, and Jake caught a whiff of the booze sweating out of his pores. His lungs were full of the gun's scent, breathing in its prickly stench with each muffled gasp. The empty whiskey bottle rattled on the table when he jerked back, propping himself against the chair's duct-taped vinyl back.

1

"Just do it, Moore," he whispered hoarsely around the gun's muzzle. "What the fuck is keeping you here?"

His life—like his ground-floor shoebox apartment—was a jigsaw puzzle of others' bits and pieces. The dinette set he sat at was salvage like everything he'd scattered about the far end of his tight rectangular space, a discarded bit of flotsam from someone else's life he'd gathered to shore up his own existence. His light blue couch was a thrift-store pick, too stained with magic marker childish scrawls to sell but in damned decent condition, and milk crates propped up a faded red wooden door, its paint crackled from the California sun. Only his welding gear, set up by the front door, and his bed were new, the mattress sitting on its frame in the coolest corner of the long room, tucked into the niche between the outer and bathroom walls.

Nothing that couldn't be sold or thrown out.

What people would make out of the twisted spires of metal he'd sculpted during his fits of need, Jake had no idea. The scraps he'd brought home and welded together quieted some of the snarling anger he couldn't shake, but he hadn't been able to lose himself in the shapes and fire since… forever. He was past the point of caring about all of it, but even with the press of shame spiking through his thoughts, his finger refused to squeeze on the trigger.

Such a fucking coward. His father's words hammered through Jake's drunken haze. *A fucking pussy who should have been scraped out of his mother.*

He'd grown up hearing that rant. Hell, Jake could chant bits of it in his sleep if he wanted. He never needed to. His father's words… other people's scalding-hot words… always found him in the middle of the night, creeping along on their sharp knifelike hooves to trample over his soul. He'd bled out in his nightmares, crying for mercy.

None came.

None ever came, and Jake woke most mornings drenched in the fears he'd sweated out during the storm of his dreams and aching from the tatters in his soul.

The porn magazine on his bed fluttered, snagged on a bit of breeze seeping through the canted broad windows along the long wall. Its pages were sticky, caught on the drops of Jake's releases. He'd left it where it'd fallen, sliding from his thigh when he'd stroked himself for the fifth time that week. Those pages—those damned pages—were his downfall, especially the center spread of the long-legged, blue-eyed young man sitting on a luxurious pile of tapestry pillows, naked as the day he was born, with his knees spread open and his left hand fondling the length of his pale cock.

Jake promised himself he'd burn the rags every single time he finished jerking off to the men between their covers, but each time, he simply thrust them away and reached for a bottle of booze. Tonight was different. He'd come and there was nothing but disgust for what he'd done, what he'd imagined doing to another man, what he'd wanted done to him.

His skin was too tight on him, and he ached for a release he'd already reached, but it hadn't been enough. He was going to rub his cock raw if he kept going.

He just couldn't... keep going. It was too much. Too much to fight anymore and too hard to hide anymore. Up until a week ago, he'd been able to tuck his want for other men into a dark hole deep inside of him. Years of being able to pass... of pretending he didn't get hard if another man's eyes lingered on—of being able to tell himself he was fine alone and didn't need anyone, much less a man—all of it was shot to hell the moment he'd seen a black sports car pull up to the boarded-up salon across the street from the fabrication shop he worked at.

The man who'd gotten out—God, only three weeks ago and his life was shit for it—that man did something to Jake's control, shattering it into a million pieces. He'd gotten out—lean, long-legged, and with narrow hips—and turned, as if sensing Jake watching him. Their eyes met, a long flicker of awareness arcing through them, and Jake blushed, his dick lengthening under his boxers and straining to be released from his jeans. He couldn't make out the color of the man's eyes, not with four lanes of traffic between them, but the sizzle was already more than Jake could stand. The man was sex scraped off of the pages Jake pored over, then hated himself for, a confident dark-haired trap begging to be sprung and baited with a poison strong enough to kill Jake if he ever so much as took a teeny taste.

Then the man winked and Jake fell away, swallowed into the darkness he'd fought so hard to keep at bay.

His phone rang, jittering across the table, and he jerked back, the gun sliding from his mouth, its barrel wet with his spit. Jake sucked in clean air, still damp and stinking of tar and street trash but cleaner than the oily filth of the gun's length pushed up nearly into his uvula. Shaking, he set the weapon down, then fumbled for his phone, his fingers numb and unresponsive.

The number was all too familiar, and the voice on the other side of the line sounded as tired as Jake felt. She cleared her throat, working around words she'd said more than fifty times before, always with the backdrop of clattering bedpans, intercom announcements, and the occasional screaming of the infirm.

"Mr. Moore?" The nurse—a round-faced Latina if he matched the voice to the right face—mumbled out his name as if someone else might have answered Jake's phone. In the five years since she'd been calling, no one ever had, but she always sounded… hopeful, perhaps wishing she could speak to anyone besides Ron Moore's fucked-up son. "Mr. Moore, we need you to come down. Your father's having an episode again, and we don't have the staff to—"

The buzzing in his brain drowned out her words. He didn't need to hear them. He'd heard them countless times before. His old man was breaking down, and there would be no turning back the hands of time for either of them.

"Sure." He cut her off before she could start in on his duties as Ron's son. He'd been their only child, a pregnancy his mother struggled to keep and one his father blamed for the destruction of his life. "Let me…."

Jake was drunk, swallowed whole by a cheap amber whale and being digested in its sour juices. His truck was too important to lose—hell, a night in jail was too much to risk—so driving himself to the nursing home was probably out of the question, but he didn't have jack shit in his pocket to pay for a car.

"Give me a few minutes." He eyed the coffeepot sitting on the card table he'd mended and now used as a kitchen counter. "I just need—"

"I hate to have to bring this up but…." Her sigh was long-suffering, and the guilt in her voice was mostly gilding for her lie. "If your father continues to act up, you're going to have to find someplace else for him to be. We've too small of a staff to give him the attention he—"

"I said I'll be right there," Jake growled. He couldn't afford another place, not on what he made, and his father was reaching the end of his rope. There were no more second chances. His father'd been forced out of too many homes too many times, and the old man grew more and more aggressive with each new home he moved into. Sighing, Jake pleaded, "Please. Just give me... give him some slack. He's dying, for fuck's sake."

"We're all dying, Mr. Moore," she snipped back. "Some of us just aren't being assholes about it. Now come deal with your father, or tomorrow morning you'll find him and his things out on the street with the rest of the trash."

"DAL, WHAT do you think about painting the whole building a bright pink? You know, so it stands out." Celeste took a step back, wobbling on her heels as she caught the edge of a sidewalk crack. Her meaty arms jerked up, a quick flail, but she recovered easily, patting at the blonde tower of hair she'd lacquered with Aqua Net before they'd gone out. "And for God's sake, see what the city can do about these walkways. We pay a hell of a lot to live in WeHo. The least they can do is make sure we don't break our necks walking the damned streets. So, pink. I'm thinking Gulp-Down-After-Clubbing baby pink."

"Pink might be a little much," Dallas mumbled absently, staring off toward the oversized brick warehouse across the street. "I want to make a statement not...."

There was movement in the fabrication shop, a shadow crossing over a shower of sparks and blue fire, and Dallas peered over his Oakleys, straining to make out a familiar face in the blobs of darkness. A second later his stomach tickled in excitement at the tall, broad-shouldered man striding out of the building's open bay doors.

There was a lot he didn't know about the man. Okay, he knew next to nothing about him, but there was something vulnerable in his rugged, pleasant face and bitable mouth. He'd taken a discreet photo with his DSLR while he'd idled his Tesla the first time he'd come to check out the building on Santa Monica. Dallas initially dismissed the site as unusable. It was too far from WeHo's epicenter, and its parking lot, while generous, would require resurfacing. He hadn't even gotten out of the car to look inside, simply peered up through the passenger side window and ticked off all the reasons the building wouldn't work for him.

Then the hottest man he'd ever seen in his life walked out of the shop across the boulevard, and Dallas knew he'd found the right place after all.

The man's shoulders and arms were to die for, sculpted and hard beneath a thin T-shirt, and when he'd slowly shrugged off his heavy work jacket under the scorching Los Angeles sun, Dallas spent a good minute talking himself out of running his hands over the man's sweat-dampened firm chest. Someone Dallas couldn't make out in the building's shadowy interior tossed the man a bottle of water, and there was another minute of negotiations and photo taking while the welder gulped down mouthfuls to cool himself off.

Any guilt over stalking the workman fell away when Dallas went home that evening. He'd almost talked himself into erasing the images before looking at them, a tiny tug-of-war between ethics and desire. The argument against deleting the photos won out, his barely rational logic reassuring himself the man in question wasn't as he'd seen, simply a fantasized construct he'd cobbled together in his mind.

He wasn't.

No, instead Dallas spent a good part of the evening studying one shot in particular, focusing on the man's hazel eyes and the light brown freckles scattered over his tanned cheeks and nose. He'd been caught in midspeech, white teeth behind a lush bottom lip, and the scruff over his jaw was a bit gingery, ruddier than the man's short brown hair and dark eyebrows. His slightly canted nose looked like the result of an elbow rather than a punch, just enough of a bump to push him from handsome to interesting.

And his hands.... Dallas hadn't realized he had a hand fetish until he'd stretched out onto his sofa and studied the man's roughened fingers and palms.

He'd winked at the man the next time he spotted him, stupidly flirtatious in an area not known for its friendliness, but Dallas hadn't given it a second thought. Their eyes had met, and the electric shock running between them short-circuited Dallas's common sense. Or at least that was what he told himself when the worker jerked his head back and squinted, pinning Dallas in place.

They shouldn't have had that moment. There were four damned lanes between them, four and a half if he counted the half-assed left-turn aisle at the cross street, and Dallas should have been able to do anything short of sticking his tongue out at the man or flipping him off and remained unnoticed.

Instead he'd caught Dallas in a wink and reeled back in response.

"All the hot ones are straight," Dallas muttered to himself as Celeste carried on about palm trees and coconut smoothies. "Or assholes. And sometimes, if Mrs. Yates's little boy is very, very lucky, they're gay assholes and he dates them."

"Dallas, the pink?" Celeste's peeved query sliced through Dallas's musings, a knife along the buttery wonder of what the worker's thighs would look like if stripped of his old jeans. "What are you... oh. Well damn. That's a good way to get your head beaten in, but sure, you just go on over there and introduce yourself. Just make sure you make me your beneficiary beforehand so I can paint this damned building bright fucking pink in your honor."

"Celeste, no damned pink. It's Bombshells and Beauties, not... shit, I can't even think of anything disgusting enough." The man glanced across the street at them, maybe a frown crossing his face. Then he disappeared back into the building, its shadows swallowing the welder back up, leaving nothing on the sidewalk but a few drops of spittle along Dallas's licked lips. "Shit."

"Bubblegum," Celeste offered up, and Dallas turned in confusion. Her thin eyebrows darted in, elongated tadpoles fighting for the center of her forehead, and she sighed, resting one hip on a post near the building's entrance. "Bombshells and Bubblegum. That's what you should have said, and for all that is Patsy Stone and holy, would you get your head out of the clouds and stop staring at the eye candy across the street? And while you're at it, get out of the fucking road before you get run over."

Celeste's voice teetered out of her normal husky alto and into the high-pitched tenor of Simon, the slightly overweight boy Dallas met at a New York bus stop more than twelve years ago. A string of diets and industrial-strength foundation garments shaped Simon's body into the lush pinup figure he'd longed for, but it'd been Dallas who'd styled him into Celeste Glory, shaping everything from her signature '50s naughty librarian clothing to the strong, powerful walk she'd taken on as her own. There were times when Simon's overprotective Jewish mother seeped out from between the cracks in her lush character, and Dallas found himself on the sharp end of a nasally reprimand whenever Celeste reached her breaking point.

Right now, Dallas heard every drop of Simon stubbornly lingering in his best friend's personality.

"What's the matter, C?" He stepped out onto the sidewalk, hoping it would soothe Celeste's rattled nerves, but the woman shook her head when he reached for her. "Love, nothing's going to happen to me. We're in WeHo for fuck's sake. Or at least close enough to use its zip code."

"We're not in fucking WeHo, Dallas. Look around you. We're in a fucking industrial park tucked in between the studio's secondary backlots where they make B movies about screaming stupid women and monsters." Celeste shuddered, taking a deep breath. Pressing her hand against her generous chest, she bit at her lip, worrying away a stripe of red lipstick. "Honey, I'm trying not to sound like some dramatic queen. I'm not. You and I both know I'm not, but this place... here... it's not safe."

"It's totally safe. I checked the crime stats before I made an offer on the building. We're fine. I'm fine. And even if it weren't okay, we can't keep running away, C. I'm not saying I'm going to go out and wave a red cape in front of a raging bull but...." Dallas reached for her, and Celeste let herself be folded into a soft embrace. She trembled, probably caught up in the memories of a night when she hadn't been safe and he'd not been there when the dark closed in on her. "Things are different now. Much different. You of all people know if we hide, nothing changes."

"I just don't want anything to happen to you," she mumbled into his chest, probably smearing half a ton of makeup on his white T-shirt. "The way you looked at that guy...."

"Yeah, well, I'm not the gingeriest cookie in the bag, so sometimes, I do stupid things," he teased. "That being said, I promise you, no ogling hot straight men who look like they can crush my head in one hand, okay?"

"Okay," she sniffed and pulled away, wiping at the dampness around her heavily made-up eyes. "But really, rethink the pink. It'll be awesome."

"You go on being you, Celeste Glory, and when you get your own place, you can make it any color you want," he shot back, twisting his mouth into a smile. "Because I sure as hell am not painting our lifelong dream fucking bubblegum pink. Now, grab the champagne and glasses from the car, and let's see what I've gotten myself into."

TWO

"DOES ANYTHING work in this hellhole?" Celeste's voice carried out of the bathroom, as leaden as the stagnant air they were stewing in. "Because really, Dallas, just cut your losses and open this place up as a sauna or something. Well, maybe a combination rat café and sauna, because I swear to God, I just saw a baby kangaroo climb up this motherfucking pipe."

"That was a cartoon, you deluded idjit," he called back. "And for the last damned time, that wasn't a rat! It was a possum!"

"It was ugly as fuck. That's what it was." Celeste stomped out of the back, sweat plastering her bleached curls to her high forehead. She'd gone without her normal heavy layers of makeup that morning, complaining the heat and humidity in the thick-walled building made her break out. "And we don't know for certain it was a possum. For all we know, you've got your very own Smeagol under this foundation and he's digging out a volcano to toss his ring into."

"You've got it wrong. He didn't want to get rid of the ring." Dallas shook his head in mock disgust. "The hobbits went looking for the volcano—"

"I don't know why you keep talking to me about this when you know I'm not going to pay attention." Her sneakers were semi-heels, new rubber wedges once pristine white until she'd begun to help him scrub out the bathrooms in the hopes of saving some of the original tile. "Who cares who wanted to get rid of the damned thing? The point is there's a fucking volcano in here and we're cooking in it. I don't want to die with what little makeup I'm wearing smeared and my legs flung apart because I've been broiled open like a rotisserie chicken. I want to die that way because I'm ninety-five and just was fucked to death by my twenty-five-year-old Latino lover who married me over the objections of his entire family."

"You've thought that out, have you?" Straddling one of the stools they'd found left in the back room, Dallas caught himself before it rocked forward, thrown off-balance by its uneven legs.

"No, that just came to me. Like this heatstroke."

At any other time, he'd have put Celeste's histrionics down as dramatic overlay, but this time she had a good point. The place was a cesspool, and the temperature was rising faster than he cared to admit. He'd owned the building for two weeks, and in between ducking outside to get fresh air and glimpses of the dark-haired, broad-shouldered welder working across the street, Dallas was grinding himself down to the bone to restore the one-and-a-half-story art deco structure.

He'd known it was going to be a lot of work, especially since its former owners seemed to only have a passing acquaintance with cleansers and hot water. As the place's flimsy interior walls came down, more problems emerged. The plumbing was shot, the loft space above the main floor was a trash pit, and the electrical needed replacing, but most of all, the ancient air-conditioning unit chugged one final time after Dallas opened the door with his own set of keys and died a smoking, withering death just as Los Angeles's summer kicked into high gear.

Despite the problems, Dallas did love the place. Its windowed west end had been boarded up, and after an afternoon of pulling out nailed-down planks, he'd finally uncovered their glory… and the sets of white-crackled wrought-iron bars someone'd laid over them. There'd been birds' nests in the cement marquee placard jutting up above the front door, its neon torn from its moorings so long ago there wasn't even an imprint of the words left on the paint. And to hear the floor guys bitch and moan, it would be a long three weeks before they peeled up the layers of industrial tiles covering the maybe-still-usable wood floor. With its high ceilings and the main floor opened up, he could see the building's potential, a showcase for men who longed to strut their stuff in stilettos, women aching to swing low, and everyone in between.

He and Celeste—Simon then—once spun out a haphazard dream of a stage where Celeste could sing her heart out and pretty boys could flash a bit of leg and warble for a crowd boozed up on sugary drinks and even sweeter desires. In the beat-up VW van he'd taken cross-country, Celeste was a bit of flotsam he'd picked up and never let go, a sister of sorts—probably as much of one as Victoria—and a damned fine friend. She hadn't wanted to be a big star, just have enough of a twinkle to make someone smile and laugh for an evening and maybe more. Bombshells, a nameless club back then, started off under the stars of a New Jersey spring evening, and he'd carried it with him every step until he found the spot to place all the twinkling glimmers he'd found along the way.

Thing was, Dallas just needed the people he hired to show up and do the damned job so he could get his performers up onstage and booze into paying customers, because while he had more than enough money to bankroll a dream, it was far better for the damned thing to break even.

Celeste cleared her throat, and he was pulled out of his daydream and back into the reality of the disaster lying around them. "Really, do you think you can pull this off, Dal? Here?"

"Well, if we can keep on schedule, Bombshells and Beauties will be open in six months, so hopefully by then…." He paused dramatically until she sighed heavily and waved her hand for him to continue. "By then, Ms. Glory, we shall have an air conditioner."

"By then LA will be tit-deep in freezing weather and there'll be crowds of perky-bottomed young women in short shorts and UGG boots climbing all over your pretty ass looking to warm themselves up," she groaned. "Honey, are you sure you want to do this? Can't you just live off the money you've already made making me look gorgeous?"

"No, because after that Slurpee I bought you this morning, all that money's gone." Dallas grinned at her upraised finger. "That was a compliment, love. Take a step back and look at it again."

"Well fuck you, backhanded one at best," she muttered, flopping into a paint-splattered lawn chair. "Seriously, it's too hot in here. We're going to pass out from the fumes."

"The windows are open as much as they can be." Dallas wiped his forearm against his brow, not surprised to find his skin dripping with sweat. "It's the bars some asshole put over them. They block the glass from opening up all the way. Whoever thought blocking the windows was a good idea should be shot. Or maybe skinned. Then rolled in salt. Like right before you roast a pork loin."

"That's one good thing to come from my removal from the family tree… bacon." Celeste leaned over to snatch a flyer from the ground. Fanning herself, she amended, "And men. Because really, that's why I walked away in the first place."

12

"Both very good reasons," Dallas agreed. He was tired of painting drywall, and more importantly, he was tired of the heat. More than a little disgusted at the painters who'd cancelled that morning, he'd gone ahead with it, thankful they'd at least masked off the windows and hardware. "Although unlike a guy, bacon will never let you down. Even at its shittiest, it's still bacon."

"Like coffee." Celeste pouted at him. "If you can't get me air-conditioning, can you at least get me an iced coffee?"

"Your wiles don't work on me, woman. You're on the other side of the fence now." It was steaming inside, and every once in a great while, a tiny wisp of cool air pushed through the cracked-open windows, taunting Dallas's overheated skin. Not nearly as hot as being back home in Texas but close enough and without an impending storm threatening to break on the horizon. "As pretty as you are, darling, you do absolutely nothing for me."

Celeste narrowed her eyes into slits, peering at him over her makeshift fan. Something in his expression must have mollified her because she sighed, then said, "That's the sweetest thing you've ever said to me." She gave him a quick smile, then leaned her head back against the chair. "Now fix the goddamned air conditioner or you're going to have to find yourself new slave labor."

"Considering how much you cost me in coffee alone, you're hardly low-cost," he drawled. "And the air-conditioning has to wait. They've got to install a new unit on the roof, and the engineer needs to make sure it can support the damned thing's weight. But there is something I might be able to do in the meantime."

"And what's that, beautiful?" She gave him a sidelong glance from under slightly parted lashes. "Get a hard-bodied, half-naked man to follow me around with a giant fan?"

"One better." Dallas grinned back at her. "A fully dressed man to open these fucking windows."

"WELL, IT'S not Brandt, but whoever did the original work wasn't half-bad," the hottest man Dallas'd seen in ages murmured to himself. "Not bad at all."

God loved him. If there'd been any question in Dallas's mind about how lucky he was in life, the universe, and everything, it was answered the moment every entity in the known cosmos sent his object of lust over to look at his blocked windows.

If Jake Moore, the welder from Evancho Metals, was delectable in photos, he was heartbreaking up close. His amber-flecked-green eyes flicked over Dallas more than a few times when he spoke in his soft, not-quite Californian, oddly French accented drawl. A light golden tan gilded his skin, deepening the faint scatter of freckles across his nose. His mouth was a mobile dance of curves while he studied the bars blocking the building's windows, his expressions ranging from dismay to resignation.

Jake smelled damned good—a hell of a lot better than Dallas did at the moment—and the breadth of his shoulders and chest nearly gave Celeste the vapors when he came knocking on the front door. Standing back a few feet from the welder, Dallas had a better view of his legs, thickly muscled beneath his jeans, and the denim snugged tightly against his ass as he bent over to inspect one of the grates.

Celeste had been torn between standing outside to watch Jake inspect the windows or escaping to the coffee shop across the street to get them all iced drinks to beat back the heat. A crisp twenty and a promise from Dallas to keep Jake at the property until she returned was enough to convince Celeste to totter across the street and stand in the air-conditioned store.

And while Jake's face and body stroked every single one of Dallas's nerves with a sensual lick, it was the man's soft murmured "hello, ma'am" to Celeste that might have made Dallas fall in love with him.

"Sir?" A flick of a word spoken in Jake's velvet-warm voice tightened Dallas's want, tickling his belly with a lick of desire. Sir? Not the game he'd play with the man, but Dallas was up for anything. Then it hit him the man was trying to get his attention. "Mister Yates?"

"Oh, sorry. Spacing out here. And God, don't call me Mister Yates. Dallas is fine." There was little hope he could pass off any flush across his face as anything other than embarrassment, but Dallas was going to give it his best shot. "Tired. We've been trying to get this place back up on its feet for weeks now, and it's kicking my ass."

"Yeah, it looks...." The man's assessment of the building was cloaked in a hooded glance Dallas couldn't make heads or tails out of. "Place has seen better days, but about the grates...."

"Can they come off?" Dallas shoved his hands in his pockets and rocked back on his heels. "Can't open the windows, and it's as hot as shit in there until the AC is fixed."

"Well, here's the thing, the swirled pieces? They're meant to be decorative overlays on the glass. Someone took them off their brackets and welded them into the bars." Jake ran his fingers along a piece of curved metal nearly hidden behind the horizontal bars. "This is probably original to the building. Art deco, pretty decent work. Not on the scale of some of the East Coast and Europe pieces, but still, really nice. I can take all of the bars off so they're off the windows, but after that, it's up to you what you want to do with the original metalwork."

"What's my other option?" Dallas dragged his attention off of the damp thin line of sweat sticking Jake's shirt to his back.

"I can restore the pieces and put the original overlays back over the glass panes." He pursed his mouth, deepening the dimple in his right cheek. "It'll be a lot more expensive. Don't know if you want to spend the time or money on that."

"But I'd be able to open the windows, right?"

"They're more like jalousies, but yeah, they'll open. The pieces should be welded onto these frames here. See, the original weld marks are still there. Or some of them." Jake bent his head and reached in through the bars to point at the edge of the frame. "And unless there's a stash of panels somewhere, I'm going to have to replicate about ten or twelve pieces, depending on how bad some of these are. You're missing a good chunk of them, but maybe they're somewhere in the building."

"Hell, they could be in the loft in front. That place is packed with crap." Dallas grimaced. "You've done this kind of thing before?"

"It's kind of what I do." Jake's smile was a bit shy, and he looked away, watching the traffic on the street. "I restore metalwork on old buildings. Some custom work. Depending on what the job needs. This isn't going to be cheap. It all depends on what you want to do—take off the grates entirely or put the building back to how it looked when it was first built. I'll need to do an estimate but—"

"Yes." Dallas nodded. "Well, do an estimate so I have an idea about how this is going to blow through the budget, but yeah, let's do this right. First things first, can we at least get a couple of the grates off? Because if we don't get the inside cooled off, my free labor in high heels is going to walk, and I'm shit at scrubbing down bathrooms."

IT WAS late, well past the time when Jake should have been at home, sweltering in his own hotbox of bricks and stale air. Instead he stood nearly hip-deep in debris going back decades, judging by a newspaper ad announcing a weekend sale of five-and-a-quarter-inch floppy discs at Kmart. Staring at the junk piled into the large space, Jake cocked his head at Dallas, who'd forged in deep, shoving his way into the mounds without a care in the world or caution about getting tetanus from any number of ancient decaying relics hidden in the trash.

"They just sold the building like this? Without cleaning it?" He stepped carefully forward, having already landed on his ass when he'd put a foot down on a pile of *National Geographic* magazines and they shot out like a pile of angry playing cards avenging their mad queen. "That's... insane."

"Well, to be fair, they gave me a really good deal on the place." Dallas's voice seemed to be coming from behind a stack of shelves, but it was hard to see him clearly—something Jake wasn't all that certain he was upset about. "The downside is that something up here stinks, so I'm guessing we've got a rats' nest or maybe a wheel of Roquefort someone left up here back in the '90s."

The man was... distracting. His almost shoulder-length black hair was a startling cobalt-ebony frame for his strong face and pale blue eyes. It was hard not to watch his mouth when he spoke, because Jake could almost feel the brush of his lips on his neck or collarbone. Jake might have had about twenty pounds of muscle on the man, but Dallas's lankiness appealed to him, a wiry strength to narrow hips and flat stomach.

Dallas Yates was everything Jake needed to deny himself. There was no question about the man's sexuality. As he removed a few of the wider grates from the front of the building, Jake overheard Dallas and Celeste joking about their differing tastes in men, coffee, and most important of all to hear them talk, the amount of hot sauce considered acceptable on a toasted plain bagel smeared with cream cheese.

His guts were churning, and the sensible part of his brain said to let the panels go, let Dallas and whatever friend he dragged in to help him dig them out. There was time to go home and shower, then see his dad if he left right at that exact moment.

But his feet refused to move, and his neck hurt a bit from craning to see around the piles of clutter for a hint of black hair and gentle smile.

"Shit, there's a… what are those purple-ink copying machines they used to have a long time ago? With the rollers?" Dallas called out from behind a bookcase. "There's one back here. I feel like I'm digging through some sick and twisted time capsule. What the hell is that word?"

"A mimeograph." Jake waded farther into the mess, trying to reach the window on the far wall. "You might want to consider renting a dumpster and a trash slide. If we can get to this window, we can use it to funnel a lot of the debris out. Probably not furniture but maybe a lot of the small stuff."

"That is an excellent idea, and thanks for volunteering. You don't have to do this, you know," Dallas replied. "I mean I appreciate you coming up here to help me look, but I can hire people, especially considering my help decided to bail on me. I love her, but sometimes Celeste is a fricking princess. Had the nerve to tell me it smells worse than wet puke and cat piss up here."

It was good he brought the woman—man—up. There'd been a pause in his brain when he first saw Celeste, a glitch as his mind fought to reconcile her slightly masculine features with her lush body and come-fuck-me voice. He'd never been around someone like Celeste, and his thoughts were tangled, a web where Jake wasn't quite sure if he was the spider or the fly.

"Hey, can I ask you something? About Celeste?" Jake heard Dallas grunt a "sure" from somewhere deep in the room. "She's… I mean it's she and her, yeah? I've got that right?"

"You got that perfect." Dallas's head popped out, and he fussed at a bit of sticky dust trailing across his face. "Why? What's up?"

"I've just never been around a… I mean I don't even know what to call her. Not a lot of real women in my life, much less…." Jake stumbled over his tongue. "Fuck, not real. I don't know the word. I'm fucking this up. I don't know how to talk about this. About her. About any of it."

"Celeste is definitely a real woman for all intents and purposes, and the word you're looking for is biological woman. And ask away. How are you going to know if you don't have that discussion?" Dallas swiped at his face, smearing the mess around in his hair, picking his way out of the rubbish pile he'd been standing in. "Well, even that some people will get pissy about, but discussion is always good. I can't keep up most of the time. Now I just ask what pronoun people like to use and go with that. Transgender.... It's what the *T* is in the string of alphabets we call ourselves. Well, I think there's a *T*. It keeps changing. I used to think it was transvestite, but hey, I learned."

"Okay, this is going to sound stupid, but how's that different from a drag queen?"

"Oh, loads of differences. A drag queen is... well, it's a lifestyle. Its own culture, really. Once Bombshells and Beauties is up and running, you'll see. Drag kings too. I know a couple looking for a place to showcase." He studied Jake long enough for him to get uncomfortable, then asked, "Really? No women? What about... dating and all that?"

"Yeah, no. I don't... date." There wasn't time... wasn't room in his life for another person, least of all a lie like a woman. His stomach twisted in on itself, bile curling around the desire Dallas sparked in him. "Dad's sick, really sick, so most of my spare time goes to taking care of him, doing paperwork, running things down for him. Look, about Celeste, I was just... back when I met her, I wanted to make sure I used the right words. That's all. She and her... got it."

"You're doing fine. Celeste was born male, and at some point in her convoluted, messed-up childhood, realized her body felt wrong. So, after a lot of internal debate and some... let's just say inflamed, destructive familial relationships, she chucked the idea of being a guy and decided he needed to be a she. So there you go, my sister, Celeste."

The dust bunny was still on Dallas's cheek and forehead, despite his flailing to get it off, and Jake trudged over to help him. Plucking the gummy mass was harder than it looked, and Jake steadied himself on the sliding piles, unwinding hair strands from the tacky web. After getting it loose, he shook the web off, and Dallas's smile blinded him.

"Thanks. And a life without women. I can't imagine. I'm surrounded by them, in one form or another."

"I mostly live at the shop, and there's not a lot of women who weld or do metalwork. It's really... well, guys are assholes for stupid reasons. Joan worked with us, and she finally painted all of her tools pink so the guys would stop taking them to fuck with her." He shrugged at Dallas's disgusted sigh. "Hey, don't look at me like that. It wasn't me. She was there for about three months. Then she left for a job near her parents' house in Seattle because they'd watch her kids for free. That was... about two years ago."

"So no sisters? Any siblings?"

"No, just me and my dad." Guilt gnawed on Jake, and he patted his pocket, debating calling to check on the old man. "You?"

"Well, besides Celeste...." Dallas stepped closer, and Jake stood stock-still, unsure of which way to go. "There's Victoria, my real sister—"

"Biological sister." Jake risked a light tease and was rewarded with a soft chuckle. "Because, you know... real."

"Oh hello, petard, my old friend. Let me hoist myself up onto thee." Dallas shook his head. "Ah, Jake Moore, you're turning my world around on me. But yeah, two biological siblings, my older brother, Austin, and my younger sister, Victoria. Our parents were a bit on the... wild side, so we're named after where we were conceived. Aus and I think Vick's name should actually be Telferner, based off of the stories we heard, but my mom's denying it. I think she just didn't want to name her kid Telferner. And what in God's name is that smell? It's like we're right on it."

Jake's boot nudged yet another tower of papers, and they tumbled, spilling over Dallas's feet. It proved to be a keystone in the rubbish pile as a stack of heavy boxes tipped forward, and Jake shoved his shoulder into Dallas as a five-foot-tall section of the room turned into a river of debris.

"I don't... crap. Move!" Something hit Jake's shin, then his knee, pushing the joint forward. They fell, nearly buried beneath the rubble, and Dallas fought to get free, his legs kicking at Jake's belly. "Hold on, wait. You're... oof! Stop."

"Sorry, panic. Was buried under sand as a kid... and now I feel like an idiot." Dallas turned over onto his side, slowly extricating himself from the pile. "Can you get out?"

"Yeah, I'm just...." Jake spotted something near the fallen mound. Something oddly shaped lay on the now-exposed, grimy industrial-tile floor. It was gray, a darker hue than the once-white tiles in the checkerboard pattern. He blinked, but the shape didn't change.

Instead, as the dust began to settle, the shape became more distinct, better formed in his mind.

It was curved, nearly balled up into itself, and at first he thought it was a part of a mannequin, something left behind from the building's days as a clothing store, but its toes—long, withered toes—were brown, caked with dirt, and marbled, with thick, jagged nails. The foot was filthy, a gray mass of bone and skin surprisingly plump considering its resting place. Then Jake followed the length of the foot up to a leg and the moving pad tossed over the lump beyond that, its olive green cover stiff with what looked like gallons of dried blood. He blinked, and the one mewling cell of Jake's brain still functioning picked up on the sound of Dallas's retching a few feet away when the decaying body's rank smell fully hit them.

"Okay, yeah, Celeste's right," Jake mumbled, jerking his feet out from under the fallen papers as he struggled to get his phone out of his jeans. "This is a hell of a lot worse than wet puke and cat piss."

THREE

THE DAY'S heat pressed down on Jake, leeching out every bit of energy he had left in him. The cops battered at him, coming one way, then another, trying to get answers out of him… answers he didn't have, and all the while, his eyes kept drifting over to where Dallas Yates stood, talking to a fierce-looking female detective with a gun on her hip as big as the chip on her shoulder.

California wasn't giving up its daylight, the long hours toward dark stretching out before them as if Maui hooked the sun again and held it from sinking past the horizon. Traffic was slow along the main street, cars ambling to a crawl to study the collection of cops, police cars, and yellow crime tape circling the building. There was nothing to see, nothing anyone could see. A dark van with blacked-out windows and a coroner's logo on its sides waited by the back door for someone to bring down the man they'd found. To hear the cops talk, it would be hours before that happened. Digging out the deceased was their top priority, and for all intents and purposes, they were treating the whole business as a crime scene.

Death never kissed Jake as it had that afternoon. His mother's death was brutal, and by the time he'd reached their home in East Los Angeles, the machines keeping her alive were still. His father hadn't waited for Jake to get there. Hadn't given Jake time to say good-bye. Her bed was empty and cold before Jake pushed his way into the hospital, frantic to find the small, quiet woman who'd slipped him bread and cheese when he was locked in his room and who'd washed the blood from his back after yet another zealous beating.

"Funny. Now I'm waiting for death to come get the old man, and instead it comes knocking on this guy's door." Shoving his hands into his pockets, Jake rocked back onto his heels and listened to the buzz around him. A quick call to the hospital reassured him his father was asleep, worn out from physical therapy and general bitchiness, but he worried anyway. "We don't even know who the poor bastard was."

Jake couldn't stop thinking about the drowning pool he swam in some nights when the loathing covering his soul grew too heavy. The roof of his abused mouth healed slowly. Shreds of skin were slick, tickling reminders of how close he got to the darkness, how easily it seduced him into wanting to end the aching pain in his chest. What troubled him most was no one knew who the man was. He'd died, alone and possibly slowly if the cops speculating he'd been buried alive by the rubbish were to be believed. There was too much blood for that, or at least that's what it looked like then. In the passing hours, he was now questioning what he'd seen, but one thing was for certain. He stood on the stoop of someone's passing and was struck by the loneliness of the man's death.

"That'll be me one day. Fucking dead alone until someone finds me by accident." He stared up into the canopy of a large tree behind the building. "Fuck."

He was scared. Somewhere in his soul, Jake knew there was nothing but fear in his bones. He was too frightened to act on his desires, to breathe sometimes, and just when he was ready to put an end to the paralyzing terror running through his veins, life tapped him on the back of the head to remind him it wasn't quite done with him yet. His fear peeled him apart, exposing the pulp of his pain to the raw, cold truth of the world's steely teeth.

Most of all, he was scared of living. That much he knew. He'd dipped his toe into its raging waters once, and his world became a storm of hellfire and anguish. It was asking too much to dare living again. It was safer to remain behind the glass walls he'd built around himself, but his heart yearned to be free.

A simple damned afternoon spent in Dallas Yates's company and he wanted more. Needed more.

But Jake knew, deep down inside, he wasn't going to get it, and it wasn't fucking fair.

"That kind of life… it's wrong, Jacques," his mother would murmur in her accented whisper after he'd retreated to his bedroom to lick his wounds after a long day of dealing with life and his father. He missed the weight of her tiny body against his and the smell of lavender in her long, dark hair. "You need a woman, *bébé*. It is how life is. This thing you have— this sickness you have about men—it will never lead to love. Men cannot

22

love men. You will see this. You will understand this when you are older. For men, it is only sex. Two men—it will only be about sex. You will fall in love with a man and he will only hurt you, use you, and then… he is done and will toss you away. And it will kill me to watch you do this."

She'd been right, his mother. He'd been tossed aside, just as she'd predicted.

And she'd died because he'd stupidly fallen in love.

It was hard watching Dallas. It was hard not to watch Dallas. There were parts inside of Jake screaming to burrow deep into the man, submerging himself in Dallas's warmth and vibrancy, while his mind knew better. He had nothing to offer a man like Dallas. Hell, he had nothing to offer himself.

"Yeah, remember what happened the last time? Went all that way and for what? Just to find out my mother was right… and then." God, the horrific then after he'd bared his heart, hoping to be loved, and had it handed back to him in tatters. The then that followed was… he couldn't get past that point. The tree's bark bit into his skin through his T-shirt, scraping at the keloids on his back, and Jake welcomed the bitter bite of silvery pain. "Your dad's right. That fucking asshole's right. Remember that. No one wants the likes of you, Jakey boy. Keep that in the front of your head when you get to thinking otherwise."

But the what-ifs kept rearing up, ugly-headed cobras looking for a piece of untended flesh to sink their fangs into and spread their poisons, rotting Jake away.

Dallas Yates stirred things inside of Jake he wasn't prepared for. The man's casual, sexy smile riled up emotions Jake buried a long time ago, emotions he couldn't afford. There were bits and pieces of Dallas's life so outside of Jake's norm he struggled to understand them.

And one of those outside-the-norms was heading straight for Jake, having just crawled out of a taxi cab, then been waved off by Dallas as he followed the cops back into the building. Swinging a canvas bag loaded down enough to weight its sway, Celeste smiled at the sea of blue lapping at the edges of the building and continued to stroll across the parking lot, putting every bit of sass she had in her walk.

Celeste was the definition of complicated. She undeniably was a woman, but there was something more. Nothing Jake could put his finger on. She reveled in her womanhood, saturating it to high contrast until the colors of who she was bled together. There was no one thing Jake could point at to say what pushed her nearly to the point of being too much, but it worked. Celeste threw everything she had into being… well, Celeste.

Her smile was broad, squaring off her chin and tightening her cheeks. Her hair had changed—again—but then it had every time Jake saw her. This time she'd gone for a sleek black bob, and unlike every time he'd seen her before, she was wearing flats. With her black yoga pants and button-up shirt, she was channeling a mean Audrey Hepburn… if Hepburn had Marilyn Monroe's curves.

Quite a few cops' eyes followed Celeste's trot across the parking lot over to the tree Jake took shelter under. Her hips swayed, a coquettish bump and grind of jiggling flesh and attitude meant to make a man take notice. Most men did, or at least the ones standing around waiting for the dead to be carried downstairs and taken off to parts unknown. Celeste should have stirred something in him. Jake would have killed for a tingle of any reaction to the woman, but there was nothing there.

Life would have been so much damned easier if he could scrape up the faintest bit of arousal for a woman's smooth flesh and curves, but his body craved another man's hardness and the bite of rough fingers into his hips.

"Hello, darling," Celeste purred up at him, holding out a bottle of nearly frozen solid water. "God, look at you. All hot and sweet. Here, I brought something to cool off with. You look about dead on your feet. Oh crap, sorry. Didn't mean to bring up—does anyone know the guy? The dead one?"

"No clue who he is. Or if the cops know, they're not saying," he replied. "Thank you for this… the water. It's damned hot."

The bottle was iced over, burning his hand from the cold, and he tucked it under his arm, thankful for the chill it ran down his side. Cracking, the ice shifted, breaking apart from the heat of his body against the plastic, and Celeste held out another bottle.

"Here. Do the other one too."

"I'm sweaty," he protested softly. "It'll get all over."

"Just how I like my water to taste, with a dash of a gorgeous man. Like a twist of lemon." Celeste didn't smirk, but her mouth twisted into

24

an odd smile. "Honey, you are absolutely beautiful standing there with a blush over your cheeks. It's like no one flirts with you."

"Not so much, no." Handing over the partially thawed bottle to Celeste, he shrugged. "I work with about twenty guys in a shop. Not much flirting going on there."

"It's probably all very macho, grunting and farting." Her smile still teased, but her expressive eyes went flat and guarded.

"Sometimes," he agreed, opening the other bottle. "Not always. Lots of older guys. Evancho likes hiring guys with families. Some of the guys are assholes, but most are okay. I just avoid the assholes."

"Do they give you shit about being gay? I'm going to be—"

The buzzing in Jake's ears drowned out Celeste's chattering, and the air grew too thick to suck in. Jake blinked through the numbness spreading across his face and chest, but he couldn't feel anything other than the heavy stone in his belly, pinning him in place. He concentrated on breathing, forcing himself to pull in a breath, then exhale it, fighting to get control over himself—over anything—and not be swallowed up in the surreal quicksand of panic he floundered in.

His chest hitched, and something in him broke, loosening the hold on his rib cage, but an unreasonable terror continued to claw its way through him. Drawing in a tar-perfumed hit of air, Jake mumbled around his heavy, swollen tongue, "I'm not gay. I can't be gay."

"Honey—"

"Yeah, thanks for the water." He stumbled back, his heel catching on one of the tree's roots. His feet couldn't seem to find a flat surface to walk on, and Jake ran a chilled hand through his hair, slicking it back away from his face. "Um... tell Dallas to call the shop when the cops say we can get back into the building. I'll.... Evancho.... Okay? Just... tell Dallas."

"Jake... wait." Celeste reached for him, but Jake backpedaled quickly away.

"I'm... sorry," he stammered, his heart seizing up when she pursed her mouth. Regret and shame poured into the spaces he'd carved out of himself, reminding Jake of the emptiness he carried inside. "I've got to go. Just... I'm sorry. I'm just... not what you think I am. And I'm never going to be."

"GOD, AS sorry as I am for that man, I can honestly say I wish he'd died someplace else, because this has turned into a clusterfuck and a half, babe." Dallas plopped down into the booth Celeste'd taken up as her second home. The coffee shop sat nearly empty, caught between lunch and dinner. Even the outside patio's seemingly perpetual rotation of mediocre musicians was quiet, and Dallas sighed gratefully when the server dropped off an enormous glass of iced tea. "How the hell does it take seven hours to decide a guy's dead when he's all leaked out on the floor and his head's all bashed in? And I sound like an asshole for even thinking it. Tell me I don't sound like an asshole."

"You're right. You sound like an asshole, sweetie." Celeste tapped at her own glass in a rapid-fire flurry of blue-painted nails. "Kind of as much of an asshole as I sounded when I asked your pretty welder how the rest of the guys in his shop felt about him being gay."

"Jake isn't gay. He's… fucking gorgeous, yeah…." Dallas sucked air through his teeth, recalling the curve of Jake's ass beneath his faded jeans. "But gay? I think that's wishful thinking on your part."

"Dallas, sweetheart, as much as you like dick and ass, you should be a damned dousing rod for gay boys. That one there? All he's missing is a little dog named Toto and a backup band of a scarecrow, tin man, and lion." She slapped at his arm when he chortled a denial. "Honey, your man there might be so far in the closet he's got radiation poisoning from the Fiestaware stored in the back, but he's as queer as I am gorgeous."

"You're wrong." God, as if life wasn't cruel enough to plop a sexy man who pushed all of Dallas's buttons right in his lap, Celeste was now trying to break him with the idea Jake could be tumbled back into a soft bed and spread open for pleasure. "Shit, I had to explain to him what drag queens were. That's how clueless he is."

"Clueless, yes, but closeted. Denying it with everything he's got," she continued with a flourish. "And you should have seen his face. Honey, I didn't see that dead guy you have in the loft upstairs, but I'm going to go out on a limb and say he had more color in his face than our boy Jake. Someone put the fear of God into him about liking other boys. I'd put money on it."

"Come on. In this day and age? In SoCal?" Dallas looked around them, drinking in the lazy California sweltering evening from their safe perch inside the air-conditioned coffee shop. "For fuck's sake, love, we're a good stone's throw from about twenty clubs known for their naughty back rooms. Why would he not be out?"

Celeste leaned over, her hands pressed flat against the table. "Dallas, you of all people, talking to me, know better than to ask that."

The memory of Simon's bloodied face and busted lip were never far from Dallas's mind. There'd been old bruises under all the blood, knuckle marks and broken skin barely healed into scabs eager to be discovered when Dallas cleaned off Simon's face with a wet napkin. His soon-to-be best friend shook when Dallas touched him, his body locking up and quaking in fear. Snot bubbled from one of Simon's nostrils, and he'd struggled to breathe, his nose broken by the barrage of punches he'd taken.

It hadn't been the first time Dallas rescued Simon, but it'd certainly been the first where there'd been blood. Up until that point, Dallas never worried about anything or anyone, secure in the oblivious fantasy he'd been raised in, a world where it didn't matter who he loved or where he was when he kissed a boyfriend on the cheek.

They'd shivered in the cold, spit freezing on their faces, until Simon broke down, tumbling into Dallas's frozen arms, and sobbed, railing at the pain eating away at him… a pain put there by the two people who should have loved him the most and were responsible for his shattered face.

It was the one thing they never, ever needed to talk about, and much like any tragedy, their minds drifted to its memory whenever its ghost lingered over their conversation.

"God, I hate your family," Dallas muttered. He did. He'd have loved to set the whole lot of them on fire, but Celeste refused to turn her back on them. "And don't start defending them. Not now. Not here. Hell, not ever."

"They're my family." She shrugged, but the pain remained as a dark flicker in her face. "Just like you're my family now. I can't walk away from any of you, even when I probably should. I just can't."

A plate of hot, steaming sweet potato fries joined them on the table, a drive-by drop-off by the gum-smacking server. She barely paused long enough to slide the dish between them and was off, doing a lap around the long coffee bar near the kitchen door. Dallas plucked one of the thick orange planks off the plate, blowing on it to cool it off.

"So what are we going to do about the boy?" She took the fry from his fingers and smiled sweetly at him when he protested. "We just can't leave him back there. Alone and unloved."

"You can't drag someone out if they don't want to be out." It was a hard truth, one they'd both learned during violently, regrettably sad turns with former friends. Dallas went for another fry, popping it into his mouth quickly, then huffing in cold air to soothe his scorched tongue. He chewed, then swallowed and chased it down with a sip of iced tea. "Fuck, that's hot. And yes, before you jump in, yes, so is Jake, but—"

"He's hurting inside, Dal. You didn't see him." She placed her broad hands over his, clenching his fingers. "Honey, someone broke something inside that boy. I looked at him and said shit, that could have been me if I hadn't met you."

"We can't save the world, sugar. Even if we want to."

If there was one thing he hated about Celeste, it was that she was invariably right. And righteous. She took up causes like most people changed underwear and threw herself into everything she did, including stirring up trouble.

And right now, throwing Jake Moore into his face while they sat hunched over a plate of steaming sweet potato fries was stirring up a hell of a lot more than just trouble.

He'd liked Jake, lusted after him if he was willing to admit it. There'd been a gentleness to the broad-shouldered man and a poignant something Dallas hadn't been able to put his finger on until Celeste ripped back the curtain and showed him a closed door she was certain Jake lived behind.

"Just think for a moment, okay? I'm not even one hundred percent sure you're right, so don't get that smug look on your face." Dallas offered up what he thought was a plausible scenario. "Suppose he's not gay and punches me in the face when I talk to him about it? I don't want to piss him off."

"If he punches you, I'll never speak of him again, but at the very least, he'll have us as friends. And we're awesome."

"And why exactly does it have to be me? Or us? Why do we have to save the world?"

"I'm not asking you to save the world. Just one sad, beautiful hazel-eyed man with a great ass, fantastic shoulders, and a husky voice that made me clench when he said my name," she clarified softly. "And it has to be you because I put my foot in it. Also, I think he likes you. He blushed a bit when I talked about flirting, and it wasn't my name he was stuttering when he was leaving. What's the worst that can happen? Besides a broken nose or maybe falling in love?"

"A broken heart?" There were scars left from another man's carelessness, and Dallas did not want to put himself through the same soul-shattering experience. "Look what happened the last time I fell for a guy who wasn't out. Truth? Jake… he's Fireball Whisky on an empty stomach dangerous for me, Lest. He turns out to be gay and available, I'm scared I'm going to fall for the guy. And that's just from looking at him."

"Jake's not Kevin. That asshole was married with kids and a user," Celeste huffed. "Jake's… I don't know, sweetie. I just… think he needs us. Needs you. Like I needed you but… different. Take it from one damaged, fucked-up kid—we recognize each other. I can feel him hurting, hidden where he thinks no one can hear him cry. I don't want that for him. I don't want that for anyone."

"I don't either. And I swear to God, this goes bad… I get hurt—" He cut himself off, biting down on his words. He'd fallen for Jake Moore the moment he'd seen him, standing in the shadows of a rolling metal door, a lean portrait of insouciance and sex framed in mystery and Dallas's damned curiosity. "God, I spend one afternoon with the guy and I'm picking out china patterns and curtains. What the hell is wrong with me? I'm not like this. I don't date. I don't do relationships. Serious isn't… me. I am so getting punched in the face over this."

"He hurts you, punches you, or even farts in your general direction, I will kick his ass," Celeste declared fiercely, then ruined everything with a soft little murmur Dallas could barely hear under the clink of coffee cups and the barista calling out for a pickup. "Well, as soon as I buy a new pair of shoes to do it with. Ass kicking requires some serious shoes."

FOUR

"MOTHERFUCKING USELESS piece of shit!"

Jake ducked, but the edge of the piss-filled plastic container caught him on his cheek, scraping down into his skin deep enough to draw blood. The sting made him cautious, and he circled in closer to the bed, unsure of what else his father had hidden beneath his covers.

"Dad... stop." It was a useless argument. One he'd had countless times before, but the old man in the bed, the withered shell of the blustery, abusive father he'd feared, was past the point of listening. All Jake could do was pick up the pieces of his father's destruction and wipe any crap off the walls before the attendants saw it.

White foam speckled the old man's jutting chin, a thin brush of white hair bristling along his jaw. He hadn't been shaved in a few days, but judging by the fierce disgust souring his father's face, he hadn't been willing to let anyone near him. His faded green eyes scanned the room, narrowing slightly, and then confusion filled his expression for a brief moment and guilt dug into Jake's chest.

"Stop what? What are you talking about?" He looked about the room. "Why am I here? God, this place fucking stinks. And they're rude. No sense of damned manners, calling me Ron like they're family or something. My day, you got to be a certain age and people talked to you with respect. These idiots act like I'm sitting down in their damned front room and visiting."

It never got any easier. If anything, the mood changes were hitting fast and hard with each passing day. The room certainly didn't help. There was little he could do to mask the dull institutional green-gray room for what it was: a place to wait for death to come knocking. A ventilator stood at the ready beside his father, as well as a few other devices he'd already been on and off of more times than Jake liked, and the curtains separating the two hospital beds in the room were thin in places, the fabric patched with brightly colored thread as if the uneven Xs would bring a bit of cheer.

30

The man who'd been in the other bed slipped off quietly a few days ago, alone and much too young. They'd chatted a few times before the pain took his senses. Then there was nothing to do but watch the drugs dull his body until he could no longer fight the diseases ravaging him. The gaunt, ashen man never spoke of his illness, but the snap of gloves on the attendants' hands every time they came into the room to take care of him was… dehumanizing and tragic.

"You've got a new roommate." Hoping to distract his father, Jake nodded to the snoring old man in the bed next to the door.

"Fucking loser. Look at all the machines he's hooked up to," his father grumbled. "Going to be beeping, and all those damned lights? It'll keep me up at night, that's what that asshole's going to do. Can't even talk to him. Just a goddamn vegetable they put in here to get him out of the way. This place's crap. Why the fuck can't I go home to die? Like a fucking man?"

"You're here just until you get better, Dad," Jake lied, his stomach dropping. Another fight they'd had before and the one Jake hated the most. "Doc said you've got to stay here until you heal better."

The house was long gone, sold to pay for his father's mounting bills, and what little they'd gotten for it was eaten up quickly. Healthcare programs helped, but there were still expenses, money pits Jake couldn't avoid, not while his father slowly deteriorated. Small wounds were slow to heal, and his dad picked at the lesions on his arm, bored and restless in the prison he'd grown in his mind. He struggled to breathe, fighting long-smoked packs of cigarettes and breathing in whatever chemicals he'd worked with when on the job. It was a race between the dementia taking him down in its final stages or the cancers chewing up what was left of his body, but either way, Jake was trapped in the poisonous molasses crawl toward his father's inevitable death.

A matter of time, the doctors kept saying, and as much as he hated admitting it, Jake was tired of counting off the seconds until the old man breathed his last.

Jake wondered if he would breathe his first after the old man died or if he'd soon follow, slipping away into the nothingness left behind.

He'd been late, too late to help the attendant feed his father, but from the pungent whiff he caught from the leftovers in the segmented dinner tray on the rolling bed stand, it'd been some kind of fish. His father would eat three-day-old liver but turn away anything with fins. Anything but fish, Jake'd filled in the food order time and time again, but like clockwork, he'd find mealy slabs of low-grade filets buried under lemon or dill sauces sitting uneaten on his father's tray.

The day threw more than a few curveballs, and Jake sank down into the hard-padded chair next to his father's bed, weary down to his bones. With the rolling table tugged closer, Jake picked at the food, wondering if he could convince his father the flaky light gray meat was chicken, not tilapia. Too many meals left uneaten and his father would weaken, forcing the staff to increase his care.

Or kick him out. It wouldn't be the first time, and there weren't many other places who would take the dying old man with a hot fist and even hotter temper.

"See the fucking cat food they feed me here? My wife wouldn't dare put that on my plate. I'd have knocked her clear across the room." His father's eyes were uneven, squinting in on the left and blown out on the right. His hands kneaded in and out, forming shaking fists. Spittle foamed at the corner of his mouth, and any other time, Jake would have dabbed it off with a napkin, but not now. Not when the man was ramping up into a full-out fury. "She'd have known better."

"Yeah, I know you don't like fish." He dug through some of the food, wishing it were at least hot. "There's potatoes and green beans. You need to eat. You'll get sicker if you don't. I'll talk to them about the fish."

"Fucking son should be in there talking to them. Son of a bitch dumped me here and took off. Boy turned out to be a faggot, you know?" His father ignored the food Jake poked at. "That's what you get when you let your wife coddle a kid. Taught him good, though. Caught him pulling his dick over one of my bodybuilder magazines and I beat the shit out of him. It's what you've got to do to queers. Only way to fix them, but my wife, she was always protecting the little bastard. Went queer anyway. You got kids? You and your wife?"

It was always a shock when his father forgot him. Jake'd been a pinpoint target for all of Ron Moore's rage and violence, the one constant his father focused on nearly every waking moment he was home. Nodding mutely, Jake worked a fork into a mound of cold scalloped potatoes, hoping to get his father to eat even a single mouthful.

"No, no kids." There never would be. Not if he could help it. There was too much bad in his blood, a wicked cruelty flowing straight from his father's veins into his. "No wife either."

"Yeah well, you're young. Some hot young thing'll catch you. Same as me. Mind you, did the best I could with that kid. Just too fucking… queer." His father chewed around the forkful Jake slipped into his mouth when he'd opened it to talk. Swallowing, he nodded toward the water glass, waving at Jake with the limp fingers on his left hand. "Give me some of that water. Bastards here won't give me a beer."

Jake held the straw tightly while his father sucked on its end. Smacking his lips, he pushed Jake's hand away, jostling the water glass. Another mouthful of potatoes at the ready, Jake kept his voice steady and calm, keeping his attention on the man's slackening fists.

"She trapped me, you know. The wife," the older man muttered, eyeing Jake. "She'd gotten pregnant before, but a few good kicks and I took care of it. It's a woman's job to take care of a man. Wasn't going to have her distracted by a kid, but the bitch didn't tell me the second time, not until she was well past showing. Hell, thought she was just getting fat."

"Could have left," Jake replied without thinking, and his father's hateful snort splattered potato chunks across the blanket. "Didn't she have family she—"

"Her family was shit. Mostly drunks."

The irony of his father condemning his mother's family for drinking heavily while he died slowly of cancers he'd brought on himself didn't escape Jake.

"Would have dumped her if I'd known. I was up in Montreal doing shipyard work. Walking off would have meant me losing the work. They take care of their own there, those Frenchies. The yard boss came after me the first time she tried to pop one out, but he couldn't prove I did anything, and I made sure she didn't say nothing." He slapped at the next forkful, sending a long green bean to the floor, then continued on as if nothing had happened. "So then, I was thinking, maybe it's not so bad. Maybe she'll give me a kid who'll make something of himself, and instead she gives me a faggot for a son. Nothing but grief."

It would have been so easy to stab the metal fork into his eye. Every single cell in his body begged Jake to sink his fingers into the soft meat of his father's face and pop out whatever bits of flesh he could peel from the man's bones. He tasted blood, startled at the metallic hit in his mouth, then realized he'd bitten his tongue, a sharp dig of teeth through the spongy flesh.

"Sure, your wife did her best," he finally choked out. "Your son too."

Jake had to stare up at the ceiling. His chest hurt too much to look at the man he'd promised his mother he'd care for. Rage consumed him, flaring into a maelstrom of pain, and Jake strained to pull his mother's face out of his memories, shuddering with each long, tortured breath. His father rambled on, swearing about long forgotten imagined slights and running a tight house. Blinking, he tightened his hold on the fork, determined to force another few mouthfuls into the man.

"Boy was a disappointment from the first day he drew breath. Knew he was wrong from the first moment I laid eyes on him, but she wanted him something bad. Put the kid ahead of me in fucking everything, and that's not right. Man should come first with his wife, with everyone in the whole damned house." The man squinted again, frowning across the bed at Jake. "What I should have done was take that cast iron skillet to his head instead of hers, right from the very fucking beginning. That's what I should have done. Life would have been a hell of a lot better without that damned kid."

HOME WAS a welcome relief of stale air and cold beer. Jake stripped off his shirt nearly as soon as he got through the front door and tossed the balled-up fabric into a laundry basket, then stretched his arms out, feeling every second of the long day sweating out of his skin. Cranking open the windows helped a little bit, but the gaps let the street in, a chatter of Korean and the smell of grilling meat from the restaurant behind the building.

"God, what a shitty, shitty day." The whiskey on one of the shelves lining the long wall called to him, promising to numb the prickle of emotions eating at his insides. Rubbing at his face, Jake gave the half-empty bottle a long look, then headed to the bathroom. "Weekday, Jakey boy. And you're talking to yourself again. Great."

His shower was a cold one once he let the water run through. The heat of the day kept the water warm, and he had to flush the pipes out before climbing in to stand under the tepid stream. A handful of citrus-ginger liquid soap on a pouf frothed up enough for Jake to scrub himself clean. Ten minutes into the shower and the water finally turned cold, sluicing the heat from Jake's body. He stood under the pounding showerhead, thankful for the old building's powerful water pressure, and let the water's cold prick phantom needles into his skin.

"Fuck, I'm going to have to fix... that thing with Celeste. Jumped down her damned throat, and for what?" The yellowed bathtub enclosure was cool against his skull when he rested his head back against the sidewall. "Shit."

Mingled in with the flush of shame about Celeste was a heavier, thicker longing for Dallas. He'd spent most of the day trying to ignore the emotions Dallas brought out in him. His body ached with echoes of the beating he'd gotten from his father the last time he'd acted on his desires for another man, and he rubbed at his chest, wishing the burning in his heart would go away. He'd lost too much giving in to his needs—his dignity, his sense of self, his mother—and Jake wondered if the pain of that night would ever stop slicing through him. One damned wrong turn and he'd lost fucking everything... except his father.

His damned sick-in-the-head father.

"No. Done with him right now." Slamming his fist against the stall wall, he swore, biting out a bit of French he'd learned from his mother. He got out, dried himself off, and padded back out to the main room.

He wasn't going to think about his father. He couldn't. Ron Moore belonged in a box on a shelf Jake only took out when it rattled for attention, and the guilt of putting him back there every day was getting too heavy to carry. Tomorrow was going to be another day of hot metal and cold rage, choked down with a mouthful of beer and a sandwich. His stomach growled, reminding Jake he'd forgotten his lunch at the shop. It was nine o'clock, and ordering a pizza was a luxury he couldn't afford, not until he took a good hard look at his bills.

"Should have grabbed one of those five dollar pepperonis," he grumbled at his open fridge, tugging on a pair of shorts while trying to keep the door open with his shoulder. The half-eaten box of pad thai was probably still good. He thought back to when he'd brought it home from the shop's month-end lunch. "Yeah, only two days old. It's fine. Hot sauce. That's what it needs. Just some… juice."

Since the beer came from the same luncheon, the selection was odd, the bottles and food hastily packed into a box and shoved at him by Evancho before Jake'd left for the day. He wasn't convinced about the pumpkin-spiced ale, so it stayed in the back for the day when he was ready to brave its taste. Evancho liked the idea of beer, always bringing in microbrews from places around Los Angeles, but the man drank anything, including fruity concoctions packaged in brown bottles and sold as the next best thing.

"Raspberry Moonrise IPA." Jake studied the label. "Brewed and bottled in Glendale. Huh. Okay, how bad can it be?"

It wasn't the worst he'd ever had, but it definitely was raspberry, a splash of Otter Pop in a fairly decent beer. Armed with a fork, the beer, and the box of pad thai, Jake flopped down onto the couch with every intention on eating, then crashing immediately afterward.

But if the whiskey bottle whispered his name, the curls of metal and arc welder dominating the far side of the long room screamed it.

The shapes called to him, begged to be molded into a waterfall of beaten silver and russet. His mind crawled with the need to create the spaces between the forms. It was different at home. Work was… work. He had to follow form there, rigid lines of design dictated by other people's imaginations. Sure, there were times when Evancho told him to go wild with a project or, like that morning, nodded to a bunch of scrap and told Jake to make something out of it. But those things were… not his. Never would be his. There was nothing in those pieces but a craftsmanship he was proud of, but still, not enough of Jacques Moore poured into them.

At home he was the only thing the sculpture knew. His hands, his mind, his soul set fire and hammer to the metal and turned it, forging something beautiful from the discarded chunks left to rot in forgotten places. The stupid thing was he understood his father's drive to shape something, to mold something and dominate it. That obsession burned in Jake, a need he couldn't slake any other way than forcing his vision onto scraps of metal.

His father. No, that had to be shoved away. Buried for the rest of the day at least. And if Jake was lucky, the old man wouldn't come riding in on his nightmares.…

Jake almost got up from the couch, abandoning both the food and the beer on the coffee table, drawn along the threads connecting him to the unfinished piece. Almost. Halfway through leaning forward, his phone burbled and sang, vibrating on the arm in a happy dance to catch his attention. The number was local, at least in the same area code, but unfamiliar. His heart flickered and pulsed with worry. Hardly anyone called him. Evancho a few times and mainly the nursing home and doctors. Unfamiliar meant something bad on the horizon, something he hadn't prepared for.

"Or it's someone trying to sell you something. Get your shit together." Tucking the phone against his ear, he growled, "Hello?"

"Hey, Jake." Lightning poured across the phone and into Jake's ear, curving down through his spine and straight into his belly. "It's—"

"Dallas," Jake choked out. He was going to lose the job; Jake was sure of it. He should have kept his mouth shut… hell, probably shouldn't have even taken the damned water from Celeste and just walked away because he couldn't talk to people. Sadly, his brain couldn't stop his tongue and mouth from blurting out, "Hey… um. Hi."

"Sorry, I know it's late. I just dropped Celeste off and—"

"Yeah, about Celeste," he cut in. "I was a shit to her today. I should have—"

"Hey, don't worry about it. We found a dead guy under a pile of stuff. We're going to be a little bit off," Dallas reassured him. "She gets it. I just wanted to see how you were doing. Okay, I was pretty much calling to see if you were coming back and working on the place tomorrow, because well… dead man under a pile of stuff."

"Yeah, I'm fine. Um… just got in and having some leftover Thai food." Relief at not having to tell Evancho he'd screwed up eased the twisted pangs in Jake's chest, and he tamped down the tickling beginning in the back of his brain when the thought of spending three weeks around Dallas began to sink in. He caught a quick whiff of the open box, a sour, malignant odor wafting up from the now room temperature noodles. "Or not. I think it went bad."

"Yeah? You said you were in K-town, right?" Dallas rolled on, not giving Jake a chance to reply. "I'm right on Oakwood and Western. Wanna grab something to eat? I split some fries with Celeste—which means I got like two fries—so I'm starving. My treat."

"Sure. Okay. And I can get dinner—"

"You kidding? Did you miss the dead guy under a pile of stuff thing? I owe you, man." His laugh was a soft, rolling pour of gold through the phone. "Tofu House sound good, or something else? I can come grab you or we can meet."

"I can walk to the one across the church on Wilshire. If that's good." It would take him about two minutes to put on actual clothes and find clean socks, then another few minutes to sprint down a block. Eating with Dallas was insane. The thought of sharing a table with the man, being up close, was probably the dumbest thing Jake would ever agree to, but the insane part of his brain appeared to be in full-steam-ahead mode. Swallowing his last objection, he offered, "Five? Ten minutes?"

"Ten's great. I'll see you there." A siren cut through the line, drowning out Dallas's voice.

"Sorry, what?" Jake rubbed at his ear, soothing his ruffled eardrum. "I couldn't hear you."

"I said it'll be great to see you, Jake." Dallas's voice dropped, growing husky. "Ten minutes, man. Or I'm coming to hunt you down."

FIVE

IF THERE was one thing Dallas loved more than grilled meat, cold beer, and great music, it was men.

He loved everything about them. How they felt against him, the slick of smooth skin or the soft prickle of a lightly furred belly. He adored how they smelled, a musk of soap and masculine aroma with the occasional hit of a sweet-pungent clean sweat from a hot day and a bit of exertion. He enjoyed the taste of a man, the savory hints he found on their bodies, loving the range, from the powdery whispers along a muscled inner thigh to the slick coolness of a taut throat.

But what he adored the most about men was the way they moved.

And no one moved like Jake Moore.

There was an innocent gracefulness to Jake's walk, a silken prowl tempered by a velvet politeness. He wove through spaces, focused on the people around him, at times stopping to let someone get by him first. His strides didn't eat up the distance so much as pull through it, his expressive face flowing through a range of apologetic embarrassment for nudging someone's head with his shoulder to a bashful, sweet shyness when the restaurant's older Korean hostess beamed up at him.

And when Jake spotted Dallas sitting in the far corner of the Tofu House, the gentle, tentative smile he let slide over his face nearly broke Dallas's heart with its uncertain beauty.

At some point in Jake Moore's life, someone made him… less. The broad-shouldered, beautiful man he watched cross the room should have been a bit more cocky, more sure of himself. As little as Dallas knew of the man, he suspected Jake held back nearly everything of himself. Jake was a bit too tucked in, too folded over into himself, and a part of Dallas ached for him. Dallas recognized the look Jake'd given him. He'd seen it in countless faces, a slap of something brightly sharp against the flat of someone's tender soul. Someone broke Jake, convincing him he was smaller, worthless. It stood out in the way he spoke of his craft, of his talents, and it wasn't

Evancho. The older Ukrainian couldn't heap enough praise on the man, assuring Dallas no one could do the work like his Jake.

A craftsman, Evancho called Jake, an artist who could do things to metal that would make God weep.

"Who fucked you up, Jake?" Dallas wondered softly. "Who reached into that pretty soul of yours and tore it apart?"

Despite the hesitant interest flickering in Jake's smoldering hazel eyes, Dallas resigned himself to the possibility of never knowing the taste of Jake's mouth or the glide of his hands over Dallas's body. There was too much pain hidden in those burnished amber-and-peridot-flecked eyes, and there was no certainty Jake would ever work past the walls he'd bricked himself behind.

"Kinda need to try here, Yates," he muttered to himself, standing when Jake drew nearer. "At the very least, be a damned good friend to the man. Looks like he needs one, but fucking hell…. God, save me from hot men in old Levi's and thin T-shirts."

It was a difficult journey through the long, crowded restaurant for Jake. Open around the clock, the Korean eatery was hopping at eleven at night, with a small line forming at the hostess stand and a promise of a wait for those in the back. Most of the crowd was young, mainly women clustered tightly around food-laden tables, chattering away. Dallas watched with a smirking bemusement at the ripple of reactions to Jake weaving between the tables, turning more than a few conversations into a wave of ducked-down heads, hooded eyes, and whispering giggles.

The man was liquid sex and vulnerability, a dangerous combination for Dallas. Jake threatened a lot of Dallas's boundaries, flowing over lines in the sand he'd drawn a long time ago. If he were gay—something Dallas now wondered about—he didn't so much as set off a tingle of desire in Dallas's direction. He didn't know what would be more devastating, Jake Moore being straight or the man just not being interested.

Dallas chanced another peek at Jake's progress through the restaurant, and his stomach clenched at the nearness of the man. A few feet away and blocked by a trio of servers with trays of food, Jake quirked a what-can-you-do look at Dallas while he towered over the short women hustling to unloaded close to twenty bowls and plates of food.

"Hey, sorry I'm late." Jake slid into the chair across of Dallas, jostling the table. The chili oil, shoyu, and vinegar bottles clattered together, and he grabbed at them to stop the glass containers from rattling. "Sorry. Shit, I'm knocking everything over."

"I did the exact same thing when I sat down." Dallas patted the napkin-wrapped bundles of spoons and metal chopsticks on the table. "This is our second set of utensils. I caught the water with my elbow and soaked everything. Surprised they didn't put a trash bag under me like they do little kids in high chairs. Waitress said it's going to be a bit before she comes back. Place is starting to get crazy."

"Yeah, Friday nights are nuts around here," Jake murmured into the menu, the LED lighting picking up the chestnut strands in his rich brown hair. The dimple in the man's cheek was distracting, especially when he flashed Dallas a quick apologetic grin as he jostled the table again. "Crap. Sorry. Feels like this thing's on wheels or something."

A few minutes later and a brief stop by the server to grab their order, and they were left chatting about the weather and the astonishing amount of *panchan* dishes being placed on the nearby tables. The conversation was awkward only for about a minute. Then Dallas decided to take the pink elephant standing between them by the trunk and shake it loose.

"I'd like to promise you we're all out of dead men in the loft space, but I can't. Chances are good we're clear, but you've seen that room," Dallas began. "They're going to send a hazmat company out tomorrow to help with the clutter. Since it's a crime scene with dried bodily fluids, the police suggested we use someone who specializes in... well... dead people showing up in unexpected places."

"It was... interesting." Jake topped off Dallas's glass of iced barley water, then filled his own. "I um... left before the cops did. Any ideas who he was? How long he was there?"

"Honest? I wish we knew. Shit, I hate to think the guy's a John Doe or something." He chewed on his lower lip and picked up his glass. "No one deserves to die without someone knowing they're gone. It's just not right. Cops said they're going to have to see if they can fingerprint the guy."

"He was kind of...." Jake sucked in his face as if he'd tasted a sour lemon. "You know, a bit dry. That make it easier or harder?"

"They have ways. Don't get me going. I watch all that kind of shit on TV. My mom calls me a ghoul. I could talk your head off about crap like that."

"Afterwards… when the detective was talking to me… it got so I was beginning to question what I'd seen up there," Jake confessed. His hands were large, dwarfing the small tumbler of light amber water and ice, and Dallas caught himself following the trail of Jake's thumbs through the condensation on the glass. "Like was that blood we saw on the floor, on the rug and papers. It could have been anything, and my brain made it… bigger, darker."

"It looks… bad, not going to lie. The guy's head was crushed in, but the coroner who looked at the body said that might have happened after he died. There was a lot of stuff on top of him, some of it pretty fucking heavy." It'd been an odd conversation to be witness to, a pair of detectives and a man in a white medical hazmat suit discussing a dead man he'd found upstairs. "They kept asking if anything'd been moved since I was up there last. Couldn't tell them anything other than we'd stuck our heads in, took a look at the mess, then turned tail and ran. Only reason I went up there today was to look for those extra panels."

"They going to let you know when they find out who he is?" Someone laughed, a boisterous spark of bright noise, and Jake turned toward the sound, a somber flower seeking the light. "I'd like to pay my respects once they get him… settled."

"Yeah, the cop said she'd call me. And that leads me into asking if you want to talk about Celeste. Or we can just leave her on the street corner where she's more comfortable." Dallas caught Jake in midsip of his drink, waiting to see if the small coughing fit that followed required more than a bit of sympathy and a napkin. "Sorry, I'll time it better next time. Need me to pound your back?"

"No, no. Shit, give me some warning before you do something like that." Jake gave one final cough, then took another swallow of tea. The bashfulness was back in full force, and Dallas deeply regretted putting the wariness in Jake's thoughtful expression. "Celeste. Um… what'd she tell you?"

"You want the unvarnished truth, or do you want me to pussyfoot around and feel out what to say?" He moved his utensils out of the way for the deep-fried whole mackerel being placed in front of him. They were silent for as long as the taciturn server bustled about, sliding tiny plates over the surface of the table. Then Dallas cleared his throat when she was gone as quickly as she'd arrived. "Do you eat the head off these things?"

"Head's the best part," Jake replied softly, the odd thrum in his voice deepening. "Fins too. You don't?"

"The crunchy bits are the best," Dallas agreed, more than a little bit concerned over the amount of chilies and oil Jake spread over his fish. "So what's it going to be? Hard or soft?"

"Hard's better." His shrug was an elegant lift of broad shoulders and slight grimace. "Is she pissed off at me?"

"Concerned. Probably worried you're pissed off at her," Dallas corrected. "You've known me for what? A day? We haven't had enough time together to figure out how to talk to each other, and she's had even less time, wandering off to the coffee shop. Seriously, useless as a teenager, our girl. She's... enthusiastic, and unfortunately for you, likes you a lot. So in her mind, that means she can meddle. So yeah, I'd get it if you were pissy about her shoving into your life without asking."

"Shouldn't have snapped at her. Wasn't warranted," Jake argued gently, his hands engulfing the glass again. "I mean, people you guys know probably wouldn't blink at her saying stuff like that, and I go and get into her face? It's not right. As much not right as that guy dying without anyone knowing about it. I don't know why I was an asshole to her, but... she didn't deserve it and I'm sorry for it."

"Jake, Celeste's been my best friend for years, and she stomps all over me every chance she gets. She assumed, and well, she goes from stranger to intrusive friend about five minutes after an introduction." Dallas chuckled when Jake snorted a quick laugh, his half smile lifting a few of the shadows from his handsome face. "Look, she'll probably apologize like hell when she sees you the next time, so I ask you, ride her hard for it because she never says she's sorry when she does it to me."

"Truth is, I don't want to lose the job. Evancho would kill me for one, but mostly I want to fix those inlays. You can't see it now, but it looks like that building used to be really sharp. Like downstairs? I think there's some nice wood floors under that crap that's there now." Jake stifled a yawn, and the restaurant's lights saturated the purple tones under his eyes. "It'll be nice to see it looking how it did back in the day."

"I should find some pictures. Talking to you made me want to do something cool with the place. Bring it back." Dallas's stomach flipped over with glee at Jake's dimple making another appearance.

"Archives at UCLA might have something. Or the historical society. I know some people who can get their hands on stuff like that. I reach out to them when I need to do vintage restoration." Jake picked at the fish, expertly peeling back the flesh and skin from the central bones with his chopsticks. After digging the cheek meat out, he dipped it into a pool of chili oil and shoyu near the fish's belly, then popped the morsel into his mouth. Catching Dallas watching him, Jake mumbled around his food, "What?"

"You tell any of my Texas relatives I said this, I'll deny it and call you a liar, but just so you know, my mouth would be on fire with that much hot sauce," Dallas admitted with a shake of his head. "And if it makes you feel better, I'd kick Celeste to the curb before I fired you. Okay, maybe not to the curb but tell her to stay home. You're a hell of a lot more useful than she is. One rat and she goes screaming blue bloody murder. She's from New York City. Rats should be nothing to her."

"Like I said, she's got nothing to say sorry for." Another shrug, but this time, Jake relaxed afterward. "It's just been shitty lately and... I guess I wasn't ready for her to ask me if I was gay. Not something the guys I work with talk about. Like ever."

Dallas picked at his own fish, trying out some of the peppery oil on the soft white flesh. "So not a lot of male bonding and backslaps over at Evancho's? And like the last time I pointed something like that out, I am teasing."

"Yeah, I get that, but no, not a lot. Couple of guys there are dicks, but really, Evancho is cool. He cuts me a lot of slack on things." Jake crunched through a fin, slowly working over the fried tidbit. "What about you? You work someplace other than... whatever it is you're doing over there?"

"Ah, I have degrees in business management and a few other stupid things that basically say I can run something into the ground and know why I'm doing it but am helpless to stop." Dallas chuckled. "I buy properties and fix them up, then either rent them out or run a business in them. This is the first time I'm doing something historically valuable... or personal. Most of the time it's houses or apartment buildings, but I've got a couple of clubs down in WeHo. Those are run by people who know what they're doing. Same here, once we get Bombshells and Beauties looking pretty, someone will come in to manage it. Hell, Celeste might even come out of retirement to do some actual work."

"If you're going to neon the old marquee on the front of the building, that name's not going to fit." Jake held a bowl of salted bean sprouts out for Dallas before taking some for himself. "Well, you could, but it'd be hard to read."

"Good point." Dallas took tidbits of *panchan* from each of the plates as Jake lifted them up from the table. It was an odd courtesy, an unconscious one by the distracted look on the man's face as he continued to mull over the building's front signage. "It's a working name. I could just call it Bombshells. Nothing's engraved in stone… or neon just yet."

Their food arrived, mounds of fragrant charred at the edges short ribs and a scoop of rice in a metal bowl for each of them. The soft click of steel chopsticks on plates chimed under the murmur of discussion around them, and Dallas studied Jake as he ate.

"Kinda weird having a guy watching me while I eat," Jake said between bites, not looking up from his food. "Not as weird as finding a dead guy under shit but still… weird."

"Most people I come here with pick food apart. They don't eat fins, fish eyeballs…." Dallas tapped a bare rib bone he'd cleaned off himself a few moments before. "And they leave a lot of the meat around the bone. It's kind of cool to be with someone who just… eats. Chew everything off a chicken wing?"

"No other way to eat them," Jake grunted, digging into the kimchee. "Maybe it's from growing up poor or your parents being poor? You eat what you've got."

"And sometimes you don't know when you're going to get it again," he murmured. "We were… I don't know if we were poor, but there was a lot of blue box mac and cheese growing up. 'Course, that could have also been because my mom worked nights and my dad's a shitty cook. Then my grandpa died—my mom's dad—and well, he was pissed off she married some trailer trash kid she'd met at college, but I guess he figured he was dead, so might as well divide things up evenly. Oil. Land. Crazy kind of shit. Life got a hell of a lot easier after that.

Dad got to finish his degree, and Mom got to stay at home and raise chickens and us. Okay, and hold mini-revolutions. She's kind of a… tie-dyed hippie sort of mom slash activist who throws bake sales."

"What's your dad do?"

"He's a rocket scientist." Dallas laughed at Jake's incredulous scoff. "Seriously, he loves it. Hasn't blown anything up in years, though. I think he's losing his touch. He's a menace, and well, Mom saves… well, fucking everything. Whales, kittens, one-eyed jaguars, you name it, the ranch has it. Five million damned chickens, ducks, pigs, and cows, and we go grocery shopping for our meat. That's my mother and father. What about your parents?"

"Mom's… dead." Jake swallowed, and Dallas knew there was a story behind those two words from the hitching breath he took before he continued. "Dad used to be a welder. Not like me. Shipyards. Big stuff. He got sick… years ago. Docs say he doesn't have long to live, so he's in hospice now. I go to see him after work."

"Dying sucks."

"Living's worse. The old man's not… he's not real popular with the staff. He needs the care, but… he's got dementia now. Makes him act… worse, and he wasn't a treat before he got sick." The murmuring grew softer, and Dallas had to strain to hear. "It's like a fucking death march, and they keep moving the finish line."

The stall in their conversation wasn't comfortable, but not as prickly hot as when Jake'd sat down. Dallas asked for a refill of fish cake, then added the jalapeño cabbage pickles as well when Jake finished off the last of the spicy dish. The server returned in a few seconds with heaping bowls of both and left with instructions for them to shout out if they needed something because she was going to be busy with a table of ten.

"Usually they're trying to shove me out the door." Jake nodded toward the hostess at the entrance. "Not her. She's always stuffing extra food into my bag when I do takeout. Last time I came home from this place, I had about six fish wrapped up in plastic shoved in between about a gallon of kimchee."

"She's very generous." This time Dallas beat Jake to the *panchan* dishes, tilting them up for him to take his portion first. There was a slight hesitation, as if he didn't know what to do, and then he hurriedly moved some food onto his plate. "If you're still hungry, grab something else. My treat, remember?"

"Nah, I'm good," Jake replied as one of the younger servers plopped a plate of steaming fried mackerel onto the table. "Okay, so obviously we're having more fish. You take what you want first."

Ignoring Jake's protests, Dallas dumped the largest fish onto Jake's dish, then helped himself. The meat was tender, fragrant with only a dusting of salt to season it, and his stomach made a little protest when he drizzled hot sauce over the crispy skin.

"Can I ask you one thing?" Jake ventured, taking the oil from Dallas when it was offered across the table.

"Shoot. Open book here," Dallas assured him. "Ain't nothing I haven't heard, done, or said myself."

"Celeste... what she... said." Jake shredded a bit of his fish into his rice bowl, mingling the white grains with the meat. "How'd she know? About me, I mean. About me being... that."

SIX

"DO YOU want to have that discussion here?" Dallas asked softly, mindful of the noise and chatter rising up around them. "Because we can go elsewhere."

He wanted to reach across the table and put his hands over Jake's, to give the man some kind of physical contact simply to reassure him. It was a human thing to do, something he'd done countless times before with friends and even strangers, but Dallas held back. Jake Moore trembled and shook under his skin, as fragile and delicate as antique glass, overheated by emotion and stress.

"I don't want to have this discussion at all." The brittle reached Jake's face, stretching his skin taut over his cheekbones and tightening his mouth. Shaking his head, he looked everywhere but at Dallas, his throat moving as he gulped in a mouthful of air. "Stupid I brought it up. Just forget about—"

"Jake—" Dallas clamped down on the "sugar" that nearly followed the man's name. "Shit, listen to me, man."

Habits were hard to break, even harder when he was stepping back into a world he no longer lived in. A world where people didn't touch or console one another for fear of it being taken as a sexual overture. Dallas clenched his hands into fists under the table, frustrated, but Jake would view them as a sign of aggression. He was certain of that.

"Look, you and I… shared something today that not a lot of people ever run into," Dallas began gently. "We stumbled upon a man who should have had a better end, and sometimes that leads a guy to thinking about the what-ifs or the I-don't-knows. And that's good. It's okay. Doesn't mean you have to look at everything that it brings up.

"Shit, it doesn't mean anything other than maybe you and I can be friends for a bit if you don't feel like dumping everything you're carrying, man, but the short answer to your question is, I don't know what Celeste saw or thought she saw." The conversations at the tables

48

next to them pitched up as a group of young men slid into an empty spot. Jake flinched, and Dallas tucked a few bills into the billfold the server left on the table. "And I really think we should be having this talk someplace you can get pissed off at me or something. Although I would appreciate it if you didn't punch me in the face for talking."

"You don't… hit people. That's just…," Jake mumbled. "Fuck, I hope you don't let a guy hit you."

The look of horror on Jake's face was comical until Dallas saw the pain shining through his eyes. This time he did reach for the man, placing his hand on the table next to Jake's, his fingers close enough to feel the heat of Jake's body but far enough away not to make contact.

"No, I don't. No one should. Okay, some people are into that, but me? Not so much." He grimaced at the thought of someone striking him with a paddle or a belt. "I couldn't even take my mom scolding me when I was a kid, and I'm going to ask some guy to whack me? Not my thing. Now, how about if I ask them to pack the food up and we go grab a coffee or something? We don't have to talk about anything you don't want to. Deal?"

"Look, I'm beat—"

"Then I'll drop you off at home and we'll see each other Monday," Dallas replied. "No harm, no foul. Look, Jake, at the very least, I like you. You're a good guy, and from the sounds of it, could use a good friend. That's it. Nothing else. You want to talk about shit, I'm here. Grab a beer? I can do that too. Life just seems kind of… tightly wound around you, man, and you look like you're about ready to pop."

"Yeah. I think… I am," Jake whispered softly. His words were buried under the noise in the restaurant, and he chewed on his lower lip, contemplating God only knew what, but Dallas hoped it was at least the offer of friendship. "Decaf would be okay. I've got to get some sleep tonight. Saturday's kind of when Dad needs the most… help down at the place he lives. I need to be awake enough to drive down there if they call."

"Easily done. And besides, we've had a fuck-ass long day, you and I." Dallas mimed a clamshell opening and closing at one of the servers near the front, and she nodded, reaching for some Styrofoam take-out containers. "Pack everything up for you? There's got to be at least three more mackerel here. She must love you something fierce."

"Only if you don't want it." Jake ducked his head down when the server slid her arm over his shoulder, dumping the take-out trays onto their table. "Screw the teach-a-man-to-fish thing. Someone offers you a free fish, you better damned well take it and eat another day."

THEY WALKED, crossing a couple of blocks in silence while Jake fought with the demons pulling him down into the dank mire he'd brewed inside of him.

Leaving the leftovers in Dallas's car, they'd set out for a coffee shop Jake knew would still be open. A couple of giant iced lattes to go and he found himself walking shoulder to shoulder with a man who'd made him want more than what he had, leaving Jake with a regret that grew with every step he took.

Koreatown on a Friday night was busy without being intrusive, pockets of energy contained within bubbles of parking lots and dots on the sidewalks. The streets were lit up with signs, flashing and sparkling to draw in the eye and potentially a customer or two. Most places had their doors thrown open, but a few were more discreet, closed and guarded by large men wearing all black and humorless expressions. One cocked an eyebrow at them as they drew near, reaching for the entrance's doorknob, then dropping his hand when Dallas shook his head before his fingers touched the metal latch.

A low-slung Toyota ambled by, its windows rattling from the bass thumping out of its speakers, and its driver, a flat-eyed Korean teen, quickly looked away when Jake glanced his way. The car stopped in the middle of its left turn, letting a pack of elderly women shuffle across the walk, their hands waving quick thank-yous as they hurried against the light. Hands clutched tightly around plastic bags, they bobbed and wove around Dallas and Jake as they passed, a flight of colorful birds gliding over the winding cement path.

"There's a… it's not a park, but there's places to sit if you want. Over there, on the right." Jake couldn't think of what to call the spot of grass with benches in front of a bank building set back away from the street. It was a raised courtyard of sorts, accessible on either side by gradual sloping ramps, and he'd driven by the place during the day, stopping to grab lunch from one of the many food trucks surrounding the block. "Lots of lights and no one bothers."

"Sounds like a plan." Dallas nodded his chin toward a busy Korean BBQ restaurant, its door blocked by a crowd of people. "We just ate and that still smells fucking great."

"Yeah, it's good. Evancho's taken a couple of us there after a job. To celebrate." Jake's stomach clenched at the thought of any more food. His nerves were fried, scraped raw from the walk and the worry chewing on his mind. "Gotta cross here."

They did a quick run across the street, catching the final seconds of the red flashing numbers before the light turned against them. He reached the other side seconds before Dallas, his longer legs eating up the asphalt. The cerulean glow from a spa's neon sign turned some glass shards pebbling the sidewalk the same color as Dallas's eyes. Jake's heart skipped more than a few beats when an SUV turned the corner too tightly. The car jerked to the center of the intersection, but Jake'd already made a grab for Dallas's arm and dragged him to the curb. The breeze from the car's passing kicked exhaust fumes and the sticky tar aroma from overcooked streets into Jake's face.

"I'm good," Dallas murmured, his shoulder brushing Jake's, holding up the drink carrier in mock salute to the retreating SUV. "Fuck, that was close... but the lattes are fine... and the crowd goes wild with the save."

"You're kind of nuts. You know that, right?" The contact burned, but he was reluctant to let go. Dallas's arm was firm in his grasp, sinewy muscles moving beneath his fingers. Releasing Dallas seemed like a great idea, but his hand had other thoughts. Letting go... hurt, but he let his hand drop to his side, then shoved it into his pocket. Taking the carrier from Dallas's hand, he headed up the slope, and the LED clock on the bank's front side flashed the time, nearly into the single digits and ticking. "Shit, it's late."

"You want to head back? I'm good if you are."

Jake didn't know how to take Dallas's question. Face value meant concern for Jake wanting to get enough sleep in to deal with his father the next morning, but a very large chunk of his brain whispered malevolence, assuring him Dallas wanted to be rid of him.

"No, it's okay. I'll be fine." He was going to be fine even if he only got fifteen minutes of sleep. "'Sides, we're right here."

Something odd burbled in him, something Dallas somehow tapped into, and now nothing Jake did could shove it back down. It started the day he'd first seen Dallas get out of his car to inspect the old, worn building across the street from Evancho's, and then everything went to hell and gone as soon as he'd looked up from studying the windows' ironworks to find Dallas watching every move he made.

Surprisingly, one of the benches overlooking the street was not only clean but cool to the touch. A lingering heat remained over the city, a blush of warmth trapped by a thin layer of clouds hanging above the streets. The sky was the peculiar citrus-tinted gray of a typical Los Angeles late summer, a few hardier stars gleaming through the patches in the overcast. Built a few feet up off the street, the courtyard leveled out a slight hill and stretched back a quarter block before ending at the skyscraper's front door. The enormous round fountain near the entrance dribbled a thin tickle of water from its spout, more of out of a need to keep the lily pads filling its bowl alive than provide a cooling spray.

"This must be a great place to people watch during the daytime," Dallas said, sitting down next to Jake on the bench. "Okay, maybe not during the summer, because hell, you'd cook."

"They bring out tables and umbrellas during the day." Jake handed Dallas one of the lattes. "Lots of food trucks in the area come here for lunch. Place gets crazy."

"Damn, I needed to just sit and breathe after today." Dallas's soft groan of pleasure when he sipped the cold drink did funny things to Jake's belly. "And you live around here?"

"Yeah, about a block north of the Tofu House. I'd have said we could go there for coffee, but I've got shit in the fridge."

"Except for bad pad thai."

"Man, that went in the trash." He wrinkled his nose at the memory of the rancid noodles. "It wasn't that great to begin with, but you know, a quick dinner, can't argue that. The fish should be okay, right?"

"Yeah, we won't be gone long, and there's nothing in there that'll spoil. Not like anything's got mayo or something." Dallas chuckled. "Shit, worst case of food poisoning I've ever had was because my sister, Tori, left some potato salad out for a couple of hours, then put it back in the fridge before the family got home. Me, my dad, and my mom got sicker than shit, and Austin was all, 'No, I'm fine. Why are you all puking?' That asshole can drink five-week-old sour milk and nothing. My mom calls him her garbage disposal."

"Must be weird having sisters and brothers." There'd been no chance of a sibling after him. He'd never once thought about having one. It would have been too problematic, another person for his father to use against him, against his mother. Leaning forward, Jake rested his weight on his palms, curling his fingers around the end of the seat. "I can't imagine growing up with other kids in the house. It was always just me."

"Wasn't too bad. Austin was an asshole, but that's an older brother's job. Like Tori was a brat. The shit we used to do to her…. I'm surprised my mother didn't skin us alive and leave us out for the coyotes." Dallas stared off across the street, seemingly drawn by the crowd gathered around the restaurants. "Not like she was an angel. Any chance she got, she tossed us under the bus. She's Dad's favorite. He says no, but she's the baby… and a girl. Can't imagine growing up alone. Who would you blame things on? What about you? You always live around here?"

"Nope." He shrugged uncomfortably. The conversation was bringing up old memories, soiled images of a childhood he'd rather have left behind him. "My dad moved us around a bit, but I went to high school in LA. He got hurt on a job, so working was out, and where we lived was cheap. My mom started cleaning houses, that kind of stuff."

"I did that in college." Dallas nodded when Jake shot him an incredulous look. "Hey, my parents paid for a lot of my school stuff, but spending money? I was on my own. Got hooked up with some guys who ran a cleaning service, and I swear to God, I'd rather work my parents' ranch than scrub another sorority toilet. How old were you when your dad got hurt?"

"I was… fourteen, I think." Those years were hazy, lost behind nights spent moving out of motel rooms in the early hours of the morning and living in the back of a run-down camper one of his dad's friends loaned them. It was also the first time he'd noticed how a man looked, his young, hormonal body flushing with uncontrollable urges at the sight of a bare-chested bricklayer working in the hot sun. "Dad could do some side jobs out of his friend's garage, under the table kind of stuff. I helped him for a long time, then… went to school for a bit. Came home when he had his first stroke and then things kind of went… bad after that, so I stuck around."

He'd come home from a few months of college to find his mother worked nearly to death and beaten bloody by the man who'd claimed to love her above everything. They'd fallen back into the same routine, a still too skinny Jake bent to his father's will to protect his mother and his mother promising to do better, to work harder for a husband who did nothing but cause them both pain.

There were cold mornings, deeply cold behind heavy brick walls, when the bones in his hands crinkled and ached so much the shock of pain woke him up. Times when he woke up screaming because he couldn't grow up fast enough in his sleep to get away from the shadow framed in his bedroom door. It was hard to reconcile the looming monster who'd terrorized his life with the sunken-in albatross of a man now slung around his neck.

"You okay, Jake?" Dallas prodded quietly.

His face was wet, probably damp from something, Jake couldn't imagine what. Then he wiped at his cheek, smearing a drop of salty tear over his lips. He was crying. Jake didn't even think he had any tears left in him, but something about Dallas, the easy warmth of the man plumbed into grief he'd buried a long time ago. He didn't want to think about his mom, or the dried splotches of her blood on the kitchen floor he'd found when he'd come home after… that night.

The cast-iron skillet fell, his father told the cops. She was short. It was too high, and he'd found his wife much too late to do anything for her. If only their son had been there to help instead of abandoning his parents when they needed him the most. He'd felt the cops' censure, stood in the fire of their condemnation, and bit his tongue raw to keep from screaming at the old man who played the system as easily as most men pissed.

He'd failed her… failed the small, quiet woman who'd silently borne his father's fists during the worst of his beatings. It was another nightmare he'd never wake from, a very real terror whose poisonous claws were sunk deep in him, so deep he'd never shake it loose. Jake owed her everything, even if it meant denying who he was—who he wanted—because when everything was said and done, his mother's death was on his head.

"Yeah, I'm good." If there was any moment he should be longing for the bite of the gun into his mouth, it should have been then. But Dallas's fingers brushing over his knee changed something inside of him, and the only desire he felt was for another lingering touch, an arm around his shoulders or maybe even a quick embrace to get his heart going again. Wiping at his face again, Jake stammered, "Shit, sorry… I—"

"Don't apologize for crying. Hell, only thing you should apologize for is feeling nothing." The bench grew smaller under Jake, because it seemed like only a moment ago, there was enough space between him and Dallas for him to breathe. Now he couldn't seem to catch enough air to get around the hard lump in his chest. Dallas shifted, and for a second Jake was terrified he'd sling an arm around Jake's shoulders, but he only turned, their knees suddenly touching. "You miss your mom? She passed away how long ago?"

"Years," he snorted with a hard huff. "I didn't get to… say good-bye. She was gone by the time I got to the hospital. Then all I was left with was… him. And now, swear to God, man, once he's gone, I have no fucking clue what to do."

"It's hard when you're close to your parents." Dallas moved the drinks to the ground, setting them under the bench. "Going to kill me when my mom or dad goes. I can't even imagine what life's going to be without them. It'll fucking break me. I know it. Your dad… shit, I can't imagine."

"See, yeah that's the thing, I'm not going to miss him." Jake shook his head, hoping to loosen the pressure squeezing in on him, but all it did was make him a bit dizzy. "But I've been so wrapped up in making sure he's taken care of, there's nothing of me left. Oh, it'll break me, all right, only because I won't have any clue what to do after he's gone… and I'm finally fucking free."

SEVEN

FOURTEEN DAYS.

It'd been two weeks since Jake's emotions punctured through the thick membrane of politeness and quietude he donned as armor, then just as quickly shut everything down again, pulling back into himself so quickly it made Dallas's head spin. A few glistening tears across his cheeks and Jake Moore was done, hidden away before Dallas could do anything other than warble a few words of sympathy.

But every morning, Jake showed up for work, a soft-spoken, gorgeous reminder to Dallas that the world wasn't always his oyster and he wasn't going to get everything he wanted out of life.

"You moon over that boy more than I do chocolate," Celeste grumbled in his ear, jerking Dallas out of his thoughts. "Seriously, just… do something. Anything. Go get laid. Buy one of those rubbery flashlight things. Get a dog. Better yet, get a cat. Easier to take care of, so when you die of boredom and sighing, I'll inherit something I like."

"You're getting jack shit from me," Dallas grumbled back. "Not one damned glass. Not even a fricking coaster. Don't you have a bathroom you were painting? You know, the one you started back when your chest still had hair?"

"I'm taking a break," she sniffed imperiously. "Besides, I'm being meticulous. You can't rush genius."

"The damned Sistine Chapel was done quicker than that fricking bathroom." He laid down another piece of blue tape on the edge of a one-way mirror partition separating the bar area from what had been a kitchen. Stealing a quick glance at Jake's silhouette on one of the front windows, he hissed at Celeste, "And I'm not fucking mooning. He's not… look, he needs a friend, not some asshole hitting on him. Don't give him any shit, sugar. He doesn't need it. He's got plenty."

The heat wave cracked that morning when a pressure front broke and pulled in a marine layer cold and thick enough to clash with the

56

oppressive hot air sitting over the city. A brief, torrential bit of rain hit the streets, steaming the neighborhood with a black-tar-scented haze, dropping the early-morning temperature to something less than hell's doorway, and Dallas silently mourned Jake eschewing the tank tops he'd been wearing all week for a T-shirt.

After a week of removing all of the random wrought-iron bars inside the building, Jake spent his mornings scrubbing down the windows and prepping the clunky bars for removal. Frustrated by the delays, Jake was ready to take a torch to the offending bars on the outside and begin working on restoring the original ironwork. His boss, Evancho, visited a few times, pulling Jake off of the job when the temperature soared too high, curtailing Jake's protests with a sharp grunt to get back into the shop where it was cooler.

It was sure as hell saying something when a fabrication shop was cooler than a SoCal afternoon, and Dallas grew used to shutting down at noon every day, then eating lunch with Jake under the huge tree in the parking lot behind the building. Despite the air being hot enough to blister the inside of his lungs with every breath he took, Dallas enjoyed the hell out of sitting on the open tailgate of Jake's old Chevy truck. It'd become a standing date, and they'd spent the hour talking about every stupid thing on the planet, from movies they adored to which superhero was the best.

Sometimes they touched on darker things. It was hard not to press, especially when Jake grew quiet and still beside him. A gentle nudge with a soft word took away most of the shadows on the man's face, but the soulful retreats and silences were bumps in their conversation Dallas hoped to eventually smooth over.

"He's got plenty of something. Have you seen that ass? It's like—"

"Cee, I love you with a deep love I only reserve for chocolate chip cookies, but I'm going to ask you one last time, stop. It's Jake. He's not...." Dallas took a deep breath, shoving down the irrational anger growing inside of him. He had no right to be possessive, but Celeste's ogling was getting on his nerves. "Look, please. For the love of God, *Serenity*, and TV dinners, just stop."

"Oh, sugar," Celeste groaned softly. "You've got it so fucking bad."

Trapped between needing to lie to himself and always telling Celeste the truth, Dallas chose the only thing he could say to his best friend.

"Shut up, Celeste."

Celeste's laughter continued to mock him as she sauntered back to the bathroom she'd abandoned earlier.

"She okay?" Jake pushed past the semiopen front door, nearly getting wedged against the wall. "Sounds like a hyena from outside."

"Sounds like one inside too." Dallas shook the feeling back into his fingers, cramped from laying down what seemed like miles of tape. "Explain to me why I'm doing this myself again?"

"Because it's cheaper, and all of the good painting companies are scheduled out until October?" Jake cocked his head at the guitar riff erupting from Dallas's phone lying on the scratched bar top. "Shit, it's noon already?"

"Crap, it is. Hey, what'd you bring for lunch?" After watching Jake eat peanut butter and jelly sandwiches for days on end, Dallas was hoping for a break in the routine. "Please tell me PB and J again."

"Yeah, why?" The suspicious look on Jake's face made Dallas grin. "What? It's cheap."

"Because it'll keep. Come on. I'm buying us lunch today." Dallas waved away Jake's impending protest nearly as soon as the man frowned at him. "Man, we've been working in this sweat hole without a break for almost two weeks. You're here all day today. I can at least grab you a lunch someplace with air-conditioning. Let me see what Celeste wants to—"

"Celeste has a hair appointment," she called out from the bathroom. "And I'm not coming back. We're going to bleach me out and go for a full red this time."

"Isn't her hair already blonde?" Jake made a face at Dallas. "Right? I thought it was blonde."

"Wigs," Dallas whispered back. "She's been growing hers out after a tragic perming accident. I haven't seen her real hair in months. It's like a Kinder Egg every time I see her. I never know what I'm going to get."

"What's a Kinder Egg?" Jake's smile when Celeste joined them in the main room lit up his face, and the grimace he gave her when she kissed his slightly dirty face was pure teasing. "And what's the matter with your hair?"

Patting his face, Celeste murmured, "God, it's good you're beautiful. I'll be back tomorrow to finish the bathroom. Don't wait up for me."

"We don't live together, you dork." Dallas watched his best friend sashay out the front door, then sighed. "She didn't have a drop of paint on her. Want to bet when I go in there, the walls are going to look exactly the way they did when I walked in this morning?"

"Sucker bet. Not taking it," Jake replied. "And what's wrong with peanut butter and jelly sandwiches?"

"Nothing. If you're five." Dallas dusted off his jeans, then tossed Jake a towel. "Clean your face off, Moore, and bring your shit inside. We're going to go have some ribs."

"EVANCHO'S GOING to kick my ass," Jake muttered from the passenger seat. "I get an hour for lunch and you're driving us to La Brea?"

"I already told him I was grabbing you for a long lunch. You know what he said?" Dallas shot Jake a quick look, amused at the slightly grumpy frown on his friend's face. "Go on, guess."

"I'm guessing he said he didn't give a shit what I did because you were paying me by the job and not by the hour." Jake peeked at his phone, then slid it back into his pocket. "Evancho must love the hell out of you because if it was anyone else, he'd lose his shit."

The squat, barrel-chested Ukrainian Jake worked for was a pushover where his hazel-eyed, dimpled craftsman was concerned. One mention of taking a long lunch to get actual food inside of Jake and Evancho was practically shoving them both into the car and waving them off as if they were going on a honeymoon cruise. The effect was ruined when the older man rubbed at his silver crew cut in frustration and began to swear at one of his workers about handling the shop equipment properly, so Dallas beat a hasty retreat while he could.

It felt kind of like asking a man if it was okay to date his son.

Not that he was going to mention that to Jake, but still, exactly that.

"Here we are. I'll go grab the food and sit out back. There's trees and shit. Okay, so it's a park but better than inside. Damned place is like an oven during lunchtime. See if you can snag us a table." Dallas pulled into a spot in front of the tiny restaurant. Jake's soft chuckle brought Dallas up short. "What?"

"Celeste said you were bossy," he replied, unlatching his seat belt. "She's not wrong."

"You have a mission. Go forth and conquer." Dallas trotted around the end of the Tesla, then thrust a fist into the air, shouting after Jake as he headed to the back of the building. "Don't let the moms back there give you any shit. It's good for kids to eat on the lawn. Builds character. Kick them into the dirt where they belong!"

"You know…." The older woman sitting at the walk-up window shook her head when Dallas approached her, the dark locs piled up on her head glistening silver near her scalp. "There is something seriously wrong with you, boy. Yelling at your man like that."

"Not my guy, Lana." Dallas leaned on the short steel counter in front of the window, thankful for the cooler weather. "How are you doing, sugar?"

"I'm fine. Got your order right here." She looked at him, a lifetime of handling messes and managing her children shining through her steady gaze. "And if that ain't your boy, you'd best be pulling back some of that smile of yours. From the look of those teeth, I'd think you were measuring your fingers for rings or something."

"Never going to happen." Dallas dug out his wallet. "He's… complicated."

"Not so complicated I didn't see those dimples of his when he looked back at you." Lana pursed her lips into a disapproving line. "Don't know what it is with kids these days. Back in my day, if you liked someone, you hooked in and made your life. Weren't no complicated anything. Telling you, son, the way you two look at each other? Better if you just accepted your shit and got on with it. Make life easier all around. Now, how about you give me a couple of twenties for all of this food and I'll be grabbing you a couple of slices of cake. Maybe a bit of sweet will help things along for you."

"Can't hurt, love. God knows I need all the help I can get in life." Dallas passed over the cash, then stared off toward the end of the building where he'd seen Jake last. "So, really? You think he's got something for me?"

"Honey, I look at cake the way he looks at you," Lana remarked, shoving a load of bags across the counter at him. "Just do me a favor. Invite me to the wedding when you two boys get around to it. I'll even give you a deal on the food."

"OKAY, THAT cake is blue." Jake eyed the pair of two-layer monstrosities sitting on the table, their electric berry bodies trapped in a Styrofoam and cling wrap prison. "Why is it… blue?"

"Because it's not red." Dallas opened a lunch plate container, and the smell of BBQ sauce slapped Jake across the face. "Just shut up and try this. I got you a combo plate. Some ribs, some brisket, side of greens, and some mac and cheese."

"And blue cake." Jake sniffed at the dessert but couldn't smell anything beyond the smokiness of the cooked meat.

"Just… eat." A bunch of napkins and a plastic fork were shoved at Jake next, and Dallas shook them under Jake's nose until he took them. "Swear to God, sometimes it's like eating with a five-year-old kid."

"That another crack at my PB and J?"

"Yep," Dallas shot back. "And tell me this isn't better?"

At the first mouthful of sauce-slathered brisket, Jake had to agree. He made it halfway through the sliced meat, gnawed one bone clean, then contemplated trying one of the chunks of bread tucked away in a folded-over white paper bag. Dallas chatted through most of his lunch, giving slightly sarcastic commentary about the other people in the park, mostly judging parenting techniques and oddly enough, sneakers.

Half-full of food and sitting across of Dallas at a park table under the cool shade of a thickly leafed tree wasn't a bad way to spend a Friday lunch. If he was lucky, they'd get back before two and he'd be able to work on removing the stalls someone'd welded together in the men's bathroom, something Dallas talked about getting done before he took out any more grates so the walls could be readied for painting.

The park was a stretch of rolling green hillocks amid the gray and glass buildings. A small playground provided a muted rumble of shrieking childish laughter with the occasional burst of shouting, mostly about some kid named Andy who wouldn't share the slide.

"We should kick those kids off the swings and see which one of us can go higher," Dallas said around a mouthful of food and grabbed Jake's wrist, shaking it once before letting go. "Betcha I'd kick your ass."

Dallas smirked. It was something Jake had learned about him. A full smile was rare, precious in its unguarded glee, but he mostly smirked and said outrageous things to tease. Being with Dallas—spending time with him—was a barrage of half smiles, snide remarks, and generous effusive comments. He touched constantly, giving small taps with his fingers on a forearm to draw attention to something or a glide of a hand along a shoulder blade to commiserate over a crappy turn in the day. There was nothing sexual in his brushes. He touched everyone, playing an unconscious game of tag with everyone he met along the way, anchoring himself in his world.

Jake tried not to see more in Dallas's light caresses than what was there, a deepening friendship with a playful, laughing man who made his soul boil with a want he couldn't quench.

"You've got something against kids?" Jake laughed at Dallas's confused double take. "First you want them eating off the lawn, and now we're kicking them off the swings?"

"Little bastards need to be taught how life really is." A fork full of macaroni and cheese made a precarious pointer as Dallas waved it around, gesturing toward the playground. "You want to swing, you've got to claim your territory. Defend it against all takers. And for God's sake, quit playing with the bag and just eat some of the bread. There's butter in that other one. Real butter. None of that good-for-you shit. If it doesn't harden your arteries, Lana won't want to serve it. Now eat some bread so I can go back to heckling kids."

The inside of the bag was foil lined, keeping the bread warm. Its fragrance hit Jake, digging into childhood echoes of his mother pulling loaves out of the oven and admonishing him to stand back from the door so he wouldn't get burned. The slices were thick with a thin, crisp crust and airy white center. Jake spread pats of butter on the two slices he chose and moaned when he took his first bite. The creamy, salty smear of melting butter on the fresh yeasty bread was something he hadn't known he missed, not until Dallas shoved a bag at him and Jake discovered a memory he'd nearly forgotten.

"Okay, I haven't had sex good enough to make me do that face you're doing right now." Dallas broke into Jake's reverie. "What the hell is in that bread?"

"My mom used to make bread like this. Same kind. It's... hell... been so damned long since I've thought about that." He didn't know why he'd forgotten her working over flour-dusted boards in the early hours of a Saturday morning. Her small hands would work the dough, pale sticky dots speckling her tanned arms. "Hell, I think we were still in Montreal? I don't know. I was a little kid. It was way before... Dad got hurt... and she'd take me down to the food bank with her because they gave out stuff like flour and sugar. Baking things.

"She'd say people didn't cook anymore, so no one took that stuff. They'd load up a huge bin, and we'd go home. Then she'd make bread. Tons of it. She used to sell it. I don't know if they knew she was coming or what, but she'd be walking down the street and people would come outside to get bread." He chuckled, remembering the long walks up and down a narrow street, struggling to carry a small basket of wrapped loaves while keeping up with his mother. "I must have been four or five. I probably bugged the hell out of her while she worked, because she'd give me a little bit of dough to mess with and tell me I was helping. Best part was she'd always save back some for us and cut off one end while it was hot, cover it with butter, and give it to me."

Shaking the piece of half-eaten bread at Dallas, he murmured softly, "That's what this tastes like right now. Like Maman's bread. Like a piece of love she's sent me from wherever she is right now."

Dallas's hands were hot on his arm, a tight clench around his forearm, and Jake blinked away the wetness stinging his eyes. He couldn't lose his shit in the middle of a park, not in front of Dallas. Not again. His emotions were sticky, clinging to him and muddling his senses. A hard swell expanded inside of him, a bubble of crackling anger blended with hot sorrow and something else he couldn't identify. Dallas's hands moved, his words a soft string of nonsense and comfort against Jake's raw, bleeding memories.

"So fucking stupid, you know?" Jake shook his head, wanting to climb over the table so Dallas could hug him, fold him into a tight embrace, holding him until the poisonous storm raging inside of him died down. "I'm getting worked up over a damned piece of bread."

"Not stupid at all, man." Dallas's smooth voice poured into him, a honey salve over the roughened edges of Jake's abraded emotions. "Hell, my mom can't toast a Pop-Tart without burning it, so now that's the only way I can eat them. It's stuff like that… that kind of crazy, happy stuff that keeps us going sometimes."

Dallas's hands felt good on him, awakening a tide of confusing, conflicting wants Jake desperately longed to let free. His fingers stroked along Jake's forearm, probably an absent caress, but it left a trail of fire behind, scorching the edges of Jake's control.

"Have you talked to someone about this kind of stuff?" Dallas canted his head, forcing Jake to look into his cerulean eyes. "Maybe a therapist can help you work this out, J. Because there's some unhappy inside of you, and it's okay to get some help to get it out."

"No therapists. Not again. Not after that one they sent me to because I was gay—"

Jake threw up the bread.

It came in a sour rush of bile and fear out of his belly and seared his throat. He couldn't see past the swirling gray panic flooding him, and just when he hitched in a breath to cleanse away the gut-wrenching fear ripping through him, his stomach rebelled again.

Clutching the edge of the table, Jake panted, frozen to the long seat he'd somehow straddled in his anxiety. He needed to run, but there was nowhere to go, nowhere he could tuck himself into where those words wouldn't come back to haunt him. A tight mewling whispered out of his burning throat, the strangled thread of air carrying along his horror in a reedy dirge.

"Hey, J, it's okay." Dallas was next to him, behind him really, his long hands rubbing at his back. He leaned against Jake, pressing into his side and shoulders, wrapping around him just enough for Jake to feel… safe. "Dude, I know… I know, man. But it's okay."

"I shouldn't have…." Jake gasped. "Fuck. I can't—no one at the shop. My dad… just no one—can know. Not… shit."

"Right now, that's just between us." More honey, more salve on the hot terror gushing through Jake's mind. "You tell me what you want me to do. Whatever you want, Jake. We leave it all here, and nothing… changes. Or if you need someone to be your friend while you figure shit out, we can do that too. Whatever you need, okay? No one is going to make you do or be anything you don't want to be, okay, Jake? Least of all me. I'm your friend, despite the PB and J habit you've got. Whatever you need."

"I just can't… I'm tired." The shock was still there, simmering and burbling, a cauldron of wicked shame and guilt waiting to be sipped at, but its scorch eased back, its toxic splash soothed away by Dallas's weight on his back. "I'm just tired, Dal. I just want to… be. I'm tired of… running, but there's so much crap I can't fucking deal with. Not now. I want to… fuck… I can't… but I want to. With you. I just need someone to know. Someone I know won't hurt me with it."

"Then that's how it'll be, then. You've got me, Jake. However long you need me with you." Dallas leaned in, tightening one arm around Jake's shoulders. His breath was warm on Jake's cheek, scented sweet from BBQ sauce and iced tea. "No one's going to hurt you. I'll fucking kill anyone who tries."

EIGHT

THE ICY bottles of craft beer clinked against one another, a chiming counter beat to Dallas's footsteps across the moist, lush lawn. The grass gave beneath his feet, its fresh scent an odd brightness framing the cloying patches of heavy floral aromas interspersed in the muggy afternoon air. The city kept its distance, its bustle and clamor held back by a surround of chain-link fence and sparse evergreens, but tiny trickles of sound penetrated the quiet, bits of a world blunted by an expanse of lawn and trees.

He was always thankful for the wide-canopied tree and bench placed on the curve of the lawn. It made things... easier, calmer, and Dallas sank down onto the shadowed, cold stone seat and sighed, feeling every ache and stretch in his work-abused body. Bending over was nearly a mistake, because at some point since his last visit, the bench lost a mooring, and it rocked forward, not enough to do any damage but enough of a shift to make Dallas panic.

"Jesus. That'd be fantastic, me having to explain why I broke...." He paused, reading the name inscribed on the brass plaque mounted to the bench. "Joyce Whitamarker's bench. Hell, all this time and I haven't even thanked Joyce once." Popping open one of the cold bottles, Dallas smiled at the long hiss of air escaping out from under the dented cap, then saluted a passing cloud. "Thank you, Joyce. You've made my time here much more comfortable."

He risked another bend, lodging two of the bottles into the sprinkler-softened grass and dirt near his feet. There were leaves—there were always leaves—crisped from the hot sun and damp from the long-reaching spray heads used to water the grass.

Brushing bits of leaves and dots of moist soil aside, Dallas patted the engraved black stone in front of him and murmured, "Hello, Kevin."

They'd been casual but exclusive lovers for over a year, drifting toward something more serious when one Valentine's Day Kevin admitted to being married. An hour later, he'd bared his soul, revealing not only a perky blonde wife named Renee but also four little Kevins of varying sizes. Dallas spent the rest of the night numb, then drunk, once he'd gotten enough tequila in him to stand hearing Kevin's 3:00 a.m. voice mail apologizing for hurting Dallas... for leading him on... for needing to go back to his wife and try just one more time to be normal.

Seven months later, he'd gotten a call from a soft-spoken woman going through all of Kevin's phone numbers, reaching out to people he'd known to tell them he'd never woken up after a handful of pills with a fifth of bourbon chaser.

"Hey, looks like Andrew's mastered his *N*s." Dallas studied the arrangement of sheet protectors taped to the headstone, looking over a spelling test, an essay on batteries, and a crayon drawing of either a Pikachu or a duck with a serious case of shitting yellow feathers. "And I know you probably love your kid and all, but man, I've got to tell you, Stevie's got shit for artistic talent."

The carnations in the white vase permanently mounted to the base of the headstone were faded and a bit brown along the edges, but Dallas supposed that was more from the rolling heat waves striking the city rather than neglect. From what he could figure out, Renee came fairly often or timed her visits to hit right before Dallas's infrequent wanderings. He was pretty certain the beer he left every time he visited was picked up by the lawn crew and gone way before Kevin's wife could wonder who was leaving booze at her dead husband's grave, but it'd become a ritual of sorts, a remembrance of times they'd spent arguing about stouts versus IPAs.

Taking a swig of his beer, Dallas choked on the foamy liquid coating his throat. "God, I don't even really like pale ales. Why am I drinking this shit? Oh, and I'd tell you Celeste said hi, but see, I've never told her you did... this. And now it's like if I did, she'd feel like crap, and... fucking hell, how the hell do I get past one small not-truth? I'll tell her. I promise."

A bit of sun struck Kevin's gravestone, flashing on the mica specks in the black rock, and Dallas rested his elbows on his knees, cradling his beer between his legs, recalling his promise to always be there for Kevin despite everything between them. As Kevin'd promised to always be just a phone call away.

Dallas never made that phone call.

And now he was talking to a chunk of black stone, splattered with schoolwork and letters to a daddy who'd never, ever come home.

"Kind of a lot's happened since the last time, Kev." Dallas picked at a corner of the bottle's label, peeling back a bit of the top layer. "There's this guy... I met. Catholic, I think. What is it with you Catholic boys, huh? So many jokes I could make right now, but... hell, you'd just get pissed off if I start talking about priests."

Kevin always had been touchy about priest jokes, but Dallas told them anyway, sometimes just to see if he could make the man smile.

"His name's Jake. Well, Jacques. His mom was Canadian, and you can hear it sometimes when he talks. Especially when he's talking about her. Problem is, he's... got issues, man. Like serious fucking issues, and sometimes I look at him and I just want to... hold on to him. Make it all better for him." Dallas took another gulp of beer, hissing at its soft sting. "See, most people would think I come here to talk to you because, well, I've got a thing for you. Which I almost did. But we never got there, did we, Kev?"

A car drove by, burdened with a pair of stern-faced women who stared straight ahead, their eyes pinned to the winding cemetery road. He watched the vehicle go by, wondering how many times they'd driven to the middle of Los Angeles in their angry silence. One of the lawn men rode a tractor mower up over the sloped curb a few hundred yards away, kicking on the blades once he hit grass. It was a peaceful, lazy afternoon, the heat buffered by the sprinklers going off across the way and the tree—Joyce's tree—covering Dallas with its thick shade.

"See, Kev, about a week and a half ago, this guy—this incredibly gorgeous, sweet guy—told me he was gay. And he's scared and he hates being gay. Hates it with a passion because... well, I think for the same reasons you did. Someone made him feel dirty, fucked-up to the nth degree, and I'm so pissed off about it." The beer was beginning to taste good, a sure sign he should stop drinking it quickly or he'd have to run through the sprinklers to get it out of his system before he got into his car. "I see the pain in his eyes, like you had when you told me you were married and needed to go play house. God, I wanted to save you. I wanted to tell you not to go back because...."

"This." He slapped at the headstone, a hard, sharp sound, and his palm stung from the smack. "I can fucking feel this on him, and I'm fucking in love with the damned asshole. And I can't...."

Dallas's chest shook with his shuddering gasp, his heart seizing under his ribs. The reality of his feelings toward Jake stunned him. It was a lost cause, a kamikaze mission into a darkness he might not survive, but Dallas wanted to plunge deep into Jake and stay there, burning away the poison his family forced him to drink.

"I didn't want to fall for him. Fuck, I've never been in love, Kev. This thing I have with Jake, how I feel? I question it, you know? Because really, who the hell knows what love really is?" He sighed, rubbing his face to scrub off the doubts he had under his skin. "I think that's why I came here. To talk to you. Because you did something you didn't want to do because you loved your kids. You fucking loved your kids, but this didn't go away and...."

"I just want him to heal. Honestly. Even if he never even looks at me, even if he doesn't want me—Lana thinks he does, but she's... well... full of shit most of the time—I want him to be... okay." Dallas shook his head, throat closing with his rising emotions. "Truth here, Kev, I just want him to start living. Because he's... so fucking gorgeous inside. So goddamned beautiful, it makes me want to cry when I feel his soul flinch.

"So that's what's going on, Kev. I've landed in some kind of fucked-up Wonderland, and my Mad Hatter is really fucking torn up inside." He turned his head, drawn to the rattle of the mower coming closer. "I need to figure out how to make it work. How to help Jake not end up like you, Kev. I can't come to another graveyard and talk to a damned stone. Not his stone. It would fucking kill me, and then we'd all be here, sharing a bench at the worst croquet game ever."

The lawn guy turned around, lining the mower up with a stretch of grass several rows up from where Kevin lay. He'd avoid the grave and Dallas; that much Dallas knew after visiting Kevin before. The man nodded, straightening the mower, then chugged down the lawn. He slowed when he drew abreast of Dallas, bringing the tractor to a stop, and pulled his headphones from his ears.

"Hey, you the guy who keeps leaving beer here?" Shouting, the groundskeeper left the mower's engine running, but the blades were stilled, vibrating in time with the motor's rumbling.

"Yeah," Dallas replied, holding up what was left of his beer. "You the guy who keeps taking it?"

"Maybe." His smile could only be called shit eating where Dallas was from. "Just do me a favor. How about bringing round some normal beer instead? 'Cause it's not like he's going to drink it, and what you've been dropping off tastes like shit."

JAKE ROLLED his shoulders back, the slow ache forming in between his blades spreading out and grabbing his spine. His eyes hurt a bit, strained from chasing sparks and lines, but the twists of foraged aluminum and copper seemed to be holding. Brazing was difficult sometimes, and he tapped at the curls, waiting for the whole thing to tumble down to the ground.

He'd left the workshop's rolling doors open, hoping for any hint of a breeze to soften the heat trapped in the building, and there was a shift in the street noise as evening fell, the rumbling rasp of passing cars and foot traffic slowing down to a trickle, then silence, except for the occasional chug of an engine rumbling by. Light shifted around him, dimming as businesses around the fabrication shop closed, but the distant scrape of chairs and rattle of crockery kept him company as the twenty-four-hour coffee shop a few doors down kept up a brisk business on its patio, a busker serenading customers from a corner spot under an awning.

It was late, probably heading around the hump of the night and curving up into double digits, and Jake hummed along with a tune coming from the musician's acoustic guitar, walking around the sculpture he'd cobbled together from the shop's scraps. The bin full of pieces had taunted him for a week, and Jake mentally calculated how much it would cost him to buy the cuttings before his boss kicked at the large container and told Jake in his thick Ukrainian accent to lock up when he was done fucking with whatever he cobbled out of the mess left for him.

And when Raoul made sucking noises behind Jake's back, Jake simply flipped him off and pocketed the shop's keys.

There were possibilities in the tangle of metal Evancho left for him, shapes teasing him with their long lines and liquid forms. It would be a woman's shape, something barely hinted at perhaps and perfect for Bombshells' reception area, or so he hoped.

"Something right for the time period," he murmured to himself, pulling up the shield on his mask so he could look at the form he'd tentatively built out. "And... drag queens. Definitely... drag queens."

It'd been a long, hard week. Shuffling between Dallas's building during the day and a few hours at Evancho's doing fine metalwork the boss didn't trust anyone else to do. He'd finished the massive gate piece destined for a driveway no one would ever see, but the delicate rose-and-lily scrollwork was finally completed, and he'd done one last check to make sure both sides matched before leaving the twelve-foot-wide work for Evancho to inspect in the morning.

A thin strain of slightly out-of-tune guitar strings chased down a few lines of a song, a young man's unsteady voice valiantly fighting to hit the husky dive in one of Jake's favorite songs. He winced when the strumming went wild, then sighed at a missed line in the chorus. He hummed along anyway, filling in the words he knew and mumbling through the ones he—and the busker—couldn't remember.

"Probably one of their harder songs," someone said behind him, and Jake nearly jumped out of his skin. "I can never tell if I'm supposed to be angry or sad listening to it."

"Jesus fucking Christ!" Jake spun about, one hand clenched tightly around a thick metal rod. Dallas stepped back, his hands raised defensively, and Jake lowered his arm. "Sorry.... Dallas. You just—"

"Scared the shit out of you." Dallas's smile was a heartbreak waiting to happen. Up close, there were teeth and laughing eyes... and an artlessness to his disarming shrug. "Sorry. I came by to grab Celeste's purse because she left it in the bathroom. Evancho's got you working late here after dealing with my stuff all day?"

"No, I finished up Evancho's stuff a while back. I'm working on my own stuff now." Jake lightly kicked the bin of scraps. "When the discard bin's full, he usually lets me buy it to take home and work. I wanted to do something... heavier, so he told me I could have this corner of the shop for a couple of months, but I don't know. I think I need to just take all this stuff home and hammer at it there."

"Couple of months seems like a long time to be working on something… said the man whose windows are going to take another three weeks. Still, seems… long." He whistled softly, circling the bin, then looked up, the stark light from the shop's overhead fluorescents marbling Dallas's face with streaks of white and shadow. "I have no idea what you're talking about or what I'm looking at. Clue me in, J."

"I do… sculptures sometimes, mostly at home. Just to play with. Nothing… major. Scrap metal because the shit's expensive, but junkyards are a good place to get stuff." He shrugged at Dallas's appreciative smile. "Harder now because they're paying people for scrap, so I've got to get there before someone cleans out a place. I know a few guys who'll hold things for me until I get there to look through what someone dropped off. Evancho… I don't know… he told me to just take what's here, so…."

"But you're looking kind of confused." Another circle, this time around the framing Jake'd thrown together so he could get an idea of how the piece would work. Sketches were all well and good, but he never knew how something would look from all angles until he did a scaffolding. "You don't like this?"

"It's okay. It's just so I can look at it and see how it flows in real life. How the angles work." Nodding to the sheaf of curling papers on his workbench, he laughed. "Things can look great in pencil. Then when I pull things together, it goes shitty real fast. It's like a three-dimensional rough sketch. That's all."

"So you built this here and now want to take it home?" Dallas's confused scowl twisted his mouth into a moue, and Jake forced his attention away from the man's face and back to the form.

"All of it, including the bin. I don't feel…." It was hard to explain what he felt. There were too many complications with working at the shop, but Dallas looked like he was expecting more than what Jake was giving him. "It's too… personal, you know? I think that's the biggest reason. It's not the only one, but definitely the biggest. And there's other guys who work here, guys who don't get special assignments or Evancho giving them free shit. I don't want them to feel like—"

"Like crap. No, no. I get it. Totally get that." Any more of Dallas's grins and Jake was sure something in him was going to burst. "You going to take this home now? I was going to see if you wanted to grab some food, but I can help you get this stuff moved if you want."

And suddenly there was panic.

No, not panic, he decided after poking at the tightness in his belly and the freefall of his emotions before they turned into red-hot pinballs careening around inside of his chest. What he was feeling was something else, something darker or more exhilarating than panic. An anxiety of some sort chopped in with a desire to bring Dallas to the place he laid himself open to bleed or cry. It was asking for more than sex, especially not the mindless, body-purging fucking he'd had in the past. Dallas's casual, nonchalant offer was a door to a part of Jake's life he'd never shared with anyone before, and he wasn't so certain he was ready for it now.

Everything in Jake screamed at him to say no. His broken, fucked-up life was in that four-walled brick shithole. There was nothing there to offer, nothing Dallas would want behind that humidity-swollen door. He'd cowered there, marinating in his own sweat and fears, painting the apartment's mortared walls with the reek of his existence, and Dallas simply wanted to walk in, carting with him metal offal Jake hoped to turn into something beautiful.

He was frightened. No other way Jake could look at it. He was scared of… what Dallas would see, how he would be seen. It wasn't about how run down the place was or how cobbled together he lived, it was about Dallas walking into the long stretch of space and seeing the thing Jake was pulling out of his depths and forming out of metal and captured lightning.

"Hey, we don't do anything you don't want to do, J." Dallas was nearer, reaching out for him, his fingertips on Jake's shoulder. Again with the touching, forever with the tactile stroking, but Dallas's skin on his felt… right, a drench of soothe over the heat rash of Jake's panic. "No harm, no foul, okay?"

"No, it's…." He quirked his mouth, debating what to say, then finally settled on the blunt, bald truth.

This was Dallas. He was safe with Dallas, and for the first time in his life since that night, Jake was tired of hiding and worn-out from walling himself away. He wanted to breathe and to laugh and maybe, just maybe one day be kissed by another man. And God, he wanted that kiss to come from Dallas.

"I've never had anyone over," he murmured softly, startlingly aware of the drift of Dallas's fingers over his shoulder and the flecks of cobalt in the other man's gaze. "Ever. It's where I—"

"It's where you're actually you." Dallas nodded. "I get that. I do."

He could study Dallas's face forever, drinking in the play of emotions through the subtle shifts of his skin and flesh. It would be enough for him. Jake knew that even as he was too paralyzed by the shit in his brain to take the first step toward being someone other than Ron Moore's disgusting, perverted little boy.

"But you know, Dallas," Jake continued, patting Dallas's hand on his arm, "I'd like you to be the first."

NINE

THERE WAS a glorious tumble of stars caught in a cosmic storm sitting right in the middle of Jake's brick-walled apartment.

It snagged Dallas as soon as he went through the door, hands full with a heavy bin of metal tidbits, and his attention more focused on Jake's firm ass than anything else. The long, narrow main room—true to its industrial roots—was a step down from the street, and he tripped over his own expectation of an even surface, nearly face-planting into the sealed cement floor. He pulled the bin up against his chest right before it tumbled with him, then dropped it anyway when Jake's flight of fancy grabbed him by the balls and stole his mind.

He'd grown up around artists, or at least people his mother dragged home with slight inclinations toward ceramics, macramé, and sculpting. There was the odd musician, and once a man who made baby dolls out of shit—any kind of shit—which prompted Dallas's dad to kick him off the ranch when he found the guy eyeball-deep in the old septic tank behind the barn.

Much like her cooking, his mother's tastes in artistic expression ran to the mediocre, where participation was as good as a masterpiece. He'd drawn the line at her friends' projects decorating his room, especially after watching the trash-bag hammock installation put up in Austin's bathroom as a protest to corporations' misuse of public lands.

Jake's sculpture—his pouring of his soul into shapes and curves—would blow her mind.

It towered over him by a few feet, swirling up toward the very high ceiling, and the room's lights played with the whorls' edges, throwing rainbow dapples over Dallas as he walked around the piece. He couldn't figure out what he was looking at, drawing deeper into the lines shaped out of what looked like silver but firmer and sharper in tone.

The piece was definitely a storm, an epic battle of matter and void, balancing precariously on the edge of a twisted churn of metal. It was a slice of chaos, bursts of energy exploding outward to splatter the viewer with an unimaginable power except… for the cage around it.

It took Dallas a good minute to realize why he felt so… disquieted by the structure. It was a celebration of expansion and energized motion, but instead it infused him with a sense of being contained. The longer he studied the work, the feeling of being trapped grew, raking a subtle prickle over his thoughts. He couldn't shake the sensation, and he stepped back, trying to find the disconnect between himself and Jake's sculpture when it hit him. The fine threads of silvery filament swirling around the upward fling of metal spurs and mesh storm formed a partially open net around the piece, subtly creating a barrier between the storm and the viewer.

"Shit," Dallas whispered, barely aware of a metallic clatter to his right. "Fuck me, it's…. Jake."

The revelation struck him as hard as the piece itself. He now understood what Jake meant about intimate. The sculpture peeled apart Jake, exposing how he felt about life and the surging need to be free of the cage he'd been put in. Staring into the worked metal shapes discomforted him. Standing in front of Jake's stark, hard mental prison beaten and forged into physical form dug into Dallas. It brought Jake's torn soul to life and laid him out for all to see.

Dallas was torn between covering the piece with a blanket so he wouldn't have to share Jake or turning around and giving the man a fierce hug, then never letting him go.

"You okay?" Jake's rough voice pulled at Dallas, shocking him with its rolling warmth. "Dallas? What's wrong?"

Everything was wrong. As beautiful as Jake's work was, what Dallas felt from it rubbed hard on every tender bit he had. His soul smarted where he'd shoved his fondness for Jake, hoping he could ignore his rapid-fire pulse and stomach butterflies every time Jake was near. Friendship was what he offered. It was all he could give Jake. All he should give Jake because that's what was needed the most. Dallas knew that. He knew Jake needed a friend more than he needed anything else, but still, the part that wept at the base of Jake's artwork screamed to protect Jake from any more pain.

"Yeah, um… shit, sorry." Jerked out of the sculpture, Dallas stumbled back, striking his heel on the bin he'd dropped. "I… um… the door…."

"No, I'm sorry." He flashed Dallas a rueful smile. "That's my fault. Should have told you there was a step down."

Standing in a now-open slender bay door with his backed-in truck idling behind him, Jake was a mouthwatering vision framed by the light coming off the street behind him. His jeans were slung low on his hips, a little too big for his narrow waist, and his T-shirt rode up on one side, giving Dallas a hint of a tight, muscled stomach and a deep V cut angling toward his powerful thighs. He was a bit grimy from a long day spent working, and his dark hair stood up over his forehead, probably from Jake's habit of running his hand through it while he contemplated how to do something.

Dallas was familiar with that habit, as well as a few others. The hair tugging was usually accompanied by Jake biting at his lower lip, his hazel eyes glazing over while his mind turned over, then rejected possible solutions. He tapped his pencil or pen on walls or pads of paper when frustrated, sometimes chewing on the end of an eraser only to spit out tiny bits once he realized what he'd done.

And the one Dallas loved the most, the soft contented sigh Jake made when something he envisioned turned out exactly the way he'd imagined.

There were slices of his heart hoping for a day when he'd bring Jake to that sighing contentment, hopefully with their bodies drenched with sweat and aching from a long, languid stretch of muscles and pleasure. As hard as Dallas tried to keep those whispers as forcefully boxed in as Jake's star-glutted storm, they kept slithering out, reminding him they were there with a clench of his throat or a tight ball of want in his belly.

"Not for you," he reminded himself with a dark mutter. "Not—"

"I think I'll be able to get the frame in, but if you can grab the other bin, I'll be able to move the truck out of the way. Building manager doesn't like me parked up on the sidewalk for some reason." Jake grunted, wrestling with the metal scaffolding he'd cobbled together at Evancho's. His arms bulged, straining his T-shirt when he hefted the framework, lifting it from the truck bed.

"Shit, let me help you." Dallas leapt over the bin, hurrying over to the open tailgate before Jake could pull the frame out any farther. His shoulder nudged into Jake's, their sides brushing several times as they began to unload the piece. "Where are we going?"

"Over there. That table." Jake grunted again, a whistle of air followed by a huff. "Fuck, tailgate caught me on the leg. I've got that side. I'll go backward. Just tell me when to stop."

The walk was awkward, a few missteps, then a cloud of laughter when Dallas got his foot stuck in the bucket Jake'd left on the floor. Positioned on the table, the frame rocked a little but steadied when Jake shoved a block of wood under one end, mumbling something about a stand or a base.

"It looks like… I don't know." Dallas tilted his head, seeing a hint of something in the curves Jake had quickly soldered together. "Like… is it a woman? It is, isn't it? Like a pinup. She's got that… 'paint me on the side of a plane and send me off to war with your boys' kind of pose."

Jake stared at the frame, seemingly stunned, then whispered, "Crap, I know what to do with this now."

When Jake's following silence stretched a bit too long, Dallas glanced over at him, not surprised to see Jake raking his hand through his hair. Endearing but frustrated, Jake shot him an apologetic grin, his dimples deepening, then cleared his throat. The desperate look on Jake's face was a priceless struggle between politeness and obsession. A fervor ran through him, one Dallas recognized instantly. Jake was itching to work, probably on the frame they'd brought in, and Dallas sighed, pretending to be frustrated only to get Jake going.

"Um… can you give me a minute? Just one minute," Jake begged softly in his husky, sinfully rough voice. "One. Maybe two."

"Don't worry about me. You go and—"

"There's beer in the fridge. And some cider. Really, not long. I've just got that one part figured out." Jake cut him off and reached for a black composition book sitting on the table, then grabbed a pencil. From the disconnected haziness in Jake's expression, Dallas knew he'd lost Jake to the tumbling ideas knitting together in his mind.

"And Jake has left the building." The urge to nudge Jake was strong, probably a leftover reaction following years of being a little brother. Even if none of the feelings he had for Jake were even remotely brotherly, he'd grown to enjoy the playful irritation he could bring out of Jake with a little teasing. "You go be… creative. I'm going to pick up the shit I dropped."

Dallas crouched over the bin, sliding the fallen pieces back in, then retrieved the other one out of the truck. After stacking everything together, he closed the tailgate, then contemplated Jake's hunched shoulders and bent back, his hand scribbling furiously over a page. Glancing up at the trapped star-cloud one last time, Dallas stared at the ass end of Jake's truck and the open rolling door it blocked.

"Okay, building guy doesn't like trucks on the sidewalk, but shit, Jake's the only one on this side of the building. Does it really matter? So, move the truck? Don't move the truck?" Asking Jake would jerk him out of whatever he was working on, and Dallas rather enjoyed the passion roiling through the man's body while he sketched. "Well, back home, you just don't drive a man's truck. Not so sure what the rules are here in SoCal, but I'm willing to bet, still a sacred thing. Let's just turn the thing off and close it up. Someone wants it moved, we'll move it."

He shut off the engine and closed the truck's solid tailgate, almost pocketing the keys before remembering they were Jake's. Another grunt from Jake gave Dallas carte blanche to bring him a beer or put the keys in the fridge, Dallas couldn't tell which, but the beer sounded great. So did collapsing on the enormous beaten-up couch sitting next to a coffee table on the other side of the long space.

But the urge to poke around was growing stronger with every moment he spent inside Jake's place. The kitchen was a good place to start, mostly because he was warm and there'd been a promise of something cold to drink in the middle of all of Jake's mutterings about lines and pressure points.

"There's a reason you get other people to do the reno." He groaned at the ache in his thighs when he banged his knee into the metal leg of Jake's Formica table. "Because it beats the shit out you. Get the beer. Then maybe sit. Man, this place is stuffy, but the space is awesome."

He liked the brick. It was warm and in some places more honey than red. More importantly, there seemed to be a ton of books, sketchpads, and oddly sized sculptural pieces everywhere. The long room had a softness to it. Despite the spill of metal and welders taking up half the space, Jake's place had a gentleness to it Dallas enjoyed.

"Probably projecting, Yates." He risked a glance at Jake, wondering if he'd mind if Dallas poked at the bookshelves for a bit. Curiosity would not only kill the cat but strangle Dallas on its way out, his mother was fond of saying, and standing in the middle of Jake's apartment, the urge to investigate every square inch overwhelmed him. "First, to the fridge."

The beer was an odd collection of fancy microbrews, ciders, and a single dark stout, leaving Dallas with a wish he'd thought to stop by a store and grab some food to put in the fridge before he'd headed over. He'd been too excited, too thrilled to see Jake's space, and as silly as it sounded—as it seemed in his mind—the stuffy, kind of worn around the edges felt more like home than the sparkling modern apartment he'd purchased twenty floors above LA's busy streets. He grabbed a couple of blue-labeled glass bottles, closed the fridge, then popped them open.

"Beer." Dallas nudged Jake's side when he left an open bottle of Primo on the long worktable. "Don't knock it over."

"Almost done," Jake promised softly, his eyes never leaving the paper. "I just… almost done."

"Take your time, J. Mind if I look around?"

He got a rumble from Jake, and Dallas took it as a yes.

As much as he wanted to, Dallas refused to look at the sketches scattered over the tabletop, and God, he wanted to. It was one thing to see the piece Jake had standing in the middle of his work area but quite another thing to peer over his shoulder. The rawness in Jake's face was… erotic, a glimmer of something special and wonderful Dallas didn't have the right to plunge into. After patting Jake on the shoulder, he went back to the beat-up couch and took in all he could of Jake from the space around him.

He could hear the city seeping through the now cranked-open windows. It had taken him a minute to figure out how the windows worked, but once he had, they moved smoothly, letting the somewhat cooling air outside into the humid apartment. Now with a slight breeze blowing and a promise of a brisk morning in the air, the place was rather nice.

The furniture looked rescued, more frat house than *Better Homes & Gardens*, but it suited Jake. Unpretentious, serviceable, and clean, with the living area laid open to the workspace and flowing straight into a sleeping space dominated by what looked like a soft king-sized bed with rumpled sheets Dallas's brain reminded him would smell of Jake. Dallas put the bed—and its Jake-wrinkled linens—into the back of his mind, where he kept the memory of his mother's horrific attempt at corn chowder and the time he'd splashed astringent on his freshly shaved balls on a dare.

"You've done some stupid things, Yates," he grumbled, wandering over to look at the bookcases lined up on the long wall. "Let's not add another one to the list tonight."

"Almost done... I feel like I'm losing this idea. Almost," Jake promised again. Dallas kept his chuckle to himself right up until the moment Jake's head jerked up and he swore, "Shit! The truck. I've got to move it—"

"Keys are on the table. Right next to... I'm assuming that weird thing you've got holding your napkins is a flamingo," Dallas called out, cocking his head to read the titles of the books on the shelves. It was an odd mix with a few surprising choices. Tugging at the top of a tall, slim volume, Dallas tried to extract the book from its tight prison. "Huh, who the hell owns an actual paperback of *Buckaroo Banzai*?"

The truck started, a chum of rattles and roars, when Dallas finally got the book loose and started an avalanche of novels, knickknacks, and a wooden box Jake'd lodged in sideways between some cookbooks and a retrospective of Middle Eastern metalwork. Panic made Dallas grab the first thing he could, snatching an old chisel out of the air before it struck the floor.

"Crap, not the box."

It was too late to grab the small wooden rectangle, but he tried anyway, lunging a bit too far and throwing himself off-balance. He got the corner of it, and it tumbled sideways, bouncing off the back of the couch. Then its lid flew open, spilling everything inside to the floor.

Something hard and solid struck the cement, then skittered across the floor, coming to a rest at Dallas's feet. His heart stopped, and the warm laughter in his throat turned to sharp-edged ice he couldn't swallow to save his life.

A gun. A handgun at that. Not something he'd ever have thought Jake would own. Not uncommon, especially considering where Dallas grew up, but still, not something he'd have placed in Jake's possession. The area once was a flashpoint for a horrendous riot, but that'd been decades ago. Koreatown was now an urban sprawl with gentile and familial leanings, not the hotspot of potential violence it'd once been.

If anything, the gun felt as personal as the sculpture, and Dallas felt dirty handling it, as if he were eavesdropping on Jake's secrets. Bending down, he picked up the gun as Jake walked through the still open rolling door.

"Hey, sorry. I—" Jake came to a dead stop when Dallas straightened, holding the gun up, its muzzle pointed to the floor.

The apology in Dallas's mouth never left his tongue, his words frozen at the sight of Jake trembling in place. The blood left Jake's face, and he swayed, stepping back either in fear or shock. Dallas placed the weapon on the couch's arm, lifting his hand away from it for Jake to see. He'd grown up around guns. Anyone who lived on a ranch as a kid had to at least know which end was dangerous, but he hadn't figured Jake for someone who'd want one, much less keep one in a box, hidden away between books.

Jake was terrified, and Dallas feared he was the one who'd put that fear inside those big hazel eyes.

"Hey, I was looking at the books and…." Dallas struggled to get his words out past the odd squeeze in his lungs. "I just knocked the box off the shelf and it fell out. I'm really sorry. I mean, I shouldn't have—"

"Jesus, Dallas, the damned thing's loaded," Jake blurted out, and his hands shook when he put them on his thighs, then bent over, hyperventilating slightly. "God, you could have—fuck… you could have died."

"Hey, Jake, it's okay. Come on, they don't just go off like they do in the movies, but still… I'm kind of used to having you around." He walked around the couch, reaching for Jake, but he pulled away, his back heaving with every struggling breath. "The loaded part isn't okay because that's not smart to do. Something could happen and things could go south fast. Suppose someone breaks in? I don't want someone to kill you with your own gun, J."

Jake looked up, his lip bloodied where he'd bitten it. His face was bloodless and drawn, and he struggled, spitting out each word as if speaking hurt. "See, that's the thing, Dallas. That's what the gun is for. To kill me."

TEN

HE WAS falling apart, tiny ashen flakes of Jake carried off on the shifting breeze, his charred core disintegrating with the weight of Dallas's worry.

The couch was a drifting raft of sanity in the churning tempest of Jake's mind, manned by a cross-legged Dallas with gentle, too-warm hands on Jake's thigh. His body thirsted for Dallas's touch, burning with need under his jeans, and despite the achingly tight clench of worry and panic in his chest, his heart skipped and sang when Dallas inched closer, his knees brushing Jake's leg.

"I want to be this guy who waits and doesn't push, Jake," Dallas finally murmured. "But this time, babe, I'm going to push. Talk to me about the gun and then tell me what we're going to do about it."

His voice was harsh, worn, and strained. Jake couldn't risk looking at him. He was afraid of what he'd find in Dallas's face. So many possibilities, but most of all, disgust and disappointment.

It'd been easier when he only had to worry about his father dying, and then… the abyss of his life yawned before him, a darkness filled with uncertainty and loneliness. Now there were… people…. Dallas… for God's sake, and now Jake didn't know what to do, how to feel, and Dallas's fingers stroking his leg made it hard for him to think.

"Fucking talk to me, Jake," Dallas insisted. "I just can't… stand the thought of you doing this. Doing that. How bad is it, J? Am I a problem? Do I—"

"No, not you!" Jake gulped, swallowing air. Fucking hell, Dallas was the only bright spot in his life at the moment, and as much as he wanted to draw closer, he feared Dallas would pull away. "No, you're not what's wrong. It's… I don't even know where to start."

Dallas's pale eyes crinkled, a soft smile lifting his mouth and plumping his cheeks. His gentle tone coaxed but held a bit of steel, hammered down and unyielding in case Jake feinted. "Start with the gun. And why. After that, we'll figure out where it goes."

He kept his eyes fixed on the porcelain penguin salt and pepper shakers sitting on the dining table. It helped not to watch Dallas, not to want to crawl into his lap or arms. Keeping his eyes on the penguins, Jake noticed a tiny chip on Salt's beak, a little pink discoloration where the ceramic came through, and Jake briefly wondered if he'd done it or if it'd come that way.

They'd been his mother's, bought for a birthday or a Christmas when Jake'd been a kid. He'd mowed lawns and washed cars for a couple of months to buy her something nice. He remembered that part of it. He'd thought they were clever, his eight- or nine-year-old mind amused by a pair of black-and-white birds being used for black-and-white condiments. She'd had no particular love for penguins, but she'd exclaimed over them, murmuring in French and petting his hair back. There'd been a moment of innocent joy, and he'd held on to those shakers after selling off practically everything else to pay his father's mounting bills.

Practically everything. He'd also kept all her books and more importantly, the gun his father'd hidden in a closet, tucked away in a wooden box Dallas eventually tumbled to the floor.

"I found the gun when I was clearing out the house. Things were getting too tight, and I wasn't bringing in enough money to pay for the mortgage, and... shit. Then Dad got really bad. So I sold a lot of it, but I kept the gun." He sighed heavily. The words leaving him were razors, slicing the soft tissues in his throat on their way out. "It just seemed.... I couldn't let it go. I found it, in that box, and my mouth itched.

"I... I wanted to die that night, when I came home after... fuck." He was going to have to go back... back to the beginning, and he didn't know if he could. "The gun... everything... everything went to shit when I... thought I could be gay. Outside, you know? Away from my parents. Away from... my mother. But it didn't work like that, Dallas. It never works like that. No matter how much you want something to remain a secret, it always comes out."

He was stretched too thin and overworked to the point of shattering if the slightest touch would undo him. Where he'd wanted Dallas to hold him before, Jake longed to put some distance between them, the recollection of that night creeping up on him, peeling away the walls he'd put up to nurture what little control he had left.

"Come here," Dallas murmured, reaching for him, then stopping when Jake shook his head. "What? You need someone, Jake. You—"

"You touch me and I'll… break." The painful ember in his soul flared, eating away at him again, and Jake tasted a sourness in his mouth as his stomach rebelled, kicking up a bilious storm. He turned, pulling his legs up so he could sit facing Dallas. "I just need to get through this. To tell you. I've never told anyone, and fuck, I still don't know if I can do this, say this. But I owe you, you know? At least…. God, you could have been hurt… died… because I have that damned gun here."

"You don't owe me anything, Jake." This time Dallas refused to let Jake push him away, gathering him into his arms and pulling him off-balance into an odd, awkward sideways hug. "But you owe yourself everything. Including some peace. You want to talk it out? I'm here. You just want to sit here and get drunk? I'll do that with you too. You want to be alone? Well, okay, that you're not getting, but the rest of it, all yours. Just… tell me what you want, what you need."

"I need you, and I'm fucking scared as hell," Jake stammered out, and Dallas drew back enough to cup his face. He was crying again—still—and Dallas's tender kiss across his forehead only made the blubbering worse. "Don't… I can't… I just feel like I'm about to crack open."

Dallas dropped his hands from Jake's face, resting them on his shoulders. "Then tell me about the gun, J. Tell me what happened back then, and let's figure out where to go from there."

Shame drowned his face in red, the sluice of humiliation and regret stinging his conscience working its way across his cheeks. His body ached from the memory of that night, the beating he'd taken from his father, then the screaming match hot on its heels. He'd run, determined to be… anything other than what he'd left behind in that house, but it'd all gone wrong. So damned wrong, and no matter how much he prayed, nothing could ever change what happened that night. But here was Dallas, asking him to probe old wounds, hoping to prick the festering blister of his memories to help him heal.

There'd be no healing. There couldn't be.

Then came Dallas's husky whisper, "Jake… please."

God, he'd do anything for Dallas, even if it meant slicing himself open until he bled to death. Jake knew he'd give Dallas anything he wanted, even if it meant losing him.

"It was stupid, you know? I met a guy—a teacher—at a coffee shop near school. He was… older, and he flirted a bit. I didn't even know what to say. I wasn't… I'd been out to clubs a bit when I'd moved away, but after I came back home, I couldn't risk it. But I guess I figured no one would find out; no one would know because it was so damned far away from everything. No one would know, right?

"So we'd meet for coffee or lunch and talk about stupid things like what I was taking, because I'd transferred back to be closer to home since my dad was getting sicker. He… this guy… taught literature, nothing I was going to take. But it was nice just talking to someone who knew what I was going through." Jake grimaced at the fumbling idiot he'd been then. "I'd talk to him on the phone sometimes. Usually at night when Mom was asleep, but he called one afternoon to ask me if I wanted to go to a party that night. And… she heard me."

"Did she know you were gay?" Dallas leaned in, strengthening their contact with a casual brush of his hand over Jake's forearm.

"She kind of knew? Maman would make these comments about how homosexuals were Satan's creatures and how I had to fight any kind of feelings I'd have for another man. She spent a lot of time praying over me—hell, I can't tell you how many priests she'd asked to say a blessing over me so I wouldn't lose my way." His nose was stuffy, and Jake's head began to throb, but he kept going, unable to stop the torrent of words flowing from him. "She was… angry. That's not even describing it. We fought a little bit. Then my dad came into my bedroom, and… he was still bigger than me then. I hadn't… I was smaller, and the next thing I knew he was beating me with the buckle end of his belt. And my mother… she didn't step in."

"Did she try to stop him? Before that night?" Dallas asked gently, prodding at the edges of Jake's pain.

"Always." Once breached, the river of pain and sorrow seemed determined to gush out, drowning them both. "She always tried to stop him, but not then. There were so many… she couldn't stand to look at me, Dallas. The things she said—she told me she hated me. That God hated me and I'd die alone, because men like me were sick and perverted. That she hoped I'd get sick and die because that's what I deserved for…. God, I couldn't listen to it anymore."

"She probably didn't realize she was saying them." He tried to reassure Jake, but his words did little to soothe the wounds left in Jake's heart. "People say crazy things when they're mad. She didn't mean them. You've got to know that, J."

"See, the thing is I, won't ever know because I left. I grabbed some of my stuff and thought I'd go over to Prescott's place and... I don't know, stay there? I wasn't thinking straight. I know that now, but then, I guess I thought I was in love with him." Jake tugged on his lower lip, dropping his eyes down before he continued. "It was late, and I was.... The party was going on, and he was so damned glad to see me. I just wanted to be kind of normal. Just once. I didn't want to feel dirty or sick."

"That's not bad, Jake. It's not." Dallas nodded, then murmured, "What happened after? At the party?"

"I...." Jake couldn't swallow any more tears. He was awash in salt and numb from the revisiting of a night he'd sooner forget. His mind recoiled, reeling from the echoes of his assaulted flesh and then the shock of discovering he meant nothing to the one person he'd stupidly believed cared for him. "I got drunk at the party, and I figured, what the hell? I was so pissed off, and I wanted to feel.... I went with Prescott into his bedroom. I knew what he wanted, and I thought I... I don't know what exactly.... Maybe I just wanted to see what it was like. But it... he... hurt. I couldn't get him to stop, and then there was...."

There'd been blood. Not a lot but enough for Jake's panic to wrap around his throat and smother him. Prescott insisted it would be okay, that the apprehension Jake felt was normal. He was nervous because it would be his first time with a man and those kinds of things always hurt in the beginning. It'd never stopped hurting, and he'd tried to get free, to push away from Prescott, but by the time Jake'd fought his way loose, it was too late.

The screaming began nearly as soon as Jake kicked Prescott off the bed and onto the floor. His clothes were buried under the bed's linens, and Prescott was up onto his feet, screaming about stupid virgins and teases. Jake'd tried to forget the battling run through the crowded apartment and the smug laughter he'd heard when he'd pushed past someone. They'd known what Prescott led him into that room for and mocked Jake with each step he took toward the front door. He'd fled to the one place he thought he'd be safe. Despite the anger and betrayal he'd felt toward his mother, he'd gone home to her, hoping for solace and forgiveness.

Instead he found only an ocean of blood and a hole in his life where his mother'd been.

"My father was killing her while Prescott… the sex we had… hurt me. She was dying while he was shoving his dick into me, not hearing me cry… not stopping when I'd begged him to. He just told me it was how things were and I'd get used to it. I'd wanted him bad enough to toss away my family and he…. Jesus I was stupid," Jake choked out, digging the heels of his hands into his eyes. "I should have been there. I should have stopped him, but instead I was so fucking full of myself and… she died, Dallas. He took her from me because… he couldn't stand what I was and lashed out at the one person he could. It should have been me on that kitchen floor. It should have been my head he bashed in. Not hers. She didn't… deserve to die like that."

"God, Jake… no. That wasn't your fault. None of this…." This time he let Dallas grab him up, falling into the man's arms and clinging to Dallas's warm body as if he would drown in his own tears if he let go. "None of what happened that night was on you. You've got to understand that. That asshole should have…. Oh God, baby."

His body rocked with his sobs, jerking quakes strong enough to rattle his bones loose and threaten to tear his spine free from its moorings. Dallas fit him into the curve of his body, molding Jake to his chest. He let go, releasing everything he'd been holding in, his skin as cold as the dried blood he'd scraped off the kitchen floor once the cops let them go back into the house. His bones were iced over, his muscles rigid when his shock at what he'd done struck him anew.

His strangled screams tore through his sobs, and Jake clenched the couch's soft cushions, fearful he'd strike Dallas when his emotions scuttled him, taking him back down into their redolent depths. Jake couldn't hold anything else in, and he gasped, struggling to swallow the damning words caught under his anguish.

"I knew as soon as I saw him… as soon as that fucker came stumbling out of the hospital room where they'd taken him… I knew he'd killed her," Jake hiccuped, arching into Dallas's touch when he stroked small circles across Jake's back. "He smiles, this sick secret grin, like he's giggling and being so fucking clever. Taunted me as the cops fussed over him like he was a weak old man. He was strong then. He had spells, but most of the time he was strong enough to hurt her... hurt me. Then a little bit later, he went... when his brain was slipping around inside of his head, he told me what he'd done, and... I wanted to take that gun of his and blow his brains out."

"I'd hate to visit you in prison, J." Dallas attempted a teasing smile, but it faded before it took hold. "You said the gun was... for you, J. What—"

"I've spent so much damned time waiting for him to die. He got so sick after, I thought he was going to die because of what he'd done... to Maman, but instead his mind started to go and he would talk, sometimes to me... sometimes to people who weren't in the room, but that's how I found out. About what he'd done." Jake exhaled, unsteady and his skull felt too tight around his brain. "When I was a kid, she'd begged me to take care of him, if something happened to her. She was so scared of getting sick, of dying before he did because... for everything he'd done to her... to me... she loved him. Probably told him she loved him as he was killing her.

"The gun wasn't for him. It wasn't. I kept it because when I picked it up, I wanted to make everything go away, and it seemed like... salvation," Jake confessed. "I wanted to make the pain inside of me stop. I could taste the gun in my mouth, Dallas. I knew what metal tasted like, and I wanted it on my tongue like I was addicted to it. I wanted to hear the click of the trigger and then taste the gunpowder right before that bullet broke through the roof of my mouth. And I want that every day, Dal. Every single damned day I come home and want to taste that bitter, hot blood so I can let everything go. I've got nothing... no one... except for that fucking old man."

"You've got me, Jake," Dallas whispered. "You're not alone. Not now. And I'm trying really hard not to... fuck, Jake, you're so damned gorgeous. You make me crazy, and you make me laugh, and I feel so damned empty when you're not around. I'm trying hard to be just your friend because that's what you need, someone to be here with you when the shit starts to swallow you up. It would fucking kill me if you weren't here. You're worth more than... anything. I need to feel your smiles against my soul, and I hate you can't see that.

"Fuck it, Jake. Punch me if you want, but I've got to do this," Dallas growled, cupping Jake's jaw with one hand, then leaned in to steal Jake's breath away.

The kiss was a salty mess of desperate hope and anguished longing. Their mouths were angled wrong, fumbling clumsily and sliding, more a smear of flesh than a long, lingering succulent brush of soft lips, but Jake caught Dallas's sigh on his tongue and swallowed it, refusing to throw away the sweetest kiss he'd ever had.

It lasted only a moment, not long enough for Jake to have more than a whispering taste of Dallas, but it was enough. The craving for the gun's acrid kiss was gone, swept away by a more powerful longing and a pair of hooded, sensual eyes the color of a sun-drenched sky.

"You can punch me now"—Dallas's voice broke, crackling around his words—"if you want, but you've got to know, you are worth so damned much. To me. To everyone who knows you. I'm scared to death for you, but seriously, punch away."

"I don't. Want to punch you, I mean," Jake admitted softly, resting his forehead against Dallas's, breathing in the scent of their mingled heat. His blood skipped and skidded, his thoughts tangled in on each other, and Jake struggled to find words among the screaming need coursing through his body. "I need... I don't know what I need, Dallas. I don't know what I'm doing anymore, and I'm scared."

"First thing Monday morning, you are going to get on the phone," Dallas replied, his breath ruffling Jake's eyelashes. "And you're going to find someone to talk to. Someone who can help you work through all of this, and I promise you this, Jacques Moore; I will be with you every step of the way. Because you're stuck with me now. No matter what, no matter what we become, I will be here with you. Because I don't want to live in a world without you in it. Might as well take away the fucking sun and stars, because my life will be that much darker. So fucking dark."

ELEVEN

THERE WAS a crick in Dallas's neck, and something hard dug in between two of his ribs, bruising the already tender muscles he'd strained reaching to strip the molding above Bombshells' antique bar. His cock was half-awake, primed and aroused. Then Dallas felt the long stretch of warm skin and solid weight behind him and he remembered where he'd spent his last couple of hours the night before... splayed out on his back, on Jake's bed with Jake stretched out next to him.

And they'd talked. About everything and nothing until sleep claimed them both.

If Dallas hadn't been mostly in love with Jake Moore before, he definitely was smitten by the time he drifted off, ridiculously happy just to hear Jake breathing next to him.

The hard thing in Dallas's ribs was Jake's elbow, and when Dallas shifted, Jake followed, his massive shoulders sliding the linens beneath him. Lying on his back with one arm thrown over his head, Jake sprawled over his side of the bed, one knee tucked up until it grazed the wall with his other leg stuck straight out, his heel nearly brushing the end of the mattress.

Dead asleep but probably worn out from the emotional upheaval the night before, Jake was a limp, handsome sprawl, his full mouth slightly open, and his lashes swept dark shadows under his closed eyes. His rich brown hair, now a mess of licks and curls, framed his strong face, and the light picked out the delicate spray of freckles across his cheeks and nose.

Darkened by a sparse stubble, his firm jaw and long throat begged Dallas to be bitten and kissed, Jake's tanned skin turned to gold from the light coming from the bank of partially cranked open jalousies above them. Every line of his body rippled with movement, muscles bunching and giving with every shift Jake made, and the peek of his flat, hard stomach from his T-shirt riding up his side drove Dallas wild.

"Okay, pee first, then food," he mumbled, forcing himself up and off the wide bed. "Because if I don't get out of bed now, it's going to take twenty minutes for my dick to go down. Fucking thing is hard enough to stir coffee right now."

After a dash out to his car to retrieve the duffel of spare clothes he kept in the Tesla's trunk and a hot shower where he was disgusted to find his arousal stoked to full force by the scent of Jake's soap, Dallas emerged clean and starving. A peek into Jake's fridge reassured him the grocery faeries hadn't visited in the middle of the night to fill the icebox while they'd been sleeping, but his stomach growled too loudly to be ignored.

Jake didn't look like he was waking up any time soon, and from what Dallas remembered of the neighborhood, there was a small market on the corner he could walk to. Eggs and bacon sounded like a great idea, but then so did biscuits and gravy. And butter. Lots of butter.

"Okay, I'm starving. And it's almost one." He grabbed his wallet out of his duffel bag and debated taking Jake's keys so he could get back into the apartment. The debate ended quickly enough with Dallas unclipping the half with the door key on it and leaving Jake a note, promising he'd be back with food. "Shit, maybe something'll be open and I'll just do takeout. I could eat a whole damned cow."

The sun was a lie, more of a watery sheet of white filtered through a low marine layer intent on fooling beachgoers to go without sunscreen. He made room on the sidewalk for a tiny, crouched-over old Korean woman, one arm slung up behind her back as she hustled by him in a power walk fast enough to rattle the overloaded wire shopping trolley she dragged behind her. Dallas caught her quick glance, an assessing, suspicious glare, and then she was off, hurrying through the gaps between the light foot traffic on the walk.

Something sizzled on a grill nearby, the scent of marinated meat toying with Dallas's senses. Any thought of bacon, eggs, and biscuits was wiped out when he spied a couple of food trucks doing a brisk business in a closed bank's empty parking lot. The lines were long, nearly long enough for Dallas to have second thoughts, but an aromatic cloud of steam slapped some sense into him, and he stopped arguing with himself long enough to study the menu.

"'Sides, it'll be cooked. Food will be all ready to go when I get back in case Jake's up." He mulled over his options, torn between a slab of ribs or Korean chicken. "Chicken can sit in the fridge and still taste decent. Foghorn it is."

His phone rang as he got to the end of a long line, a low dirge of a metal song about an iron man and if he was blind. Grinning stupidly, Dallas answered the call with a chuckle. "Hey there, Ozzy."

"Hey, Dolly. How's it going?" Austin rumbled back, and Dallas chortled when his mother shouted at his older brother to stop calling him by that stupid nickname. A dog barked in the background, followed by a howling chorus. Then Dallas heard the familiar squeak of the ranch's back screen door opening and the scrabbling chitter of his mother's pack of mutts heading outside. "Mom just doesn't get it. You've been calling me Ozzy for what? Over twenty years? It's like she doesn't even know us."

"She's just pissed off Dad encouraged it."

"She's pissed off he taught you to call Victoria Tick."

"That'll teach her to give us names little kids can't pronounce." There was an odd snorfling sound coming across the phone, and Dallas struggled to identify it. "What the fuck is that? A horse?"

"Llama. Five of them, actually. Mom rescued them from an abattoir, although I don't know anyone in their right mind who'd eat a llama."

"People eat guinea pigs, Ozzy. Meat's meat when you don't have the luxury to be picky." Dallas sighed, a twist of longing for his mother's mediocre cooking kicking in. "This is going to sound stupid, but I miss Mom's burnt hot dogs and lumpy mac and cheese. No one can put a char on a dog like Mom."

"So go fire up the grill and toss some wieners into the coals. It'll be just like home," Austin suggested. "Pretty sure that's what we're having for lunch. What're you doing?"

"Right now? Standing in line at a food truck for Korean chicken so I can take it back to this guy's place and feed him." Something crinkled in Dallas's heart, and he wished he'd not gotten out of bed until Jake had. "So if I have to put you on hold, it's because I'm at the window."

"Good boy. Because only assholes keep talking on their phone when they get to the cashier." Austin's approval tickled Dallas into a grin. "And I can hear you laughing at me, dickwipe. You're not too big for me to fly out there and beat your ass. Tell me about the guy. Someone you're bringing home to Mom and Dad or just a bed to stash your boots under on the weekend?"

"It's… complicated. He does metalwork and works across the street from the place I just bought. I've got some grates he's restoring, but he does sculptures that'll take your breath away." Dallas took a step as the line shuffled forward. "But yeah, I'd… love to take him home. Mom would…. God, she'd fall in love as soon as he opened his mouth, and Dad would drag us all down to the river so we could drink beer and fail at catching fish."

"So what's the problem?"

"He's been hurt." Three words—three small little words that held more pain than Dallas could imagine. "His father… that man fucked him up so much, it's not even funny. He's… he's a damned mess and a bit screwed up, but God, Ozzy, being with him makes me so fucking happy, and at the same time, I just want to put him into a box so no one can get to him. But with holes so I can shove cookies and hamburgers at him."

"Kind of stalkery, but if it works for the two of you, who am I to judge? Does he feel the same way about you? Except for the box thing, because then neither one of you would get fed." Dallas could almost see his older brother leaning against one of the ranch house's porch posts, shadowed by the overhang and watching his mother's dogs wrestle in the grass. Austin's tone lightened, brightening as he teased, "Is he hot?"

"So fucking hot. Built like a swimmer, and he's got these hazel eyes I want to fall into. And yeah, we get along. I'd say he's thinking fondly of me, but you know, it's going to be some work." He made eye contact with a mother carrying a baby, and her disapproving flare made him grimace. Mouthing an apology, he put some distance between them, letting a pair of giggling teenaged girls cut in front of him. "Seriously, Ozzy, no words for what he does to me, but honestly, I just like talking to him, being with him. It's just that he's had a crap life and he deserves better."

"Just be careful, okay?" Austin warned. "Sometimes people like being miserable. Make sure he's not going to drag you down into something."

"Don't think he will, but I promise I'll be careful. Mostly, he's been holding himself in really tight, Oz. Like not letting anyone see who he is, like he's folded in on himself. Watching him open up these past couple of weeks is… you know how it is when there's a soft rain after being dry for a long time. It's like that. He's like that, and I'm just sitting here waiting to see what blooms." Dallas sighed. "Fuck, I've got it bad."

"Soooo bad," his brother teased. "But if he does it for you, then helping him wade through the shit will be worth it. Look at Mom and Dad. Lot of crap they had to deal with, and they're the best things in our lives. Although I could do with less art commune. Mom's trying to talk Dad into turning one of the old barns into a retreat thing. Like knocking down some of the stall walls to make living quarters people can rent out. She's gone nuts, Dolly. Asked me if I'd ever considered buying a loom. What the hell is up with that? Oh wait, you said he does art stuff. Yeah, bring him here. Get her off my back."

"He's kind of shy about it, but damn, you should see what he can do with metal. Mom's going to latch onto him and never let him go. She's always complained the three of us can't even color inside of the lines. She's going to shit when she sees the stuff he creates."

"Time for a ring?"

"No, not time for a ring. Hell, not even time for me leaving a toothbrush." He kicked at a loose piece of gravel with his sneaker. "He's not ready for a relationship. Not yet. Maybe never but… fuck, Austin. He's it for me. I can feel it. It's just that… no one's ever really loved him before. Not really. Not without… conditions, and I'm asking him to let me in, to trust me, and that's asking a fuck of a lot."

"Relationships are hard, Dolly. And then you add kids, because you know, you have to have kids."

"Kids aren't the reason for a relationship, Oz," Dallas poked back at his brother. "You have relationships for the relationship, not anything else. That's what's got to work. Always. Kids can be like the whipped cream on top of a relationship. Not everyone likes whipped cream, and the ones who do love the taste, but they've got to work off the calories afterwards. Kids are work, delicious for the heart but a lot of fucking work."

"Taking philosophy courses out there in granola land, baby brother?" Austin shot back. "Because you sound like you're munching quinoa burgers and aligning your chakras right now."

95

"Careful there, your Keep-Austin-Weird is showing, dick," he teased back. "I don't even know what a fucking chakra is."

"Bullshit, you've probably got five pairs of yoga pants and order complicated half-caf macha-infused espresso drinks at your free-trade coffee shop slash seal sanctuary...."

"That rolled off your tongue way too smoothly to be off the cuff there, bro. That your standard order? 'Cause you know when I come home for a visit, I'll want to know what to bring you in the morning."

"Fuck you, Dolly." There wasn't any heat in Austin's curse, and his low chuckle brought a smile to Dallas's mouth. "So what are you going to do about... the maybe-relationship with this artist guy? Last thing I want to see is you getting hurt."

"I'll try not to." The line moved quickly, and Dallas craned his neck to catch another look at the menu. "I'm almost at the window. You call for something in particular or just to see how I'm holding up?"

"Just checking in on you. Mom's kind of worried about you. Want me to tell her about the guy?"

"Are you fucking kidding? She'd be on the first plane out. Any whiff of anything serious and she'll be at my front door." Dallas groaned when the girls ahead of him got to the window and asked what the food was like. "And don't think you're going to be throwing me and Jake out to distract Mom if she gets on your ass. Keep your mouth shut about this, Ozzy. At least until I know where we're going with this. Might be all he wants is a friend and—"

"And then I'll fly up there to kick his ass for breaking your heart," Austin promised. "Then I'll tell Mom so she can fly there, kick his ass, then kiss your boo-boos."

"Good to know you've got my back."

"Seriously, Dal." His brother's voice deepened, a gruffer, meaner version than their placid father's. "Take care of yourself. That's number one. In all things. But if he's worth the time and energy, take it. Do it. You and I both know life's way too fucking short not to be happy. And if he makes you happy, you fucking hold on tight and teach him how to love you right. And now Mom's yelling for some help. Love you, Dolly, and if you need anything, give me a call, okay?"

96

"Got it, Ozzy. Kiss the 'rents for me and kick the Tick." Dallas grinned when his mother's panicked cry for help with a loose pig screeched through the phone. "Have fun catching the hog."

The girls were still debating the pros and cons of chicken versus beef ribs when Dallas's phone buzzed again. Expecting it to be his mother, he answered with a laugh, "What? Austin couldn't keep his mouth shut?"

"Dallas? Where are you?" Jake's troubled voice plunged an icy knife into Dallas's gut, and he stepped out of the line, worry twisting him around. "I need—"

"What's wrong?" Dallas was across the sidewalk and to the crosswalk before Jake could utter another word. "I'm heading back. What's the matter?"

"It's my dad. I need to get over there." Jake sucked in a hiss of air, then exhaled a slow, tortured half sob. "They don't think he's going to make it... and... I think I need you."

WALKING THROUGH the sliding glass doors of the nursing home, Dallas realized he'd discovered the last place in the world he wanted to die in. Outside, the two-story building was depressing, a long narrow bit of gray-on-gray cinder block without even a hint of shrubbery to soften its hard lines. Inside was an equally flat muddle of space Dallas knew would drive him to madness if he had to live in its mushy-pea-and-shit-tinted drab walls for more than a few days.

The car ride over was tight with emotion, and more than once, he debated turning around and taking Jake back to the apartment or anywhere other than the nursing home where Jake's father lay dying. They'd rounded a corner, Dallas taking the curve a bit too quickly, and Jake flushed green, clutching at the door until his knuckles bled white. When they'd arrived, Dallas sat quietly while Jake composed himself, reaching over to hold Jake's cold, clammy hand when it looked like he was about to lose the bit of tea he'd choked down before they'd gotten into the car.

"It'll be okay," he'd promised, rubbing some warmth into Jake's icy fingers. "I'm here. We'll get through this."

Standing on the lobby's cracked tile floor, Dallas was having serious doubts they were even getting out alive.

The place smelled cleanish, an oversaturation of lemon cleanser and bleach, but there wasn't enough chlorine in the world to mask the scent of incontinence and vomit. There was a round-faced woman sitting behind a curved nurses' station placed directly in front of two hallways leading to the rear of the building. And from the sounds coming out of a pair of partially open doors to the right of the desk, residents were engaging in an exercise class being led by a celebrity workout DVD much too advanced for anyone without double joints and possibly a rubber spine.

From the far-left hallway, a cadaver-like male attendant shuffled next to a balding old woman with a walker, her too large pink housecoat dragging on the floor. The woman's hair matched her loose-fitting Crocs, bright orange and patchy, but her grim, toothless smile and wink when she hobbled by the front desk made Dallas smile.

"You better get out of here while you have your good looks, dearie," she rasped, coughing out a chuckle. "I was a Playboy Bunny before I got stuck in here."

"You're still gorgeous, Ruby," the attendant mumbled. "Got all the boys in here chasing you."

"That's 'cause I've got all the good drugs." Waving away the helper's hand, she lifted the walker up a few inches, then put it down, leaning on it to support her next few steps. "Hurry the hell up, Henry. I need to get to the damned TV before Gladys or we'll be watching some stupid gossip show with grinning idiots talking about some fat woman's ass."

"Down the right hall," Jake murmured, waiting for the old woman to go by. "He's… third door down and to the left."

Dallas kept a hand on Jake's back, hating the tremble running through the man's body. A sour-faced lanky woman sitting behind a reception desk shot them a desultory glance, then went back to reading a gossip magazine, slowly flipping a page as they approached. Jake seemed to know where he was going, but she cleared her throat when it looked like Jake wasn't going to stop.

"You need to check in and state what room you're visiting, sir," she droned, a flat scraping drawl catching on the edges of her words. "And then an attendant will be with—"

"No, I've never checked...." Jake turned, his eyes nearly wild with panic. "I don't know his room number. I just go there. There's never been a check-in."

"Go find out what room he's in and text me." Dallas ignored the woman, pushing Jake toward the door. "I'll fill out the form."

"Sir, he can't—" This time the woman stood up, reaching for a phone on the desk.

"They called him in. His father is fucking dying, and you're hung up on some stupid rule you probably just made up?" Dallas leaned over the counter, slapping at the bare wood. "Where's the damned check-in list? Jake, just go. I'll deal with this."

"Dallas, I'll meet you—" A bloodcurdling shriek came from down the hall, cutting Jake off, and he bolted, sprinting toward one of the open doors.

The howls grew louder, and Dallas was torn between following Jake or handling the woman dialing the phone. An attendant in orange scrubs popped her head out of the double doors, her blonde ponytail pulling her temples back, and she smiled at Dallas, more seduction than welcoming.

"Just checking to see who that is. Haven't seen you around here before. First day?" She flashed another smile, a piece of purple gum wedged between her teeth. When a chorus of slurs pelted the air, she made a face. "Oh, that asshole. God, hope his son gets here soon. Mean son of a bitch. Piece of advice? Suck up to Nurse Crabby back there and she'll make sure he's not on your roster."

There was a commotion down the hall, and a scuffle broke out near the door as a broad-shouldered man shoved Jake out of a room. He turned, blindly reaching for the wall to lean on, and his fingers dug into the drywall, scraping off a line of paint, scattering gray flecks on the floor. The screaming continued, a horrific wailing filled with pain and rage. Then as suddenly as it started, it stopped, bathing the area in an eerie silence.

"Fuck her," Dallas muttered, striding down the hall to get to Jake's side.

It was close. Jake stumbled as Dallas grabbed at him, their arms tangled together as the nurse at the main station screamed into the phone, ordering someone to come down and take care of things. If anything, Jake was even colder now, deadly still and white in Dallas's half embrace. He didn't seem to be breathing. Then finally he gasped, his chest jerking out once, then twice, but the color never returned to his face, not even when Dallas wiped at the tears wetting Jake's dark lashes.

"They're killing him, Dallas." He shook, fear darkening his eyes. "I think they're killing him, and… I don't know if I'm ready for him to die."

TWELVE

EVERY BROKEN inhale Jake took hurt.

The machines hooked into his father's limp body kept time with him drawing in breaths, then slowly pushing them back out again, his lungs too chilled to warm the air before releasing its hold. Every inch of Jake's body was tight and cold, his spine frozen into a slumped curve from sitting vigil at his father's side. He was submerged in the iced-over pond of his regrets and anger, his joints aching and his nerves knotted in tight.

Every rattle in his father's throat caught on death's grip, then continued along its way, fueling the limpid pulse keeping time with the beeping machinery. Every hour or so, an orderly or nurse would make a circuit of the room, a passing shadow keeping a jaundiced eye on the dying man and his silent son.

There'd been doctors and words, a constant river of information too frothy and violent for Jake to manage. He'd gone under within the first five minutes of listening, letting it all wash over him and filling his mouth with its brackish punch. In the end, Dallas saved him, throwing Jake a lifeline by stepping in and flinging questions back at the wall of brittle-faced people poking at him.

Every query Dallas made came back with the same reply: simply wait for death to come and make peace in the meantime.

There was no peace. Jake existed in a tumbling purgatory where he couldn't find a purchase to grab, nothing to hold on to as the world spun around on him. And it would continue to toss him about, bruising his soul until Dallas returned from wherever he'd gone to stick a pin in Jake's whorls, anchoring him in place.

Jake hadn't realized how alone he was until his father lay at death's door. He had no one to tell, no one to console so he didn't have to look at his own conflicted grief. Instead he could only hunch over his father's still body and count the breaths the old man took, silently praying each one would be his last.

"God, I can almost see through you," Jake whispered. His voice sounded loud slamming against the silence death held over his father's head. He no longer heard the beeping and shush-shush of the machines dragging his father's life along.

The hands that once were massive and hard were nothing more than bones and skin. It was difficult for Jake to see them curled in solid and tight, pounding into his ribs while his father's weight pressed his face into the filthy carpet. He'd been choked along the crook of that elbow, trapped in the man's then massive arms, the back of his head slapped when he'd burbled up snot and spit out of his nose and mouth.

Those hands slapped him hard enough to ring his ears, and those arms swung leather belts with enough strength to break the skin on Jake's back. The whisper of a man pinned down by bleached sheets and a thin blanket could never have kicked Jake down a flight of stairs or punched him with enough force to break his eye socket.

He couldn't see that man in the fleshy ghost lying in front of him, but Jake knew he lived somewhere inside, raging and spitting at the world and at the son he'd never wanted to see the light of day.

Touching his father was something Jake'd never done. Not on purpose and never for anything other than moving him from one spot to the next. He could never remember hugging the man or even touching his arm, but staring at his father's age-spotted, skeletal hand with its translucent skin and thick blue veins, something in Jake broke.

And he reached for his father's hand, gripped the man's cold, clammy fingers.

"I hate you with everything in me," he murmured, loathing the tears threatening to fall from his fatigue-stung eyes. "But God, I can't let you die alone. I won't let you die without you knowing someone's here for you. Because there is no one. We have no one, no family. Hell, I don't even know if you have brothers or sisters because… you never said. When you're gone, there'll be just me, and I can't… I can't keep living just to hate you. I need to be more than that, Dad."

His father's chest slowly rose, filled by forced air and electricity. Jake's thumb kept track of the sluggish push of blood through his father's veins, a weak flutter he lost every few seconds, and he caught himself steadying his breathing to match his father's.

"I should have flat-out told you I was gay a long time ago, before you killed Maman, before you tried to kill everything about me." A chuckle slid from Jake when he realized he'd been holding his breath, waiting for his father to explode even as the man hadn't moved in hours, hadn't spoken in days, and couldn't even think. But Jake tensed anyway, poised to flee a storm of fists and words. Shaking his head, he looked up through his lashes at his father's waxen, sunken face and tightened his hold on the man's hand. "God, I am everything you hated in life, and now I'm the only one to see you off.

"I was never strong enough to ask for help. Neither was Maman. You made us prisoners in our own lives. I get that now. I understand how isolated you made us. How you moved us around and kept us off-balance." Jake sniffed, refusing to cry for the man he sat next to. He'd keep his father company until death came for him, but he'd be damned if he cried for him. "What did she say to you that night? When she told me never to come home again? Did you fight with her, or did my leaving get you so angry you—"

Jake bit back on his words, refusing to go down the dark path his thoughts were leading him to. The pulse stuttered again, another chorus of beeps and whooshes, and then a shuddered sigh bled from Ron Moore's slightly parted mouth.

"There's this guy. His name's Dallas. Dallas Yates." Jake smiled despite the cold eating away his warmth. He hadn't brought a jacket. Hadn't thought to. Who brought a jacket to watch their father die? "You'd hate him. Okay, that's not saying much because you hate everything. I never realized that before now."

His father, naturally, said nothing.

"You were never happy about anything. If you made a dollar, you were angry because another man made two. Maman wasn't ever pretty enough, skinny enough, so you had to go out and fuck other men's wives. She used to cry about it. About the nights you would not come home because you were with another woman, but God, I used to pray for you to find someone else. Anyone else. Because it meant you left us alone." He watched another pace of lights jump across a screen, blue and red lines reassuring him life gripped his father still. "I get scared, you know? Of another man being next to me because it meant pain. Because the only time you touched me was to hurt me. I went out that night because I was tired of being afraid, tired of being hurt. I wanted to feel something good for a change, but everything went wrong anyway.

"But now there's Dallas, and… even if I fuck that up, if he decides I'm too much to deal with…." Jake's bitter laugh speckled his father's sheets with a bit of spit. Wiping at the damp spot, he shook his head. "Sorry, I just… I'm scared again, Dad. I'm always scared. I'm bigger than I was when you… well, back then… but inside, I'm still that little kid, and I'm scared shitless about everything."

A couple of people walked by, their indistinct conversation leaking into the room for a moment, a muddle of words and soft laughter. Jake couldn't hear the machines over a man's boisterous chuckle. Then the beeping reemerged with a woman's amused shush. It was funny to hear amusement in a sound, but there it was, evocative and poignant, a bit of shared joy in the dank, morbid anticipation filling the room.

"Dallas is…." Jake searched for the words to explain the swell of emotion even the idea of Dallas Yates brought him. "He's funny and cute. Okay, he's hot, which probably isn't what you want to hear, but he makes me feel, Dad. I've wanted to cut out every part of me that felt anything before, because it was all… so fucking horrible. Dallas makes me feel like there's something in life besides the sour shit you fed me. I feel like I could be happy. And yeah, that's what's really hard. There's a lot of 'suppose this happens' in that. But you've got to understand something. I can't become you. I can't be your legacy of hate. The first thing I need to do is stop hating myself, and Dallas… he's promised to help me learn how to do just that. So, Dad, I'm not sorry to tell you this, but after you die, you're not taking me with you."

"DAMNED THING," Dallas growled, tapping at the vending machine's lit-up front. "I just want a couple of coffees. How fucking hard is that?"

"Get out of the way, Dal." Celeste bumped his shoulder, edging him aside. Her curves strained the seams of her dress, and the orderly passing behind them eyed her appreciatively, then straightened his face when he noticed Dallas's glare. Celeste was, as usual, oblivious. "Move, move. Let Mama take care of it."

"Yeah, good fucking luck. I should go across the street to the café. I just don't want to…." He glanced down the hall to where Jake sat in a heavy silence over his father. "I don't want him to be alone, but he… he doesn't want anyone with him right now."

"Sometimes a man's got to face his demons all by himself," she replied, jiggling at the coin return on the machine's front, then tapping its side. The coffee cup remained stuck in the chute, and Celeste frowned. "God knows I do. You wouldn't understand."

"I have—" Dallas started, and Celeste cut him a fierce, telling look.

"You shut those lips, sugar," she cautioned. "You don't have any demons. For God's sake, you were born gorgeous and happy into a family that's weird enough to be cute and just the right amount of loving not to be sicko-pervy. You don't get to talk."

"Sorry, didn't know being normal meant I don't get to have an opinion," Dallas teased, then winced when Celeste kicked the coffee machine's side. "Don't break it. I can go downstairs. I just didn't want to leave him alone… in case he needs me."

"I'll go downstairs," she offered, then nodded over to four armchairs arranged in a square near a wall of windows. "Sit down with me for a bit, and then I'll grab the coffee. And maybe something for you guys to eat. When was the last time you had something in that stomach of yours?"

"This morning. I shoved a Pop-Tart at him and ate the other one," he confessed softly, the sweet sting of the frosted blueberry pastry a memory on his teeth. "I just… fine. Let's go sit down, but I'm going to be honest. There's not a lot of good mood in me right now. I need that coffee."

The seats seemed like they were a mile away, and Dallas kept glancing over his shoulder, looking for a peek of Jake in case he came to the door. Celeste's arrival complicated things. Or maybe they were less complications and more jealousy and aggravation. As much as he loved his best friend, Dallas wasn't in the mood to share. Or be coddled. He was angry, and something dark and nasty inside of him whispered to unplug every machine in Ron Moore's room to release not only the hateful old man but also his son.

Celeste showing up in a perky leopard-print baby-doll dress and fuck-me black heels did nothing to soothe away his ruffled, sharp emotions. Neither did the assessing look she gave him as they walked toward the sitting area.

"You're grumpy and probably hungry," she said primly, arranging herself on one of the chairs, tugging the hem of her dress over her exposed knee. Patting at the black bob she'd tugged over her own hair that morning, Celeste smiled at him, slightly flaring her nostrils in an imperious sniff. "So I'm going to forgive you your trespasses."

"I don't have any trespasses." Dallas made a face. "I don't even know what that means. I thought it was sins."

"Don't ask me. I'm Jewish." Celeste sniffed again. "Or was. I haven't been to temple since before I grew my mini-boobs. I always thought it meant someone being an asshole, and I'm going to stick with that, because right now, Dallas Vulcan Yates, you are on the edge of being an asshole."

"God, I wish I'd never told you my middle name." Dallas sighed, and he hit the wall, fatigue settling in. His face slipped down, the weight of his tired pulling at his skin, and he leaned over, resting his elbows on the chair's padded arms. "It's been four days since they brought Jake's dad in here, sugar. And I'm starting to feel like shit asking God to take that man so we can all get on with our lives. A man's dying, and I'm cheerleading him on so Jake can... I don't know what I think Jake's going to do or be after that bastard dies, but I'm ready to find out."

"You said he woke up once?" She inched forward, bringing herself in until their knees touched. Her stockings scratched at his skin through the hole in his jeans. "Do they think he's getting better?"

"No, they don't know why he woke up. He shouldn't have. That was...." Dallas struggled to remember when he'd pulled Jake back from his father's bed, as if distance could shield them from the man's bitter spewing. "The doctor said he wasn't really awake, and he was... something was going on in his brain, like a dump of nonsense, but sweetie, you didn't hear the shit that came out of that man's mouth.

"I'd never heard anything so damned... foul. And I've lived in some not-so-nice areas, but this.... God." He wanted to throw up after hearing what flowed out of the old man's mouth, a diatribe filthier than he'd ever imagined. "And all I could think was, that's what Jake grew up around, how he was treated. No wonder he's as fucked-up as he is. I want to drag Jake out of there so badly I can taste it. I want to shove him on a plane and we go home to my mom, where she can make us grilled cheese sandwiches and tomato soup until we're sick of eating them."

"Well, having been on the receiving end of the grilled-cheese-tomato-soup tour, I'm all for it, but…." She looked at him expectantly, and Dallas harrumphed with pure disgust. "You and I both know he's not going anywhere. And as much as I'd want him to head to your parents' place so he can live under a soft quilt, that's not going to happen as long as that man has his hooks in Jake… and death doesn't always unhook evil from a man's soul."

"And that man would give the Devil a run for his money," Dallas agreed softly. "I just want to fix things. For Jake."

"That's your mom coming out in you." Celeste angled her head, studying him. "And now I'm going to ask something that is probably going to piss you off, but what do you think is going to happen after that nasty man dies? Where do you see all of this going?"

It was a fair question, one Dallas had asked himself ever since he'd dragged Jake out of the nursing home's excuse for a bedroom so the attendants could work on resuscitating the old man. It seemed like a lifetime ago since he'd spoken to Austin and a century since he and Jake discovered the body in the upstairs loft. Jake's whole world revolved around the man dying a few yards away, and for the life of him, Dallas hadn't given himself permission to think beyond getting through another day. He couldn't risk the what-ifs, especially if it meant Jake slipping away.

"I have no fucking idea," he finally answered. "It's all a damned mess, honey. Perfect world? Jake and I go riding off into the sunset and—"

"Now I'm going to stop you right there, and I'm asking you this as your best friend." Celeste's voice dropped, and a sliver of Simon emerged from the rough huskiness. "Are you sure you're not just… wanting him because you need to be the guy who wears the white hat? You said it yourself. You just want to fix things. Have you thought that maybe—and I love Jake—but just maybe you've got this whole fantasy of how it's going to be afterwards because he's fucked-up and you need to unfuck things?"

"It crossed my mind." She'd pulled the first real smile Dallas had in him since they'd hit the hospital's front doors. "I've looked at it. Looked at me. Looked at him. Hell, I've even talked to Austin about Jake, and you know how shitty he is at giving advice. It's more than fixing things, Celeste. I promise. Yeah, I want to wash away the filth that dick father of his smeared on him. I want to scrape off the stink and guilt he'd been raised in, but not because I need to but because he and I....

"It isn't just for me. Yeah, I want him. I want to hold him and share a sunset without him tensing up with fear. I want him not to flinch when I touch him, and I want him to touch me without having to analyze it or look to see who is around." Dallas paused, searching for the words he needed to describe the delicate furls of emotion Jake brought out in him. "God, you need to see his smile when he doesn't care who is looking and how he scowls when he's working because he's beating the world into submission. There's a beauty inside of Jake I want the world to see. That's what I love, C. I love that beauty and those dimples and the rough of his hands on my shoulders when he feels safe enough to put them there."

"But he's broken, Dallas," Celeste murmured, reaching to hold his hands. "He might never ever get there. I don't want to.... I don't want to see you lose yourself."

"That's how I know I love him, babe." He turned Celeste's hands over, running his fingers over her palms. He'd first held them when she'd been Simon, and now after the long, hard battle to become Celeste, her hands never truly changed. They were a constant, a slightly bent pinky finger and a left ring finger knuckle a bit larger than the rest. "Jake's going to heal. He's committed to that, to be who he should have been. I think of the man he is now, and yeah, I'm fucking pissed off he wasn't raised by a couple of people who cherished what they had. That man in there doesn't deserve Jake sitting with him. He raised Jake to believe he's not worth anyone's love. So yeah, I'm going to love the fuck out of him—broken or not—and maybe one day Jake will believe me—"

"Dallas?" Jake's honey-rough voice tumbled down the hall, amber chips sharp with grief and confusion.

He'd not been watching the door or he'd have seen Jake come out of the room, his dark hair wild around his temples and the color stolen from his cheeks. His shoulders were bowed and his lush mouth tightened into a firm line, his jaw clenched too tight for Dallas's liking. Behind his tear-matted black lashes, Jake's eyes burned emerald, stark and hollow in his fatigue-bruised face.

"Hey." Dallas was across the hall and to Jake before he could say another word. Jake was cold, shivering and wound tight, but he let Dallas draw him into a hug. A moment skipped over them, and then Jake returned the embrace, his sinewy arms closing into an iron lock around Dallas's body. "I'm here, love. Whatever you need—"

"He's gone, Dal," Jake stammered out, burying his face into the curve of Dallas's neck. "And I don't know what the fuck I'm going to do."

THIRTEEN

"I STILL can't believe there wasn't a funeral. I would have come! He shouldn't have been alone. Or at least had someone besides you. So you all just... did what?" Celeste's mouth dropped open, and she turned to stare at Dallas, caught halfway into putting her purse away before tackling the loft space upstairs. Shoving the sleek black-and-red sling tote into the metal desk they were using in the office, she shook her head. "You just chucked him in there and walked away?"

"Chuck's a bit harsh," Dallas protested, hitching himself up on the edge of the ugly green metal monster desk he was sadly growing fond of. "He was lowered down. Sedately while some guy in a long black dress said nice things about him and in a coffin way too good for him, but there you have it. The ground is now salted and bitter and nothing shall ever grow there again."

He'd had visions of a glorious wood piece with lions' feet until Celeste reminded him the place was more dinner and drag than gentlemen's club, and he should save all the geegaws for where they'd do the most good, out with the paying customers. The metal desk probably would stay once it was stripped of its Army heritage, and the long rooms in the back would be for employees and talent to change their clothes and stash their things while on shift.

"You should feel horrible for saying that." Celeste leaned toward an old mirror they hadn't taken down, wiping at her mouth to remove a bit of lipstick, then met Dallas's gaze in its mottled glass. "I mean, the man's dead, and we should have some respect."

"I'm more respectful of the man we found upstairs." Dallas scratched at his cheek, wondering if they had fleas in the building or if there'd been mosquitoes at the graveyard. "Jake's... he's over at Evancho's right now finishing up some stuff, then heading over here."

"Man just put his father in the ground." She made a face, wrinkling her nose. "Okay, a whopping asshole of a father, but still. He jumped

110

right back into work instead of taking some time. It's been what? Almost three weeks now? He should take some time off."

"And we spent more than half a week waiting for the man to kick off before that," Dallas reminded her, then sobered, dropping the edges of his smile. "Babe, Jake's been on a death watch for years. He'd broken and beggared himself to get his father the best care he could. Yeah, I think he should take time off. Hell, I'd spring for a vacation someplace tropical with rum drinks served with little umbrellas, but he wants to work."

Celeste sniffed at him. "You've never bought me a vacation with rum drinks and umbrellas."

"I bought you boobs." He nodded toward her chest. "You wanted boobs. You got boobs."

"True." Celeste cupped her chest and smiled at Dallas, making smooching noises at him. "And they are spectacular. Haven't bought myself a drink since."

"How about if we get some work done today? We're scheduled to have the air-conditioning guys install that new compressor, so we'll need to be done painting the trim in the loft by this afternoon so we're out of the way." Spreading the plans out on the desk, Dallas ran through the build schedule in his head. "There's so much little crap to do, and I'm kind of tight on time here. Once the AC is in, we can get more workers onboard. The electricians and plumbers hit Monday, and then hopefully we'll be back on track. We're also going to have to meet with a couple of the marketing guys who handle Mars and—"

"Well, look at you." A woman's silhouette darkened the office doorway, her voice a blend of honey and peaches with a touch of steel. "I never thought I'd see the day when the little boy who couldn't even put his toys away would be running his own business."

There was always a bit of panic in Dallas's chest whenever he heard her someplace other than the ranch. An anxiety he couldn't quite shake. She was the ever-present looming authority figure who'd show up at school after he'd spent half an hour cooling his heels outside of the principal's office and the enraged Valkyrie who swooped down with a flaming temper and sharpened tongue the times he'd been arrested for protesting one thing or another. There'd been a few times when he'd been brought home in the back of a police car during his teen years, but she'd always keep her head on straight and listen to whatever nonsense he babbled out to excuse what he'd done.

He'd won some debates, fewer than he'd like, but they were usually the ones he was the most passionate about. She'd raised him to have a voice and to know when to use it, to speak up against someone's fist with strong conviction, and to turn the other cheek when someone talked shit. When he dragged the flotsam and jetsam of his world into her house, she'd welcomed each and every lost, wandering soul with open arms, shoving another chair up to the dining room table, then asked about food allergies.

She'd taught him how to be a human being, and Dallas couldn't have imagined a greater mentor, flawed, beautiful, and honest, with a sensible eye on what was necessary and a silly sense of humor. He'd grown up thinking if he could be half the woman she was, he'd turn out okay.

But she still scared the shit out of him when she showed up in his life without warning, a wild card dealt by a capricious God looking for a good chuckle and a bit of chaos.

Because his mother always brought a little bit of chaos with her.

Still, it was a delight to see her, and something happy burst into fireworks inside of Dallas as he came around the desk. "Mom!"

A few strides and he was across the room, scooping her up into a tight hug. She smelled of sunshine, root beer, and bubble gum, a mental poke for him to buy a few cases of the sweet brown soda before he got home. Her arms were thin, strong considering her slender frame, but he'd seen her sling a wild pig over a fence more than a few times. Her back was unbowed, and the embrace she'd gotten him in threatened to squeeze every bit of air out of his lungs if he didn't let go soon.

"Hey, sugar." Celeste bumped his hip. "Leave some for me. Hi, Auntie Martha!"

"Oh, look at you," his mother exclaimed, breaking free of Dallas, then cupping Celeste's face. "Aren't you simply the most gorgeous thing ever? After my son, of course."

Dallas stepped back so they could hug, digging the desk's rounded corner into his thigh for a moment as he tried to make room. They were an odd pair, a curvaceous New York Jewish girl with slightly sad eyes lined with black caterpillar lashes and a lanky, beautiful silver-streaked blonde belle who'd been raised on Texas oil, money, and cotillions, but they'd both walked away from their families in order to live their own lives, a tangible grit binding them together.

Their hug was a fierce battle of murmurs and giggles. Then his mother stepped back, pinning Dallas in place with a canny pale blue gaze, one he'd gotten from her. A graceful, elegant woman, she'd come dressed casually, worn jeans and a raglan shirt he'd worn during high school, considering the faded dragon sitting on a pile of D20s silk-screened across her chest, even though she'd been built for Chanel.

"Nice shirt." He grinned down at her. She wasn't short, not like his baby sister, Victoria, but he'd been looking at the top of his mother's head since he was fourteen. "Didn't you make me throw that out? Said something about it being indecent."

"It was indecent." She tilted her nose up at him, tugging down the shirt's hem. "On you. Walking around showing your belly like some tart. On me, it's fine. Now, I was planning on surprising you and seeing the building, but a funny thing happened while your brother and I were heading to the airport. He was telling me you'd called him a while back— how did he put it?—found someone you wouldn't mind waking up next to in the morning. So my number two son, why don't you start telling me about this boy you've been seeing. Jake, is it?"

"Fucking Austin," Dallas swore under his breath. His mother didn't interfere. No, she stalked, waiting for the right moment to sidle up to someone and weasel her way into their lives. He was sure she wasn't going to be happy until the ranch was overrun with people she'd taken in. Martha Yates was sweet, adorable, and made it her life's work to crowd in on her children, then keep track of their every move. "Swear to God, I'm going to kill him."

"Don't blame your brother," she murmured, straightening his shirtsleeve. "I'd booked the tickets two weeks ago. And you should know by now, if you want to keep a secret, the last person in the world to talk to is your brother. All I've ever had to do to find anything out is not say anything and he babbles to fill the quiet."

"Hey, at least you hadn't gotten around to telling him about the dead body you found upstairs. You can tell her that too." Celeste leaned around Dallas's shoulder, grinning at Martha. "He and Jake found a dead guy up in the loft."

"A dead man? In here? So, a maybe-boyfriend and a dead body." His mother crossed her arms over her chest, and Dallas could have sworn he heard Wagner start playing somewhere behind her. "How about if you sit your little ass right down over there on that chair, Dallas, so you and I can have a little catch-up?"

"JAKE, COME here." The intercom broke through the hissing from torches and a bit of chatter in the main workroom. "To my office."

It normally wasn't a good thing if Evancho called a guy into his office in the middle of the day. Usually. For all his gruffness, Peter Evancho was a fair man, willing to forgive mistakes if his employee learned from them, and Jake knew of at least three occasions when a guy ruined thousands of dollars of work and Evancho gave him a chance.

He'd been one of those guys, and it'd been years since he'd fucked up that royally. Still, a walk through the work area was a gauntlet of puckering lips and groans with a soft murmur of "good luck" from Brent, working on a mesh screen attachment for a custom door.

The door to Evancho's office was open, a sure sign he wasn't pissed off. He made people knock if he was pissed off at them, probably to give him time to take a breath so he could start off with a hearty yell. There was still a bit of lime-green paint on the edges of the window, left over from when a younger Jake'd been tasked to freshen up the door and hadn't masked the trim properly. Evancho told him to leave it, saying it added character to the battered old wood, but Jake itched to scrape the blob off, especially since his boss rubbed at it every time he opened his office up in the morning.

He knocked anyway, a short rap just to let Evancho know he was there, and a loud grunt shoved its way past the door, ordering Jake to come in.

The office was small, tucked behind the reception desk, barely large enough for a single man to work in, much less two. A heavy utilitarian desk sat facing the door with a short end against the wall, bisecting the space, and was rigidly clean, holding a laptop connected to another monitor and a few papers. The walls were lined with bookcases and filing cabinets filled with reference manuals and catalogs. An overhead fan turned in lazy rotations above the desk, barely stirring the air, but the air conditioner vents were open and blowing cold.

Sitting behind the desk was the first man Jake ever truly respected and, all things considered, was probably more than a little bit afraid of.

Peter Evancho was a bull of a man, nearly a foot shorter than Jake but about that much wider, with powerful muscles and a hearty personality. He'd come to California from the Ukraine with a few stops along the way, a square-jawed force of nature with a somber face and a gruff demeanor, but Jake'd always liked him. His solid, bulky arms strained his T-shirt sleeves, a wiry spread of pale blond hair peppering his forearms, and Evancho shifted in his chair, the office's fluorescent light picking up the silver in his short-cropped hair. He tapped away at a keyboard, his stubby fingers hammering at the plastic pieces as if he were working a punch press, his eyes keen on the flat monitor sitting to the side of his desk.

Stepping into the cramped space, Jake edged past a coat rack laded down with welding masks. "You wanted to see me, boss?"

"Yeah." Evancho jerked his chin toward the door. "Close that and have a seat."

Jake eased into one of the chairs in front of Evancho's work area, angling it when his knee hit the front of the desk. While rubbing at his knee to get rid of the tingles running up and down his right leg, Jake glanced up to find Evancho looking at him, the side of his mouth pulled into a wry smile.

"I keep forgetting to move the desk back," Evancho growled, clipping his words with his thick accent. "You're too tall, Jake, and too skinny. My wife sees you, you'll be eating nonstop for the next month. Quit fidgeting. I just want to talk to you, see how you were doing. What with… your father."

"I'm fine." Evancho gave him a stern bulldog look, and Jake shook it off. "No, really. I'm fine. I'm okay."

He'd spent a few days with Dallas doing stupid things he'd never done before. A walk down Santa Monica's sidewalks to taste cheeses at a specialty shop. Having pancakes and bacon for dinner and beef stroganoff and buttermilk biscuits for breakfast. Then he'd thrown himself into his routine and caught himself parked in front of the nursing home one afternoon, panicked because he was late with his father's cheeseburgers when they were serving fish that night. He'd almost tossed the burgers, then handed them off to a guy begging for change near the intersection.

Then he went home, got slightly drunk, and stared at the scaffolding he'd begun building the night Dallas found the gun in his bookcase.

That was yesterday, and in the morning, he'd gone in to work aching a little less inside than he had before, but the guilt lingered, souring his thoughts. Now, two hours later, he was sitting in Evancho's office, wondering what he'd done to deserve sitting in front of the man's desk.

"Really," he assured Evancho. "I'm fine. It wasn't a surprise. He'd been sick for—"

"Did I ever tell you I knew your father up in Montreal? Back when he worked the shipyard?" Evancho cut in, pushing his chair back in a long scrape. "Back when I was younger than you. Just getting into the business. I went up there for seasonal work. Did he tell you he knew me?"

Jake's tongue stuck itself to the roof of his mouth, and he tried swallowing around it, confused. His father never said one word about Evancho, or knowing him from before. Shaking his head, Jake replied, "No. I didn't know."

"I didn't know you were his kid when I hired you." Something on the screen beeped, and Evancho pushed a button, killing the monitor. "I found out one day when he came down here and you were working on a job up in the Hills. You hadn't been here long, I don't think, but he knew who I was. Evancho, it is uncommon, and he knew it. I did not remember him until I saw him, and then I remembered why he was not my friend."

"He never mentioned that either, sir." If he was confused before, Jake decided he'd upgrade to bewilderment and maybe even a little bit past that. "Don't know why he'd come here. Or how. The home shouldn't have let him out."

"This was before he got really bad, back when you two were still living in the house over on Hancock." Evancho pulled out a pack of gum, offering it to Jake, then taking a stick when he refused. Folding it past his teeth, he chewed at it, then said, "He was drunk. Drunker than he should have been for nine in the morning, but once I recognized him, I wasn't all that surprised. He looked like shit, but still, not surprised. He came to accuse me of sleeping with his wife—your mother—back in Montreal. And I'd hired you only because you were my son."

Jake's stomach curled, folding in on itself, and he took a sharp breath, unsure what to say. "I look like him, a little bit. More my mother but—"

"You look much like her, and I am sorry, but you are not my son, Jake. I am sorry that I am not your father. Understand this, but I never was with your mother. Your father was a jealous, angry man, and despite that, your mother loved him," Evancho asserted. Then he leaned forward, spreading his hands over the desk. "I didn't know her well. Mostly by sight. She brought him food once in a while, and I saw her belly begin to grow before I left. She was nice to me, fed me a few times. Even found me *kalach* for Christmas, but I did not know her. I am sorry she is gone. But I am more sorry she remained with him. I'd have hoped she'd left him and given you a better life.

"And you are probably wondering why I am talking about this now, after your father is gone. And why I didn't mention this before." Evancho rubbed at his face, his palm raking over the stubble on his chin where he'd missed shaving. "I've been sitting on this since you've been back, and well, I talked to the wife. Actually, I should have talked to you sooner. But here we are. Now. Thing is, you know we have a son, yes? Andre?"

"Yeah, met him. Nice guy." Jake tried to recall anything about the tall, slender blond man who'd come to the office Christmas party a few times. Other than a shy smile and a gentle hello, he'd kept to the background, letting his boisterous mother bustle around and order him about. "He was here with your wife."

"Tasia, my wife. She loves that boy. She loves the girls too, but that boy is her world," Evancho proclaimed softly. "He is like you, that boy. He likes other men, and for a while, it was hard. Hard for me. Hard for her. Hard for him. Mostly because of me because I had an idea of how my son would be, and suddenly, he was not."

If Evancho had reached across the desk and punched him in the face, Jake couldn't have been more surprised. Finding his throat closing up, he rushed in. "I'm—"

"Do not deny this to me, Jake. I know. And because there is nothing wrong how you are, who you are. I've seen you with that one across the street, the one with the loud friend, and the two of you are...." Evancho steepled his hands together, nodding. "Knitting in together. So do not lie to me. I know. And I am telling you now, it does not matter to me. Tasia and I talked… I told you this… and then we prayed, because that is what we do. Do you pray? Do you go to church?"

"I don't think you can ask that here in California," Jake murmured, trying for a smile, and Evancho shot him a reproachful glance. He hadn't thought of God or church in forever, not even when he stood over his father's grave and a priest laid him to rest. Jake's mind whirled around everything but prayer. "I haven't been to Mass in a long time. Not since before… Maman."

"Well let me say, we did not pray for your father. What I knew of him, I did not like. I prayed for forgiveness because I did not step in, step up when God sent me you." Evancho screwed his mouth up tight, then sighed. "You have been good for me. You have helped me see there are many different kinds of men and strengths. I love Andre. He is my son. And he will make me proud doing the film thing he loves, but you… you should have known how proud I am of you, of your skills, of your art. I am sorry for not saying that. I am sorry it took the death of your father for me to see those words should have been said.

"That is why I called you in here." He grabbed a set of keys sitting on the desk near the monitor, then slid them over to Jake. "Those are for the shop. They are yours. You can do your work here. You need better equipment than what you have at home. The back room is useless. Clean it out and set up there. Anyone gives you a hard time, they'll answer to me. But this place, that bay, is yours. We continue as we do. I will give you scraps, and you will take them and not complain. Make art, Jacques. Make your art, and one day you will give me your notice because you are a famous man. And we will drink heavily to celebrate that day."

Jake couldn't see the room. His eyes were too wet. His soul floundered in the ocean of savage emotions and conflicting thoughts. The keys were tempting. What Evancho offered seduced him. Trailing his fingers over the ring, he shook his head.

"I can't. It's too much. The cost of running the—"

"What I pay for that is nothing compared to how it will heal you. Because I see you, Jake. I see your mother looking back at me through your eyes, and I see how haunted you are. I told myself before it is none of my business. You are a full-grown man, but I was wrong. That is another thing I am begging forgiveness for. And now I need to make it

118

right. Do right by you. Like you've always done right by me." Evancho stood, then walked around the desk to sit on its edge near Jake's chair. Placing his hand on Jake's shoulder, he gripped him tightly, giving Jake a quick, light shake. "You take the keys and work here, where I know you are safe. And one Sunday, you bring your friend Dallas around my house for dinner. At six. I insist. Tasia insists. And if you have to, bring his loud friend too. I know someone she might like because I know him, and he will definitely like her."

FOURTEEN

THE KEYS in Jake's pocket weighed down his every step. It was stupid. He knew it was silly to think two slivers of metal would add much to what he carried, but it felt like he'd loaded a boulder into his jeans pocket, and every step forward took more effort than he had in him. Crossing the street toward Dallas's building was a struggle. He was torn between heading back to Evancho's office, to do what he didn't know, and the beckoning peace he only found when Dallas was around.

Traffic was thick, and he'd dodged a line of motorcycles zipping through the intersection, blowing the red light with a cop hot on their tail. Hot, he supposed, was a relative term, considering the cop meandered by, his siren on a low wail and slowing once he crossed into the intersection. Once clear, the squad car zoomed off, its screaming klaxon echoing between the low-rise buildings.

Celeste's car was parked on the side of the building, a sure sign she was going to bail halfway through the day, and Dallas's Tesla glistened in its spot at the curb. It was odd seeing the building stripped of the faux-adobe someone had slapped on its exterior at some point in its history, leaving it bare-faced and tippled with baby pink patching lines near the side and front windows.

The exterior grates were gone, in time for the cooler weather and the air-conditioning unit install. He'd left many of the interior mesh screens in place until a security system could be wired in, and he was done fabricating the panels to weld onto the jalousies' new glass panes. The sheer organization of everything boggled Jake's mind, but Dallas appeared to thrive on it, juggling schedules and work crews in an odd maniacal glee.

Even though he'd admitted to Jake Bombshells was probably the biggest project he'd ever taken on and probably would ask Jake to tie him to a chair if he ever considered something like it again.

"Like he'd listen to me," Jake scoffed. Taking in the reworked jalousies, Jake pursed his mouth. "Okay, maybe on a few things. Definitely not about any buildings. He likes bossing people around."

"Talking to yourself, honey?" Celeste came around the corner, hefting a pair of paint cans up for Jake to see. "Look! Goodies for the painters."

"Let me get those for you." Jake reached for the cans, then cocked his head when Celeste shook him off. "What?"

She studied him carefully, one hip canted out, her overalls and tank top as spotless as they'd been the first time he'd seen her in them. "If I were still a guy, would you grab them from me?"

Pulling up short, he considered it, then frowned slightly. She had a point, a valid point, but the urge to help her lingered. "Nope. But from now on, I'll ask even the guys, okay?"

"Didn't think so—okay, valid point. It's good to always ask. No matter who's carrying the damned things if it looks like they need help." She nodded toward the door. "You can get that for me, though. Hands are full, and there's way too much jelly here for me to make it through that crack Dallas left me."

"So many land mines," Jake muttered to himself, swinging the heavy front door open. "I need a manual or something. Anything."

"You're doing fine," she assured, slipping by him with a quick smile. "You're also hot as fuck, and that goes a hell of a long way. Believe you, me. Oh, and heads-up, we've got company—"

"Celeste! I told you I'd help you with those," an unfamiliar older woman called out, emerging from the hallway leading to the back of the building. "I was just coming outside."

She was blonde, dressed down in jeans and an old long-sleeved shirt, and she reminded Jake of his neighbor's long-boned Siamese cats, elegant and poised, with clear pale blue eyes. Very familiar blue eyes. The hair color was wrong, those eyes belonged with pitch-black hair, and the look in them lacked the smoldering humor Jake was used to, but the color—that vivid, sun-kissed sky color—was definitely recognizable.

"And the pudding thickens," Celeste murmured to Jake. "Gird your loins. Life is about to get really fucking interesting for you, honey."

"Why hello." Her smile was an echo, a bit of a quirk to the side and rich with warmth, a melted butter pat on a fragrant golden cake. There

121

was a hint of a husky drawl with a curl of upper-class tea and cut glass to her voice, for all the casualness in her stride, and the hand she thrust out to Jake sparkled with silver rings, thick bands studded with gems or flourished designs. "I'm Martha, and you must be Dallas's Jake. I've heard practically nothing about you, but I'm certain you can fix that, can't you? Let's you and I talk."

THE DAY got stranger with each passing second. It hadn't started out that way. When dawn crept into Jake's apartment that morning, he'd gotten up, showered, and headed in, only stopping long enough to grab a large cup of coffee from the shop across the street. Within the course of a few hours, his changing life went from unsettled following the death of his father to a straight-out tsunami of chaos.

Between Evancho and Martha Yates, Jake didn't know which way was up anymore. Dallas's mother was sweet, poking in a very gentle way, coaxing bits of information out with a delicate hand. Celeste mentioned Jake reworking the building's ironworks, restoring the pieces back to their original condition, and the conversation veered off into history and art.

It'd been an eye-opening ten minutes. Perhaps even fifteen. She'd listened. Like Dallas listened. Leaning in and eyes on him, intent on what he said and then weaving back in with more questions. Martha seemed at home amid the art deco faded glory, her blonde bob swinging gently about her sharp jaw, softening her chin, and when she spoke, her hands flitted about, dabbing at the air and skimming over his arm, much like her son did whenever he was nearby.

Dallas came in with a bit more of the paint, and he'd paled, setting the cans down, then excusing himself to talk to Jake in the office. He'd made some excuse. Jake was sure of it, but he'd been too entranced with Martha, much to Celeste's amusement.

"She's not supposed to be here," Dallas said for the fifth or sixth time since he pulled Jake into the office, closing the door behind them. "I'm—"

"Don't apologize again," he cut Dallas off. "She's your mother. Don't apologize for having a mother. It's fine. She's fine."

"But are we fine?" Dallas stepped in close, hedging Jake into the desk. "Are you fine?"

122

It was hard to think with Dallas standing next to him, and he rested his ass on the desk's edge to give him a bit of breathing room, but that only made things worse. With his legs stretched out, Dallas straddled his shins, the lingering heat of Dallas's body traveling up Jake's length and burrowing into his center. He couldn't not respond to Dallas anymore. Every glance, each touch, and sometimes even simply the sound of his laugh tickled Jake's senses. There was a brightness about the man, a lemony drop of color on the gray of Jake's thoughts, and he instinctively seemed to turn toward Dallas, a rain-drowned flower seeking the sun as it crested over the horizon.

Then Dallas leaned over, shuffling closer, and put his hands on the desk, his thumbs brushing Jake's hips. "I just want to make sure you're okay."

Jake wanted to drown in Dallas's eyes. He'd never thought about anything like that before he'd seen the man climbing out of his sports car and lowering his sunglasses to stare at the battered art deco building on the corner. When he thought of his world before Dallas pushed his way past the thick membrane Jake lived behind, he had to admit the changes were startling. He woke up in the morning… anticipating the day. Took time to have a cup of coffee, then study the sketches he'd done for the pieces he wanted to work on later. He looked forward to the text he'd get an hour later from a groggy Dallas, a half-kidding demand for a bagel with cream cheese and a gallon of hot, sweet coffee to be delivered to his apartment before Jake went over to Evancho's.

The day he'd walked across the street with a cream-cheese-slathered bagel and an enormous cup of java earned Jake a brush of Dallas's lips across his cheek and a smile he still carried inside of his heart when he was feeling down.

"I'm okay." There were needs in Jake, lingering threads whispering to him, begging him to respond to Dallas's casual touches.

He risked lowering his hand, trailing his fingers over Dallas's palm, then hooked a thumb around his. Jake felt Dallas's heartbeat pulse through where they touched, and he nearly drew away, except Dallas crooked his finger, tightening the bond Jake'd begun.

"Evancho… he did something today." Jake dug the keys out with his free hand and dangled them for Dallas to see. "He gave me shop keys.

Told me to clean out the back room so I don't blow my apartment up. And he invited me… us to dinner at his house this weekend. Or any weekend. Celeste too. I think he's going to set her up with someone. Hopefully not Frank because—"

"Wait, let's go back to the keys." Dallas's grin stretched wide over his face, plumping his cheeks. "Tell me everything he said. Slowly."

They stood, barely touching while Jake spun out every detail he could remember of the conversation. There wasn't much. He'd stammered through most of it, and when Evancho began talking about his mother, his thoughts flatlined, taking in nothing more than the fierceness in Evancho's voice, then the tenderness when he spoke of his son.

"He told me he was proud of me." Jake turned the idea of Evancho's pride over in his head. "He likes the things I do, and he talked about me with his wife. I don't know how to take all of it, Dal. It's not real, you know. This conversation I had with him confuses me, and at the same time, I feel tight in my chest because I'm scared of failing him, of failing his trust. I like the man. He's been good to me. Better than I deserve—"

"You deserve everything, Jake." Dallas slid in a butterfly of reproach. "You've got to—"

"Remember that," he finished the litany he heard from Dallas's lips at least twice a week. "I know. I know. It's just… too much sometimes, this time. Everything he said to me, layered on top of the next like he was gilding pot metal, and pretty soon I couldn't tell what was gold and what wasn't. My head's not on straight, and after I'm done here, I've got another therapy appointment."

"Want me to come with you?" His thumb tightened again, pressing into Jake's.

"It's got to be as boring as hell waiting for me." Jake liked walking out of the therapist's office and seeing Dallas's smile. He loved Dallas's hand on his back when they left, and he exulted in the feel of Dallas's arms around him after a couple of the tougher sessions, but asking the man to wait forty-five minutes just so Jake could get a hug out of the deal seemed a bit too much to ask sometimes.

"I don't mind, besides not like I don't work on stuff while you're in there." His grin was fleeting but deep. "Okay. I kind of work, then read or watch an episode of something. It's like a bit of downtime for me, and being there for you is as important to me as you being there for you. Tell you what, we go to the therapist—well, you go and talk to her—and afterwards, how about if you and I go out?"

"Go out?" Jake's brain glitched.

"Yeah, like a date. Okay, not like a date. An actual date, J." Dallas's expression changed, growing somber and tender. "Since we've been kind of dancing around each other for the past few weeks, and I've been thinking, let's go do something fun."

"A date?" He'd been wrong. The day could get more overwhelming. It all became too real, too quickly. He'd turned a corner someplace, before his father passed and after he'd seen Dallas's sexy curve of a smile. Now Dallas opened a door, leaving Jake to walk through it.

He didn't know if he was ready. Didn't know if he'd ever be ready. It was a trust moment, something his therapist challenged him to experience. Today had already blown through so many of those goddamned moments he wasn't able to choose to take, and now Dallas was dumping the most important, most real moment right in his lap to keep or throw away.

"Yeah, J, a date," Dallas repeated. "Might be kind of fast. I don't know. I just feel like today… with everything… we've gotten to a point where we decide what we want to do… what to be."

Jake took a breath, and his fear found its own voice, slithering out of the darkness inside of him. "Suppose I fuck it up. Suppose I fuck us up? I don't want to lose you, Dallas. I don't want to risk you."

"Babe…." Dallas rested his forehead against Jake's, bringing their noses together, the barest of touches. "You're not going to lose me. No matter what happens to us… there will always be an us. I will always be your friend first. Even when or if we become lovers, I will always be your friend. I just… hope for more. I want more, and I'm kind of hoping you want more too. So… a date. Doing something fun with maybe a lot of fried food and possibly cotton candy."

It was still in his lap—that moment he'd longed to take—and Jake swallowed, unable to meet Dallas's eyes. Trust. Having faith in someone, believing they wouldn't do anything to hurt him on purpose, was more frightening than a set of keys, a weekend dinner with a man he respected, or the mother of a man who made him joyful inside.

"I've never had cotton candy," Jake confessed, his breath rippling through the space between their mouths. "Or I don't think I have."

"That's just a crime, babe." Dallas's voice dropped, roiling with a deep velvet promise Jake felt down to his toes. "We are definitely going to have to get you some cotton candy."

"Okay, then." Jake exhaled, letting go of the knot bundled up tight inside of his chest. "You've got a date."

FROM THE outside, Doctor Val Shiga's office looked like every other door along a long corridor of doors. The building was a standard cement-and-glass office structure, perhaps with more parking and a bit more landscape, but it didn't stand out from any of the other thousand buildings dotting Los Angeles's busy streets.

It was hard for Jake to believe the seventeen-story building next to a taco joint and a muffler shop would become a Mecca and his salvation.

There was nothing personal in the waiting room. It was simply four walls with thick carpet, comfortable wide chairs, and a music system quietly playing soothing rainforest tracks on a continuous loop. The space's colors ran to cool, the carpet a tumble of grays, chiseled granite and marble pile soft enough to sink into when stepped on, and the chairs were padded heavily, broad enough to sit cross-legged if he'd wanted to.

Dallas said the chairs were damned comfortable, but Jake hadn't spent more than five minutes in one. Dr. Shiga—Val—shared the office with two other therapists, and instead of a receptionist, they'd installed a bank of buttons with their names below for their patients to push when they came in.

"It's kind of weird, you know?" Dallas whispered to him once as soon as they sat down. "It's like we're in purgatory, waiting for St. Peter to come out and give us a cat so we can head on over to heaven."

"You think there's cats in heaven?" Jake eyed Dallas.

"No, I think there's dogs in heaven, but in order for people to get in, they have to take a cat," he'd replied. "Only assholes don't love dogs, but true, pure souls love cats. You refuse the cat, you don't get in."

"Now I feel like I need a cat," Jake grumbled to himself as he sat down on the couch in the doctor's inner office. He gave the older woman a gentle smile, reassuring her of his sanity, which made him chuckle. "Sorry, something Dallas said a couple of times ago when we came into the waiting room."

"How are you doing with him? With your relationship?" She took up her position in a broad chair much like the ones in the waiting room and tucked her feet under the table sitting between them. "Or do you want to talk about something else?"

"Something else." Jake schooled his face, then remembered his promise to her about being open emotionally. "He and I are going to go on a date tonight. I'm not sure I'm ready to deal with that yet. Well, talking about it. I'm kind of...." Words were sliding around in his belly, refusing to rise to his tongue and dancing about with razor-sharp edges. "Scared? Apprehensive? I'm excited about it. I'm not scared of Dallas. I think I'm more scared of myself. For myself. I just... I guess I want to keep Dallas to myself for a bit. Because it's like... a birthday cake. He and I. And I don't know what it tastes like, but... it's cake, so I know it's good."

"That I understand perfectly." Her smile reminded him of Martha's, a warm chocolate chip cookie smile dipped in soothing, calm vanilla ice cream. "So what do you want to talk about?"

He liked her. Liked her a lot. She was more approachable than the first therapist he'd found, a man who'd resonated disapproval when Jake began talking of his feelings regarding Dallas and his attraction to men in general. Dallas insisted he find someone he liked better, and Val was... comfortable. He needed comfortable.

"Let me tell you about the keys," Jake began. "And Evancho."

He spent nearly thirty minutes talking about his parents and their loose connection to Evancho, then segued into Dallas's mother and how she made him feel discomforted at first. Jake poured everything he had inside of him out, at one point standing up to pace about the room, conflicted over using Evancho's back room for his art because it would be seen as favoritism, only to sit back down again when he was overwhelmed by his emotions when he talked about Evancho being proud of him.

Jake finally came to the end of his words, a skein of muddled colors and bright clashing metallic threads. The clock on the wall ticked away, and he caught himself before he glanced at the time, forcibly rejecting the guilt he felt for taking up her afternoon.

"You almost looked at the clock again, didn't you?" Her tone was light and teasing, not the verbal slap he'd come to expect from people. If he took anything away from their sessions, it was the understanding he was worth someone else's time. It was the hardest lesson she intended to guide him through and the one he knew he needed to learn the most.

"Almost." Nodding, he let out a short laugh. "I feel bad asking Dallas to wait for me outside, but he says he wants to. And now's when you ask me how I feel about that and I tell you I don't know. But this time I think I do. He makes me feel... good. Him waiting for me. Like I'm worth his time.

"That's kind of flipped around, because I've always been the one looking at the clock, making sure I'm somewhere early so no one's mad I'm late, and... it feels good. I've never felt this good about someone else before, and... I just want to take care of him. Like he takes care of me." The couch gave when he pushed back against it, settling his shoulders into its cushions. "Paying attention to what he needs, waiting for him sometimes. Not like I've got to keep track, but I don't know how to explain it. Equals, I guess. That we're worth each other's time."

"That's a big step for you," she acknowledged. "No matter what happens from this point on, you need to hold on to that, remember it for when things feel bleak."

"Like when I want to press the trigger on that gun?" He rubbed at his face, then stretched his legs out. "I need to get rid of it. I haven't, and I should. I don't need it. I don't want it, but... why do I keep it? It's not... right. It doesn't feel right anymore."

"Probably for a lot of reasons. No one can answer that for you, Jake."

"That gun's a part of my past," he asserted, hating the way the roof of his mouth itched when he spoke about it. "I need it to stay there because I need a future where I'm not tasting gun oil and whiskey in the morning before I brush my teeth. That gun's like watching the clock. It's me thinking I'm not worth the time or space. So I need to get rid of it. Maybe even today."

"If that's what you need to do, then you should," Val agreed, giving Jake a small nod. "We've talked about how to surrender it. The detective I know said she'll take it from you whenever you're ready to give it up. You just need to take it down there and give her a call. If you're ready."

"Yeah, I am." The weight of the keys grew lighter in his pocket after he'd accepted Evancho's pride in him, but the gun—that damned gun his father'd left behind in the house—was an albatross around his soul. What it was, what it meant now dragged him down. "Because I think I'm in love with Dallas, Dr. Shiga…. Val… and I can't do that… love him or learn to love him… with that piece of metal in my life. So it's got to go so I can move forward. So I don't have to watch any more clocks, waiting for the seconds to end. I think I'm ready. I think I'm ready to be in love."

FIFTEEN

"PRETTY BIG thing… doing this." Dallas angled the Tesla into a parking space, cranking the wheels slightly into the curb. "She knows we're coming, right?"

Jake shifted in the other seat, craning his neck slightly to look at the square glass cubes dominating the block. There was a bit of sunlight left in the day, catching on the red tints in Jake's rich coffee-brown hair. It was a pleasure to watch him, even as he struggled to turn over a piece of destruction he'd carried with him, an escape route for when life grew too sharp and dangerous for him to live.

The day was showing on Jake's face, deepening the shadows beneath his hazel eyes. What they were doing was necessary, but if he could, he'd have spared Jake the trip. The air inside the Tesla was hot with pressure, and Jake's limbs were stiff with stress. He'd been mostly silent on the trip over, his eyes drifting to scan the streets during their conversation, but Dallas suspected he saw nothing beyond his own thoughts.

"You don't have to do this. Today's been kind of big for you. If it's too much, that's okay," Dallas said for the tenth or so time since they'd packed the gun and ammo up into a box. "I can go in and hand it to her if you want me to."

"No, I've got to do this." Jake's long lashes dipped down once, his gaze falling to the box at his feet. "I don't understand why I want to not do this. It doesn't make any sense. I've…."

He trailed off, and Dallas reached for Jake, letting his fingers brush Jake's thigh. He twitched when Dallas touched him, his muscle jumping under Dallas's fingertips. The freckles were out in full force across Jake's cheekbones, their light scatter burnishing his paling skin. The longer they sat under the pepper trees' shade, the paler Jake got, until Dallas was worried he'd pass out from lack of circulation if they didn't start moving soon.

They were squeezing the last bit of the afternoon out, wringing the dregs from the day, and Los Angeles's streets were thickening with

130

traffic. The rush of cars passing them was a waterfall of sound, and coupled with the fragrant spicy green of the nearby trees and the faint breeze flowing through the coupe's partially open windows, it was a nice, serene spot to sit and watch the world go by. It should have been peaceful, sitting in front of a long stretch of lawn and pathways with odd sculptures crawling up into the air from their circular stone pedestals.

Dallas hated Jake being denied that peace. Hated knowing Jake's solution—a finite, horrific solution—to the turmoil raging in his gentle soul lay in a box between his feet. He also hated knowing Jake was the only one who could walk that box up to the detective and hand his death wish incarnate over to her.

It would do Jake no good if Dallas handed the gun over. Dallas knew all the reasons why he shouldn't—good, solid, valid reasons—but they battled with Dallas's longing to grab the box and chuck it as far away as he could... because Jake didn't need any more pain in his life. Yeah, Jake had to be the one to hand the gun over. It was the only way he was going to heal, but Dallas still didn't have to fucking like it.

"Hey, look at me." Dallas inched closer, or as much as he could in the Tesla, twisting in his seat so he faced Jake. When Jake turned to look at him, Dallas was struck by the guileless trust in Jake's face and the sweetness of the man's soul shining out of his troubled gaze. "I want you to know something, and you don't have to respond or react. You just have to sit here and listen for one minute, and when I'm done talking, you can either punch me in the face or get out of the car and we'll go do this thing together, okay?"

"I worry about you and your thinking I'm going to ever punch you. Don't you think I've had enough of that kind of shit from my father?" Jake tilted his head back against the car seat, sighing. "Sorry, I.... God, I can't seem to shake him off of me. He's like dried snot I can't scrape off my skin, and I feel... guilty for being happy about being free of him. And pissed off because I'm guilty."

"Okay, all of that? Valid." A bicycle whizzed by, nearly clipping the Tesla's side mirror, and Dallas shook his head at the courier's back, then turned his attention back to Jake. "I'm not a doctor. I don't play one on TV. I don't even pretend to know what to take when I've got a cold or the flu. I don't know what to starve or what to feed, and most of the time—and I'm not too proud to admit this—I call my mother to ask her. So, I'm probably the last person you should ask advice from about anything related to your body or your brain."

"But?" Jake mimicked Dallas's slight drawl back at him. It wasn't a bad mockery. Celeste did a terrible impression of him, especially when she spackled on a country accent so thick it grew hayseeds. "You're going to say a but."

"But I think this gun here is like a piece of your father, and it's comfortable to you because at some point in your life, you knew your father was going to kill you." Jake flinched—visibly flinched—but Dallas pressed on. "I think you keep that gun—want to keep that gun—because it's what you've always expected would happen. He would kill you. And now he's dead, and that's all of him you have left that can do the job.

"You're stronger than that, J. I know you are. And he didn't deserve you. Not one fucking bit. I know you've got to go hand that thing over because it's something you need to do in order to move forward, but I'm telling you this...." Dallas cupped Jake's face, feeling the strength of his jaw on his palm and the softness of Jake's lower lip on his thumb. "I'm not going to let that asshole take you from this world. If I've got to follow some short, hairy-footed guys to the edge of a damned volcano to do it, that thing's going to burn. You're special, beautiful, sweet, talented, and so damned gorgeous you make my teeth ache, so yeah, one way or another, that gun's leaving you today. And then, so help me God, I'm going to get you some cotton candy."

"It was nice up until the cotton candy." Jake's reproach wasn't serious, or at least it didn't seem to be judging by the dimple creasing his cheek. "And I don't think you're wrong about the gun. Any of it. I do have to be the one to hand it over, and I like that you want to do it for me. I also want to tell you thanks for... well, everything.

"For being here. For everything. Just... for being with me." Jake turned his head, his mouth leaving a slightly damp imprint on Dallas's palm in a gentle, lingering kiss. He leaned into Dallas's hand, then pulled away, bending over to grab the box by his feet. "I like you a lot, Dallas. Probably more than I should or... I don't know... I've never been in something serious with anyone before. Not really. I don't know what to do with how I'm feeling, and I don't think I'll begin to understand what's inside of me until I get rid of this. Because I'm ready to put this part of my life… of whatever I was living… behind me."

"But then cotton candy?" Dallas poked at Jake's side, finding a ticklish spot between his ribs. "Because, Jake Moore, I cannot wait to see how you taste with a bit of cotton candy on your tongue."

"I really don't care about the cotton candy, Dal." A shyness filled Jake's expression, endearingly sweet and unexpected. Then he whispered back, "I just want to taste you."

It was over too quickly. Oddly anticlimactic and without a fanfare or heavenly choir descending to part the clouds and drown the Earth in their glory. Instead a handsome, somber-faced Latina detective in jeans, black T-shirt, and a shoulder harness with a gun in her holster met them in a flat-gray interview room and took the box before Jake could slide it across the table to her.

Detective O'Byrne greeted them at the front desk, and Dallas laughed when he saw her, telling Jake she'd been the detective called in for the body found at Bombshells. They'd both stopped short when she came downstairs, shaking hands and murmuring about how it was nice to see each other again, and then Detective O'Byrne led them down a hall, asking a passing uniformed officer to grab her three sodas from the vending machine and bring them to the interview room.

"I just need to ask you a few questions, Mr. Moore," she said, finally sitting down after the cop who brought the sodas in took the box out with him when he left.

And that was it. That part of his life was gone. The darkness of its presence and its foul oily metal taste were no longer going to be hovering in the back of Jake's mind. He didn't mourn its loss. If anything, he felt freer than he had when his father exhaled his last rattling breath or when he watched the gravediggers toss the first few shovels of dirt over the coffin.

It was done. He was done. And the first inhale Jake took when the box left the room eased away the barb he'd nursed in him for way too long.

O'Byrne cleared her throat, catching Jake's attention. "How long have you had the gun in your possession, and do you have a license to own a gun?"

"Sorry. I've had the gun in my apartment for a few years now, but… it was my father's." O'Byrne's fierce expression concerned Jake, especially when she began taking notes. "I don't have a license… um… its registration is in the box."

"His dad just passed a few weeks ago," Dallas interjected. "He was in a home right up until he went into the hospital."

"Did you bring a copy of the death certificate?" She looked up from her forms to take the piece of paper Jake'd copied for her. "Thanks. Normally we do a quick sheet during gun buybacks, but since you're here instead of doing it through the program, it's a bit different. I just want to make sure there's no questions I haven't covered with you. Okay?"

"Sure, fine." He glanced over at Dallas.

"Gun buybacks are something the cops organize for people to drop off weapons like guns. Usually in exchange for cash or gift cards," Dallas explained. "You could have waited to turn it in then, but—"

"Yeah, no. I don't want anything for it." Jake raked his hair back from his eyes. Dallas's hand snuck into his, and Jake took it, thankful for the touch. "I just want it gone."

"Not a problem. Just a few more questions." The cop gave Jake a quick glance. Her unreadable dark eyes and flat expression were hardly reassuring, but her tone was gentle. "Do you know if it's been used in a crime?"

"A crime?" That shocked him. He hadn't ever imagined his father using the gun, especially since he'd never told Jake about it. Finding it was as startling as O'Byrne's question, and he didn't know how to answer her. Clearing his throat, he shook his head. "I don't know. I don't think so?"

Jake tightened his hold on Dallas's hand. He had questions as soon as he found the gun. Where'd it come from, and why did his father kill his mother with a cast-iron skillet instead of a bullet? Opportunity and rage? There'd never been any question in his mind about his father's duplicity. There'd been too many signs, too many sly confessions alluding to his killing of his wife, but the gun…. Why hadn't he used that instead, and where had it come from?

"I don't know," he repeated, then sighed. "Look, my father? He wasn't a good man. There are things he did… pain he caused… I can't undo. This gun, I've had it with me because… it was his. A part of him I never knew, a violence way past what I thought he had in him. I think the only good thing I can say about him is that he didn't use this on me or my mother, and that's the only good thing I can say. If it was used on someone else, I don't know. Maybe because I wouldn't put it past him. So… maybe."

"Maybe is good enough. I'll have ballistics check it out." O'Byrne jotted something down on the paper, then flipped it over. "Has it been fired recently?"

"No, I've cleaned it. I learned how to do that to take care of it but…." Dallas's fingers squeezed in, a velvet band around Jake's hand, and his breath caught in his chest. "But I've never pulled the trigger."

And now he never would.

"That's it, then." She patted at the paper. "Do you have any questions for me?"

"No, I think I'm good." He was about to get up when Dallas tugged at his hand.

"Actually, I've got a couple. Not about the gun," Dallas assured her. "It's about the man we found in the loft space. Have they identified him? Thing is, if he doesn't have family, I don't want him to end up in some hole without a marker. I spoke to someone else about it, one of the coroner people, but she told me I'd have to talk to you. Was going to call, but…."

"Since you're already here?" O'Byrne tucked the paper into her pen's clip. "You seem a bit too invested in this, Yates. Something you want to tell me?"

"Just want to do what's right by this guy, Detective," Dallas replied. "He died in a building I purchased, and no one knew he was there. The previous owners don't know him, and unless you've got a family you're going to send him off to, he's going to get put in a numbered box and buried on top of other people whose lives were so shitty they died without anyone knowing who they are. I don't know about you, but I was raised better than that. I might not know the guy, but it doesn't mean I'm not responsible."

"I work homicide, Yates. Having someone do the right thing isn't a common occurrence in my day to day." She glanced at the door as someone knocked. Then a handsome Hispanic man popped his head in, glancing over Jake and Dallas quickly. "You need the room, Montoya?"

"Captain just wanted to know if you're wrapping this up. He's got a couple of questions for you on the girl they found the other day."

Montoya spoke with a smooth accent, a lush roll of simmer and spice, but not the Mexican Jake heard around him at work. "I can go back and say you'll be a bit."

"About ten minutes, tops." This time her smile reached her eyes. "Don't want to keep the old man waiting."

"I'll tell him you said that," the other detective rumbled. "The ten minutes. Not the old man."

"Nice, I'll owe you," she promised him. The detective closed the door behind him, and O'Byrne took a moment before speaking. "Okay, what I can tell you is someone in Narcotics believes he knows the man you found. Nothing's definite right now, but based on his clothing and everything else, it's a strong possibility. I can't tell you there's going to be family to pick up the remains because from everything we know about this man, he wasn't exactly the nicest of guys to be around. Coroner's leaning towards natural causes just at a cursory look, but there hasn't been time to do an autopsy.

"If it is who the detective thinks he is, then he's older, probably pushing seventy or eighty, and did most of his living on the street. If—and this is an if—we don't have someone to claim his body after the investigation, I will contact you. I'll even put you down as next of kin to be notified upon release, but it's going to be a couple of months at the earliest." O'Byrne stood, scooping the paper and pen up from the table. "Until that time, there's nothing else you can do. Just wait for someone to call you. One way or another, I'll make sure someone lets you know, okay?"

"That's all I want," Dallas replied.

The trip back downstairs turned into a surreal journey of uniforms, cold hallways, and white walls. If a blue-haired caterpillar popped out of a crack in the wall, Jake wouldn't have been surprised. He held Dallas's hand all the way down, half-afraid to let go and lose the one anchor he had to reality. Or to the dream. Standing in the middle of an elevator filled with cops and guns, he was walking out into a different life.

They pushed through the double doors, and Jake stopped at the top of the stairs leading down to the green space in front of the building. He felt different. A little worn down, but the day tore nearly everything out of him. He'd been turned around and chewed up from the inside out. He was caught on a bit of a ledge between what he needed and what he feared.

"Dal, can I ask you something?" Shoving his hands into his pockets, Jake caught himself bracing for... unpleasantness. "And this is stupid. Right now. Here. I'm scared to talk to you, and I shouldn't be."

"Nope, shouldn't be at all," Dallas replied. "But what did Val say? You're in the habit of being afraid. It's going to take time to unlearn that. Kind of like chewing on your fingernails. Just a bad habit. Well, at least with me. I'm the picture of tolerance and understanding. I can't answer for the rest of the world. But go on, please."

"There are times when I don't know how to take you." He eyed Dallas. "I just wanted to ask if it was okay if we didn't go out tonight. I know you wanted to do a date thing, but truthfully...."

"Jake, honey." Dallas drew Jake into a loose hug. "I always want you to be truthful with me."

In front of everyone. Every cop in LA. People on the street. As if grabbing Jake and holding him was an everyday thing. Jake tightened up, rigidly firm and sick to his stomach. Then... nothing happened. No one cared.

"You okay?" Dallas prodded. "Hey, I'm here. Whatever you need, J, I'm here."

"I know." He began to breathe again, relaxing in Dallas's embrace. "I just think... today's been... long and weird. Your mom's here, and... you sure you want to be around me tonight?"

"I can't think of anyplace else I'd rather be." He chuckled. "Besides, my mom's going to spend the evening with her other daughter, Celeste. She understands today's about you. If you want me to drop you off, then—"

"I don't want you to drop me off." Jake's tongue was suddenly an unforgiving lump in his mouth, and he forced it to move, forming words he needed to get out before he choked on them. "I want you to stay tonight. I think what I need... all I need... is you."

SIXTEEN

IN THE end, they danced.

Or the beginning, Dallas corrected himself, because he had no intention of ever letting Jake go.

The music was soft, instrumental and unfamiliar, but the rise and fall of notes was a waterfall of comfort while they swayed back and forth behind the couch. Jake's bare feet brushed his every few steps, an oddly gentle, surprising caress Dallas loved. They'd fumbled at first after Dallas held his hand out to Jake, asking him for a dance, and when they'd come together, it'd been a brief skirmish of elbows, knees, and chins before they found where they fit into one another. A few shuffles in and Jake finally relaxed, his arms loosening slightly around Dallas's waist, and then his head drifted down, resting on Dallas's left shoulder.

Dallas simply breathed, taking Jake's clean scent into him, then holding it there, lulled by the man's warm body rocking against him.

Outside, Los Angeles faded into the rising night, the clash of cars and people held back by the apartment's thick brick walls, and the drop in temperature meant cranking the windows closed to keep out the chilly snap and a promised heavy morning dew. There was only a single floor lamp on, an old-fashioned tree with a heavy burlap-ring shade, but the fabric diffused the bulbs, turning the light golden and warm.

"Your smile takes me to the stars," Dallas sang off-key to the music. He'd never had a talent for singing, and normally it took more than a few shots to get him in front of a mic, even for karaoke, but something silly bloomed in him. Surrounded by Jake's life, holding the man in his arms, Dallas serenaded the world with what was in his heart. "I love the feel of your kiss, the moon shining in your eyes."

Jake made a muffled noise against Dallas's throat, a garbled something resembling a snort if Dallas heard it right. "I didn't know this song had words."

"It doesn't. I'm making it all up." Dallas kissed a spot on Jake's temple where his hair stuck up in a tuft. He turned, keeping Jake close. "You just make me want to sing."

"You're a really crappy singer," he teased, then yelped when Dallas pinched his ass. "Hey!"

"Critics, like children, should be seen and not heard." He sniffed in mock offense.

"Kind of like your singing." Jake stepped back quickly, avoiding Dallas's intended light pat on his rear. "Really, you're kind of… horrible. Like dog howling bad."

"You, Jacques Moore, need a broader musical education," Dallas said, slowly stalking Jake as he backpedaled across the floor. "Come back here. I'm not done dancing with you."

It didn't take much to grab Jake, a simple snag of his T-shirt and Dallas drew him back in. They were on the edge of the shadows, cloaked in a milky gray. Dallas's soul filled with a brightness he didn't know he could take when he wrapped one arm around Jake's waist and their hips bumped, the buttons on their jeans clacking in a dull chime loud enough to make Jake laugh.

"God, I love hearing you do that… laugh," Dallas whispered. "The things you do to me, J. Just… everything you are makes me feel so good. What the hell did I do without you in my life?"

The ashes of Jake's past were falling away, burnt-off crusts they were both chipping away at. He was cracked beneath the hurt. Dallas knew that, felt that anguish sometimes when Jake grew melancholy or his hazel eyes went dark with echoes of remembered pain. But the healing was there too, bright pink bits shining out of the tragedy of Jake's injured soul. He grew stronger every day, taking small steps toward trusting others as he reached out to Dallas to steady him.

"I promised not to take advantage of you, Mr. Moore, but…." Jake's arousal pressed into Dallas's leg, a lengthening siren call begging to be answered. "You are making it very difficult."

"Can you be taking advantage of me if I start it?" He cocked his head, the shadows curling over his strong, handsome face, and Dallas's heart twinged at Jake's playful smile. "Just curious. How does that work?"

"Kinda works like this," Dallas murmured, leaning into Jake. "Let me know what you think."

It was their first real kiss. A touching of their mouths, then a deepening of their connection. It was funny how Dallas had never thought about a kiss as being important or life changing before he brought his lips to Jake's.

Dallas's existence became a small tiny sliver of the universe, holding enough starshine in its folds to set his soul on fire. His body thrummed with energy, aching with a need he couldn't let loose. Not yet. Maybe not ever. Everything he knew about Jake's experiences told Dallas to go slow, to coax and let the other man lead them down whatever path he wanted to take, and a part of him—that insane, needy part of him—cried out to quench its heat in Jake's soul.

Just from the brush of his lips on Jake's parted mouth.

Then Jake's tongue dabbed lightly at Dallas's upper lip and Dallas was lost all over again.

Time needed to slow down, crawl past each second so he could savor everything—feel everything—happening to him as Jake pressed forward. Dallas closed his eyes and drank in the single most important moment of his life.

It was the little things Dallas wanted to remember: the slick of his hands on Jake's back when he slid his fingers under Jake's shirt, the taste of lemon soda on Jake's tongue, and the feel of his teeth on the plump of Dallas's lip. Their kiss continued, a slow savoring of their bodies, and Jake tentatively explored the span of Dallas's ribs, skirting over the bone and down to the rise of his hip. Dallas held in an aroused gasp when Jake's fingers dipped below his waistband, barely gaping his jeans. There was the feel of beard scruff on his palms and the tiny thump-beat of Jake's pulse beneath his thumb when he stroked at Jake's throat.

Jake trembled as Dallas caressed his spine, a feathery exploration of the powerful strength of Jake's muscled back. He moaned when Dallas nipped at his lower lip and clenched his ass under Dallas's palm as he continued his skimming journey of Jake's lean form.

But the feel of him, the visceral feel of Jake's long, hard body fitting into his and the heat of their mouths sending shivering aches through Dallas's spine, those were delicious moments he needed to burn into his memory to hold on to for as long as he lived.

It took every ounce of Dallas's willpower to pull away, ending their kiss, and the next breath he took ran stale without the taste of Jake on it.

"Jesus," Jake gasped, leaning his forehead against Dallas's. "You're going to break me."

"Can't have that," Dallas whispered. "Not when you've worked so hard to unbreak you. Can't I just… try to make you lose your mind?"

"Yeah, that's kind of what I'm hoping for." Jake exhaled, a shudder working through him. Then his lashes dropped, hiding his eyes, and as gently passionate as the kiss he'd just shared with Dallas, he asked softly, "Will you make love to me, Dal? Right now?"

HIS BRAIN fixated on the stupidest things. Jake knew that. He dealt with it every day. From getting caught in the negative space inside a line of metal to the whisper of a song lyric surfacing over and over while he worked, his mind did funny things to cope and deal with the things he couldn't quite think about.

Like the moment he and Dallas tumbled down onto his mattress, all Jake could think about was when he'd changed his sheets last.

"Dallas, I…."

There were too many memories, faded echoes of a tongue pushing into his mouth and fingers, dry and cracked, catching on his skin, but Jake burned for the man half lying on him. Dallas's weight was more blanket than burden, familiar and erotic with a bit of mystery Jake longed to explore. Simple things were worth discovering: the softness of Dallas's skin under his jaw, the scent of his hair after a shower, and even the noises he made when he slept during a thunderstorm. All things Jake needed to know, bits of Dallas he could hold in his heart to ward off the cold fears determined to crawl up from his past-forged hell.

Dallas rose, sliding off of Jake's hips, and sat back, his knees pressing into Jake's side. One hand remained on Jake's abdomen, fingers wrapped into Jake's shirt, caught halfway up his belly. He didn't need any more light from the lamp in the living space to see Dallas's look of concern. He could feel the tension in Dallas's body, taut and alert to Jake's needs.

"What is it, babe? Are you okay?" The back of Dallas's hand brushed up Jake's stomach, following the curve of his ribs. "Do you need me to stop?"

If Jake'd needed anything more to convince him Dallas would never hurt him, gouge into him as others had, it was that moment when he heard the tremble in Jake's voice and slid his weight from Jake's body.

Jake knew the logistics of sex. Experienced it in the hands of someone who hadn't cared about Jake's pain or heard him when he cried out. Dallas's tenderness coaxed out the arousal in Jake, strengthening the rush of blood coursing into his cock until Jake wept from the tightness of his skin rubbing on his underwear. He wasn't going to let the past cripple his need for Dallas, and he certainly wasn't going to back away from wanting the one man who he'd come to… love. A man who'd taught him how to feel love when he'd spent his life crawling through a black wasteland of apathy and hate.

"I wanted to tell you…." Jake hitched in a breath, getting up onto his elbows. "Wanted to say I'm glad you're here. With me. Now."

"Babe, I'll be here forever." Dallas's kiss was stunning, an incredible burst of masculine essence with a drop of caramel-sweet affection. "If you'll have me."

"Aren't you supposed to have me?" Jake teased, then grunted when Dallas playfully beat his head once on Jake's chest. "Seriously, will you? Just… please?"

"Any time you're not feeling it," he whispered through a soft kiss. "You tell me. And I stop. Okay?"

Jake couldn't answer, wouldn't answer. Dallas's words were more for his reassurance than anything else, and he nodded, then lost his mind when Dallas's teeth lightly dug into his chest and his tongue moistened Jake's hardening nipple through the thin fabric of his T-shirt.

"We need to get us naked," Dallas growled. Then he raised his head, staring at Jake. "Shit and hell, lube. Condoms. Shit. I hadn't planned for this, babe. I—"

"Drawer. Paper bag. White." Jake nodded toward the nightstand. "I figured we'd get around to it someday. I just—"

"When did you buy these?" Dallas dug around the drawer and came up with a book. "Hmmm, okay… some light reading. A Scottish weredog named Jeremy and werewolf princes? Sounds cool. And it's an actual book. I love that about you. You buy real books."

"I like paper, okay?" Jake pushed his toes into Dallas's shin. "Like the bag you're looking for. Grab the bag, Dal."

"Bag has been grabbed," Dallas muttered, crinkling the paper for Jake to hear. Then he sat back and let out a long sigh. "Fuck, you are so... damned... beautiful, Jake."

No one ever looked at Jake like Dallas did.

Probably no one ever would.

"Seriously, I can't even handle how gorgeous you are sometimes, love." Dallas lowered himself down slowly, stretching out next to Jake. Tucking the bag up near the mound of pillows pushed up against the headboard, Dallas chuckled when Jake bit into his upper arm. "You, Jacques, have some very sharp teeth. Let's see if we can't find something else to do with your mouth. But first, clothes. Those need to go."

They took their time, shedding fabric from their bodies and tasting the skin underneath with slow licks and tiny nibbles. Jake discovered a tiny starfish tattoo on the small of Dallas's back, a memento of a summer he spent in the Greek isles. He felt Dallas's tears hit the curve of his back when his lover saw the pale, thin scars striping his back, marks left from his father's enraged beatings, then shattered under the punch of his emotions when Dallas traced each one with a finger, kissing the end of his trails and promising Jake he would help make things all better.

"You do," Jake gasped when Dallas's oiled fingers began to dip into the recess between his cheeks. "Make it all better."

He'd never been much of a talker, but Dallas brought out the words Jake never seemed to be able to find with anyone else, not even himself. It was easy being with Dallas, a comfortable roll of personality and soul around his wounded, broken self. Then there were times—like now— when Dallas's touch set him on fire and Jake wondered if he'd ever survive another kiss.

A kiss? Hell, he didn't think he'd survive Dallas's delicate brush of fingers around his hole or the heat of his mouth right before he closed his lips over Jake's cock head.

"Let me do this for you, babe," Dallas whispered around a mouthful of Jake. His fingers danced lightly around Jake's balls and crease, finding sensitive spots to stroke and heat. "And if you need me to stop, I will. This is about you tonight, J, and I want to make it good."

Dallas's mouth left a wicked, moist trail across Jake's body, his tongue finding tingling, erotic spots Jake didn't even know he had. He wanted to explore Dallas, but he couldn't do much more than moan and fist his hands into Dallas's thick black hair, mewling and needy. His skin tightened, nearly overwhelmed by the sensations Dallas left behind in his wanderings, and when Dallas slowly eased his fingers into Jake's body, Jake held on tight and prayed he could ride out the electrical storm Dallas summoned from deep within him.

He was safe. It was silly to think passion—this deep passion Dallas evoked—was safe. Yet there he was, roiling in the drowning tide of his body's responsive keen to Dallas's hands and mouth, and lying in the middle of the tempest, Jake was safe.

There was no pain. A bit of discomfort when his body learned to give way to Dallas's light pressures and a touch of overstimulation around his cock head when his balls began to churn, needing their release, but nothing Jake didn't love having done to him. The sharp, bitter ache of being handled too much faded nearly as quickly as it started when Dallas felt him shift, the man's mouth pulling free of Jake's shaft, leaving with a sensual lick as if promising to return. The push of his flesh around Dallas's fingers yanked a gasp from Jake's throat, and his mind fought the unfamiliar intrusion for a moment. Then the shadows parted, giving Jake a glimpse of Dallas's wild blue eyes, and he knew he'd come home.

Dallas was home. A shelter in the storm Jake'd been caught in since the moment he drew his first breath. Every step up until the moment he'd lost his heart to the smirking, lanky Dallas had been a slog through broken glass and torn dreams. Dallas wasn't salvation. He was something more. A lifeline for Jake to grab, a man who'd known Jake needed to find his own strength. Dallas had thrown a rope to a drowning man, a lifeline to help Jake find the shore in what he'd thought was an endless bitter ocean.

And when Jake finally touched solid ground, he'd stood in the shaky mess he'd become and found someone who saw the person within the rot and fear.

"Love you." Jake's whisper was lost, carried off in the velvet whispers of Dallas's thickening Southern accent. He didn't need Dallas to hear him. Mostly he just needed to know Dallas was there, and when Jake reached for his lover, Dallas shot him a naughty grin.

"You okay, babe?" Dallas licked at Jake's belly button, then chuckled at Jake's short nod. "Because if you aren't—"

"Will you just stop talking and do this? Because—" Dallas's fingers slid in, filling Jake until he choked on the sensations coursing through him. "Oh... damn."

Those fingers, fiendishly erotic and deliciously intrusive, stroked and teased for a long, shuddering moment. Then Jake was empty, left gasping and aching for more. Dallas shifted his weight, his knees dimpling the bed between Jake's legs, and he slicked himself over the condom he'd put on, his gaze caught on Jake's face.

The shadows and light loved Dallas, playing catch along the lines of his muscles and burying into the depths of his inky black hair. He was a golden-pale sweep of beauty and silly, a tumble of laughter and seriousness intermingled with a pure sweetness Jake didn't know he needed until Dallas was there, filling his life... filling his body.

Oh God, he was filling Jake's body in a slow, torturous glide of hard flesh, a broad, firm length Jake wasn't sure would fit—didn't know if he could take—until he felt one of Dallas's hands along his side, stroking away the shivers. And then Dallas nestled against the rise of Jake's ass, guiding Jake's legs up to rest on his hips.

Dallas didn't ask if Jake was okay. He waited. Silently waited and stroked at Jake's belly, letting him get used to the feeling of a man's cock—Dallas's cock—buried inside of him. It was an awkward pleasure, pressing the air from Jake's chest and mottling his thoughts with bursts of tingles and building desire.

Then Dallas moved, stroking his shaft along the inside of Jake's core, and the world churned, turning into a field of stars.

Dallas's fingers were on Jake's shaft, a gentle, twisting caress until Jake closed his hand over Dallas's. Then they began to stroke in unison, a slow, steady pump along Jake's cock. Dallas's hips moved, rolling into Jake's depths, and Jake didn't think he could be stretched out any farther, take in any more. Then Dallas slid over the already too tangled spot of pleasure in Jake's body.

And Jake let go.

He fell. Or flew. He wasn't sure which. It didn't matter anymore. His body responded, a mindless need driving his hips and fueling a thirst for Dallas he didn't think he'd ever quench. Their legs grew wet, damp with sweat, and Dallas leaned over him, panting hard but pushing in, reaching for Jake's soul and cresting pleasure. Their hands moved furiously in unison until their release hit them hard, together, and the beat they'd found was lost in the crescendo of a powerful climax.

It hit Jake first. Coming up out of the frenetic slide of their limbs and joined bodies, his pleasure slapped at his mind, breaking away any threads of control clinging to his thoughts. Nothing existed but Dallas. Nothing mattered but the pleasure Dallas was driving into him, taking from him, and then Jake felt his body clench, seizing around the orgasm about to rip through him.

Definitely flying. Or maybe falling.

He was caught in the froth of their release, tumbling over the too hot too muchness of what they'd done, were doing. Jake was on the edge of a silvered emotion, seeing Dallas go over the edge in a gasping, lunging push. His lover's shoulders bunched, arms stiff and framing Jake's shoulders. Dallas rocked in, hard and fast, then shuddered, his climax shaking through him as he found his release in Jake's heat.

They tumbled over one another, a slide of bones and worn muscles, a stretch of tendon and laughter when Dallas pulled the lube out from under his hip, the skin there bruised from Jake's clenching fingers.

"You. Are. Absolutely. Fantastic. And I can't wait to do that again. Any way you want it, I'm there, babe," Dallas gasped. Dallas's phone burbled Celeste's ringtone before Jake could reply, and Dallas frowned, lifting his head up to stare at the table where he'd left it. "Shit. I am not going to get that."

"You should." Jake found his lips were numb, a bit swollen from their kissing, but he didn't care, stretching out across the sheets. "She's with your mom, remember?"

"Shit. I hate that you think of the right thing to do when all I want to do is roll around with you some more," Dallas mumbled.

He stole a quick, hot, nibbling kiss from Jake, then slid off the bed, naked and beautiful. His limp cock swung slightly when he walked, his asscheeks firm and supple, bunching as he moved. He grabbed the phone and answered with a short, playful "What?" Then the color drained from his face. The call was short, too short for Jake to do anything but get off the bed and catch Dallas when he stumbled over one of the dining chair's legs.

"Dallas, what's wrong?" Jake held Dallas close, reaching for the phone in Dallas's hand. "You're scaring me. What's happened?"

"We have to get dressed." Those pale blue eyes, filled with fire only a few moments before, were now wide with fear. "We have to go to the hospital. Someone's attacked my mom."

SEVENTEEN

"SHE'S GOING to be fine," Dallas reassured Jake all the way to the hospital, but his hands shook when he ran them through his dark hair, and when Jake pulled the Tesla up to the hospital's front door to let Dallas out, his lover stared blankly at the entrance, his lips pulled into a tight white line.

He'd parked the sports car, then spent a good ten minutes trying to find Dallas in the maze of corridors and people, finally stumbling across a forlorn Celeste sitting in the corner of the ER's waiting room, her bright-green-polished fingernails tapping at a crinkled paper cup. There was a uniformed cop hovering nearby, a phone plastered to his ear as he carried on a half conversation with one of the male nurses at the ER's admittance station. There were clusters of people, a few holding appendages in various states of injury, but the long hall was fairly quiet, a large television screen mounted to a wall softly playing a kid's cartoon with Spanish subtitles.

"She's going to be fine," Celeste murmured when he slid into the chair next to her. Her stare was hard, a flat line of dark pinned to a pair of closed swinging doors on the far wall. "She's going to be just fine."

Jake reached for her hand, and Celeste glanced at his fingers, startled when Jake touched her. Setting the damaged cup down on the floor near her feet, she took Jake's hand and leaned into him, resting her tear-streaked cheek against his shoulder.

Unless Celeste took to wearing a short retro green-and-pink polka-dotted white dress and blush go-go boots to lounge around the house, Jake gathered they'd gone out for the evening. Blood splattered the dress, a smear of it across Celeste's chest and more on her belly. Her ever-changing hair was blonde this time, teased up high in a hairdo he'd seen his grandmother sporting in the one photo his mother had of her. From its frizzy ends and wild strands escaping from the bubbled mass, Jake wondered if he was seeing Celeste's actual hair. Her face was puffy, with black runnels dappling her

148

skin, streaks of mascara and eyeliner smudged away from under her lashes, but her cold grip was strong, nearly crushing Jake's fingers.

"What happened?" He'd gotten little out of Dallas other than a knife and a lot of blood. The drive to the hospital was tense until Dallas bent over at a red light, kissed him hard, and told Jake he couldn't have borne his worry and anger if Jake hadn't been there. "What did the doctors tell you? Did the cops talk to you already?"

"Last things first, the cop—there's a ginger one, a detective—is inside talking to Martha. The kid in the uniform called, and he showed up a couple of minutes later. He told me to stay put while he talks to Martha, and then he'll come out to get my statement." Celeste sniffed, and she gave the tissue box Jake put under her nose a watery smile. "God, Dallas is... I could hate him for spotting you first. You, Jakey, are a doll. A gorgeous, sweet, loveable doll. With one of the best asses I've ever seen. If ever you decide to toss Dallas out, give me a call."

"I... I was going to say I don't think you have the equipment I like, but then... it's because to me, you're a girl. All girl. So even if you still have... that... you're a girl." He kissed her temple, smelling a whiff of powder and cherries on her skin. "You confuse me sometimes, and I don't know what to say."

"You do just fine, sweetie." Celeste dabbed at her eyes, then grimaced at the inky smears left on the tissue. "God, I must look a mess."

"You look beautiful," he reassured her. "And I don't even like women."

"Seriously, you're going to break my heart." Putting her head back down, she sighed. "And as to what happened? I have no fucking clue. Martha forgot her purse at Bombshells, so I stopped there before we went out to the show. She wanted to get it before dinner, but I told her I had it. I was going to take her out, but.... God, I should have gone then. She wouldn't have been—"

"Celeste, sometimes things happen." Jake sighed at the irony of him imparting wisdom about fates and changed courses. "It sounds stupid, but they do. I know. Looking back at the *what could be* doesn't do anything but eat you up inside. Then you've got to go find someone to talk to, someone you like, and it takes forever to get your head on straight."

"You know something, sweetie?" She looked up at him, rubbing at her reddened nose. "I think that's the most you've ever said to me.

I can't help it. Martha's like… she's like a mother. A real mother. Who cooks really badly and one time gave me food poisoning with a taco, but still, she held my hair while I puked my guts out. And she cleaned the bathroom floor when I'd missed the bowl. I wanted to crawl under a rock, and she was all… no, darling, don't worry about it. If you love someone, you don't care what is happening, you just want them to feel better. She wants to make me feel better, Jake. How can I not feel like shit for letting some asshole stab her?"

"Did you see who did it?" The worry was back, digging into Jake's spine. "Celeste, was she okay? Dallas didn't know. Should I try to go in there?"

"They won't let you. I'm surprised they let Dallas in, but… you know, an actual blood relative. Okay, maybe that makes sense." Celeste sighed, tucking her arm into Jake's. "Martha went inside, and then I heard her scream. I was so scared, Jake. Just so fucking scared. It was so dark, and I couldn't see how badly she was hurt, but…."

Celeste's voice changed, her deep contralto breaking down, fragmenting into a higher pitch, a glittery confetti of panic and fear. The chair's arm dug into Jake, but he ignored the spur in his side, leaning over to drag Celeste out of her seat and into a tight embrace.

It was awkward, a half hug with their legs sprawled out, but Celeste clung to him, burying her face into his chest and muffling her howls in the bunches of his T-shirt she'd pulled into her clenched fists. The cop glanced at them, alert and concerned, but Jake shook his head, silently assuring him she was okay. A minute later, Celeste had cried herself out, settling into a raging fit of hiccups, then sat back, patting at Jake's makeup-mottled shirt. Then in a quiet, still voice, Celeste began talking.

"She took me bra shopping." Her eyes were unfocused, drifting back to the closed doors again, and her voice dropped back down, rolling through a velvet huskiness. Celeste's fingers tore through the tissues in her hand, a rainfall of pale specks drifting down to dust the ER's tiled floor. "When I first started… hormones, you know? I was staying at the ranch, in one of the bungalows. Everything was just too much for me to deal with, and let me tell you, that shit takes months. I felt sick, and my body wasn't changing quickly…. I wanted it all to be magical, but… it wasn't. Then one day, she pulled me out of my bed, made me put on my prettiest clothes, and we went out shopping. For bras.

"I never had a bra before. But here was this crazy woman, dragging me into some chi-chi store where everything was pink and lace and telling the saleswoman we were there to get me fitted, to get her daughter fitted. My boobs were… they weren't an A cup, but a lot of that was just me being big already, but there was my fucking magical. That should have been something I did with my own mother, but Martha was there, laughing with me as we tried to figure out what was going to fit me and what I'd have to buy later when they changed… yet again." Celeste's tears ran down her face, but she left them unchecked. "We had lunch, and I got pampered the hell out of at the lingerie store. And for the first time in my life, I felt like a fucking woman, Jake. A full goddamned woman, and I can't… I'm not ready to let the woman who gave me that leave this world, and I feel like it's my fault. I shouldn't have—"

"You said it yourself, Celeste. She's going to be okay." Jake hesitantly wiped at her face with a tissue, unsure of the etiquette on smearing already ruined makeup. "It wasn't your fault. You weren't… you did nothing wrong, and Dallas will be out here in a bit, then… and wait, why didn't you go inside? Why did you stay out here?"

"Because I panicked when they asked me if I was related to her. Like an idiot I said no. I should have told them I'm her daughter." Her hands were back on his, fingernails digging into his skin. "Seriously, I heard her scream, and everything went weird. I saw someone running, and for a second I thought it was Martha, but it was the guy who'd stabbed her. I didn't even think about him. I needed to find her, and she was against the building. I just grabbed her, threw her into my car, and headed here. I think I ran every red light. I'm going to have so many fucking tickets because of the traffic cams, but screw it. I don't care."

"But she was awake? You're not helping me, C." Jake patted her face again, then handed her the tissue. "And this isn't helping you. All I'm doing is making more of a mess."

"She was awake. Complaining and telling me she was going to be fine, but…." Celeste hiccupped again. "Who knows what was on that knife or what that guy stabbed. I wasn't going to wait for someone to show up in an ambulance an hour later. She's too important to me… to everyone. God, Dallas is going to hate my guts. I got his mother stabbed. This is worse than when I killed all the fish in his freshwater tank."

"Mister Moore?" A fresh-faced woman in purple scrubs called out from behind the admittance counter, then smiled when Jake stood. "Your boyfriend just wanted me to tell you both his mom's fine and they'll be out after the detective takes her statement."

"Oh, thank God," Celeste moaned. Then she fixed a steely glare on Jake. The stress eased off her face, and she pursed her mouth at him. Making another attempt at cleaning her face off dislodged a false eyelash, and she plucked it free, leaving her looking like she'd attached a dead caterpillar to the other side. "So she's going to be fine, and he had them ask for you."

"Do not look at me. I don't know why he didn't have her tell you—"

"Screw that, sugar." Celeste sat back, crossing her legs and tugging her soiled dress down over her knees. "Tell me exactly when you became Dallas's boyfriend. And leave nothing out."

"WHAT CAN you tell me about the man who attacked you, Mrs. Yates?"

The tall, rangy detective had introduced himself nearly the moment he'd come through the cordoned-off space they'd put his mother in, but Dallas couldn't recall his name. He wore a wedding ring and a gray suit tailored to fit his lanky form, had a pleasant face and a warm, professional smile, but it was hard getting past the fiery red of his tousled hair.

If he was asked later why he had vision issues, Dallas was going to swear it was the spectral burn the detective's hair left on his eyes.

"Are you all right, Mr. Yates?" The detective's question jerked Dallas's attention away from the silken red beacon screaming at him from the top of the man's head. "Shock over someone being hurt is common, so if you need some medical assistance or a breather, we can get that for you. This shouldn't take long."

With the adrenaline leeched out of his system, the evening he'd spent with Jake was beginning to make itself known, and it wasn't that terrible to feel Jake's teeth marks tingle along his ribs. His body throbbed and ached in places he hadn't thought existed, but after the screaming panic of knowing his mother was hurt finally died down, Dallas was… happy.

The detective probably thought he was a mindless idiot, sitting next to his mother's hospital bed, her side patched up in a thick layer of bandages, and he had a goofy, shit-eating grin plastered all over his face.

"Sorry, I'm just... it's been a long day, and yeah, Mom being hurt sort of ramped up my nerves." He made a silly face at his mother. "Stop trying to scare the living shit out of me, Mom, and answer the nice man's questions so we can get you home before Dad lands."

"You did not call your father over this," she gasped. "Oh God, he must be worried sick. I can't believe you called him."

Dallas smirked at her. "I didn't have to. Celeste did."

"Mrs. Yates?" The detective pushed into the conversation. "Any description would be helpful."

"My height? Maybe a little bit taller." His mother shifted in the bed, wincing when she smacked her elbow on its railing. "Older. He was.... He wasn't all that concerned about personal hygiene, Detective Camden."

Unlike Dallas, apparently his mother remembered names mumbled through the noise of a busy ER ward.

The detective began to make notes in a tiny book. "So he smelled? Or was dirty?"

"Smelled a bit off. I couldn't see about the dirty. It was dark, and the lights in the back of the building are woefully dim, but I understand the whole city's like that because of the observatory." She straightened, sitting up on the bed. "I think I startled him. It looked like he was trying to open the back door with something. I came around the corner, and I was shocked to see him there."

"When did he attack you?" Camden asked. "Immediately after you came upon him, or did he threaten you first?"

"Immediately," she clarified, then cocked her head. "I don't think he meant to stab me. Not like, oh I'm going to try to kill this person. More like I scared him and he lashed out. I'd say it was mostly my fault for startling him. I should have backed away and called out instead."

"Mom, stray cats get scared and lash out," Dallas grumbled at her. "If you're breaking into a building, then stab someone who approaches you, that's a whole 'nother story."

"I'd have to agree with your son, Mrs. Yates. You caught this man in a criminal act. He might have been motivated to kill you so you couldn't identify him." The detective's phone chirped from a pocket in his jacket, and he pulled it out, glancing at the number. "Excuse me, let me take this. It's my partner."

The detective slipped out from the drawn curtains, leaving Dallas and his mother alone. She stared at the swaying fabric for a moment, then turned to look at him. "You didn't have to come. I knew you and Jake—"

"Mom, what part of your right mind did you leave where you believe I'd not come to the hospital after getting told you'd been stabbed?" Dallas moved his chair closer to the bed, then lowered the railing between them in a loud clatter. "Shit, if I get yelled at for this, I'm blaming you."

"Sure, blame the old lady—"

"Woman, the day you're a lady, we'll talk," he teased, parroting a line he'd heard his father say ever since he was a baby. "And Jake understands. Shit, he drove me here because I was a fricking mess."

"He's a good boy," she said, stroking the hair away from his face. "I'm glad you found him. He'll do you a lot of good and vice versa. You're cute together. You are together, yes?"

"Yeah, as soon as I talk to him about it. Jake needs... clear lines drawn for him. He needs to know how I feel said to him out loud." Dallas sighed, rubbing at his eyes to relieve the tiring ache digging into them. "Mom, his family fucked him up something fierce. We just buried his father, and if I knew that man would feel it, I'd dig him back up and set him on fire for what he's done to Jake."

"He's prettier than you normally go for," his mother observed. "And more broken. The last time... with Kevin...."

"Kevin was.... God, he was a tragedy. I wish he'd found some peace." He snorted, looking away when his mother laid a hand on his shoulder. "I hate that I couldn't help him, Mom. I know I can't save a drowning man intent on drinking the sea, but Kevin, he had so much to live for and couldn't find his way out of his pain."

"Is that Jake?" Martha's prying was gentle, a subtle brush of words lined with sharp velvet. "Is he drowning like Kevin? Do I have to worry about you showing up on my front porch broken and hurting again? And how serious are you with him?"

"Totally different, Mom. So. Very. Different." Dallas picked at a nub on the sheets, following the line it made in the cotton threads. "I can't explain it. He makes me feel something inside of me. I think of Jake at the most random times in the day and something blooms in my chest. Hell, I can't even tell you what it feels like. It's just this brightness filling me, like Christmas, birthday cake, and fireworks all rolled into one, but softer, gentler. It's the feeling you're left with when you're done with a kiss and know you're about to get another one.

"And God, the things he sees in the world. How he sees the world. For every shitty thing that's been done to him, he's a good person. Flat-out decent and nice." Dallas grinned, remembering Jake's first encounter with Celeste. "And he looks to understand how someone feels or why they are the way they are. I think that's when I first felt something really serious. He asked for help. No judging, just a need to fill the holes in his comprehension of the world, but at the same time, he challenges me to take another look at what's around me because he sees beauty in places I'd write off. So yeah, Mom, it's serious. I want a lifetime of looking at the world through his wonderment. And I want to wake up every morning to the sound of him singing while he sets things on fire to recreate the bits of his soul he wants to share. I love him. That's what it feels like."

"Well, then." His mother sighed contentedly, resting back into the pillows. "Looks like you've gone and fallen in love, my darling son. And with an artist to boot. You've made me very, very happy, but one thing…."

"What's that, Mom?" Dallas dodged another swipe of her fingers when she went for his hair again. "Stop that. What's the one thing?"

"Can he fish?" She poked at his chest, unknowingly finding a tiny bruise left from Jake's teeth. "Because if he does, your dad's going to be over the moon. So, you'd best go tell him how you feel, because I've never seen you so happy, sweetie, and if Jake's the reason for it, you'd be a damned idiot for letting him go."

EIGHTEEN

DALLAS'S FATHER was definitely not what Jake'd been expecting.

But then he also never expected to be standing in Bombshells' main room on a Thursday afternoon listening to Brandon Yates and Evancho, who he was now supposed to call Peter, quietly discussing the merits of an Aglia Streamer versus a Timber Doodle with something else thrown into the mix Jake didn't quite catch, but it centered mostly on feathers and wiggling plastics.

Dallas's father now looked nothing like the man they'd picked up at the airport, his long face lined with worry and repressed grief, who'd hugged Dallas fiercely enough to make him squeak, then shot Jake a wan smile after a short introduction. Then he'd been a pale, stretched-out crane of a man with Dallas's black hair and a wry, teasing grin, which bloomed across his sharp-edged features when Dallas pointed out he not only buttoned his shirt wrong but wore mismatched socks. The grin was still there, but the anguish and fear were gone from his eyes.

The Yateses were physical people, unafraid of showing love. Dallas's father touched his son casually while they walked to the baggage carousel, their shoulders brushing, his hands moving when he spoke, and gentle skims across Dallas's back and arms when they stopped. It was a subtle dance of affection, a grounding so instinctive between them. The Yateses touched one another to form anchor points in the sculpture of their familial ties, welded spots meant to hold up a seemingly impossibly dynamic piece, a moving, living organic construct of flesh, thought, and love.

Watching Dallas and his father gave Jake an ache in his chest, and he'd looked away, needing the sensation to go down so he had room to breathe.

That exact same ache flared up again when Peter caught Jake up into a bone-crushing embrace when he'd come into the club, the shorter man's heavy Ukrainian accent clipping off the end of his mumbled welcome. And it grew when Peter took a moment before finally letting Jake go after calling him son.

"Doesn't look like anyone can get in through here, but I can swap out the plates if you want." Other than a few gouges on the plate, the door's lock looked intact, and Jake flipped the deadbolt a few times to check its action. "When is the security company coming in to check on the connections? A week is a long time for them to blow it off, and the sound system goes in tomorrow, yeah?"

"Yep, not something I want to leave unprotected. The rep and I had a conversation about it about an hour ago. So first thing in the morning, I'm to expect a man named Steve to come look at the whole system, so please, swap away." Dallas stood to his right, just beyond the threshold, and he rested his fingertips on Jake's shoulder before turning to look down the hall toward the entrance. His father and Evancho were still talking, having moved away from feathers to mirrored scales. "The rep said the preliminary system should have been triggered, but I don't think he got in far enough to trip it. Dad suggested a guard, but I don't know if that's worth it for what we have in here."

"Might be. The copper work I did on the bar is worth a lot, less if it's melted down, but that's what some people do. Can't tell you how many times I've been called to a place to restore something someone's cut off of an old statue." He grinned, then lowered his voice. "Mostly it's hands or parts, but I've made a few dicks in my life."

"Well you certainly make mine... happy." Dallas ghosted a kiss over Jake's mouth, leaving him with a blush dusting his cheeks. "That was horribly bad, and I meant every last fucking word of it. And I love my parents, I am glad my mother's okay, and it's awesome to see my dad, but they've been here more than a week, and I want both of them out of my house."

"They're... nice," Jake offered. "Your dad's got to stop cooking and sending stuff over with you. There's no more room in the fridge."

"Hey, be glad it's Dad. Mom's idea of comfort food is refried beans and Fritos casserole with enchilada sauce. In theory, delicious." He pressed a hand to his stomach and grimaced. "In reality? It'd make Mr. Creosote go on a diet."

"Who?" There was sometimes a misstep, a piece of something Jake didn't catch, and Dallas usually sighed heavily, then promised to show him the one true way. From the pathetic, pitying look on Dallas's face, this was definitely one of those times. "Okay, yeah, we'll add that to the list."

"Seriously, did none of you alien overlords do any research before you crash-landed your spaceship?"

"No, once we got to the video of you putting ketchup on your eggs, everyone threw up and said they'd wing it," he shot back.

"Oh, the game is afoot, Pinky." Dallas gasped mockingly. "The game is afoot."

"That one I know." This time, Jake was the one who stole the kiss, a tentative touch to Dallas's mouth. "But now you're mingling things."

It felt right at first, touching Dallas, kissing him in the hall's lengthening shadows. Then the sibilant rankling began, a quick-moving fouled river eating away at his foundation. There was shame and guilt in the sweetness, mixed in with an overwhelming need to hide, to cover what they were doing. Then Dallas's fingers circled his wrist, holding Jake in place. He hadn't realized he'd taken a step back, ducking into the doorway leading to the changing room, until Dallas's grip closed in tight.

"No hiding us, babe," Dallas whispered, cupping the back of Jake's neck, pulling him in closer. "I'm never going to hide you, never going to push you into the dark. I know it's hard. I get it. But never let go of me, never step away."

"It's… fuck, I'm tired of saying it's hard. I'm tired of choking on my own shit, Dallas." Jake exhaled, forcing out a bit of the simmering fear lingering inside of him. "It's stupid. I should be able to kiss you and not…."

There was a crossroads beneath his feet, paths leading off to journeys Jake couldn't begin to imagine, and many he wouldn't take alone. For all of the ghosts looming over him, the one wearing his mother's face haunted him the most. Her words echoed behind every kiss he shared with Dallas, her blood flavoring every moment of happiness he found at Dallas's side. He couldn't live through her hatred of who he was, any more than he could thrive in the shadow of his father's rejection.

Clearing his throat, Jake searched through the barbed tangle of emotions wrapped through him. Dallas drew closer, a faithful touchstone Jake could anchor himself to until he steadied. It didn't take him long, not as long as it had before, and the brittle glass-threads of pain piercing him whenever he thought of his mother slipped away into the darkness he'd always hidden in.

"Maman—my mother—I think I spent so much of my life trying not to be," he started shakily. Huffing out a breath, he tried to smile off the sour in his throat. "She always used to tell me to be quiet, be smaller. I used to hide in the cracks of everyone else's lives because we lived in fear of my father noticing anything wrong.

"And you know, Dal, it took me so long to realize it didn't matter what I'd done or how small I was, he'd always find something," he whispered, refusing to let the shadows rise up between them. "It was how he kept us under his control, how he could break us with one word. He owned me, owned her, and the moment it looked like one of us was going to slip loose of his leash, he'd choke the other one."

"The man was… I'm sorry you were born to him." Dallas kept his voice down, stepping into Jake until their hips brushed, his thumbs hooked into Jake's pockets. "There's a lot of shoulds, babe. I can't even begin to say them all, but the one thing I know for sure, someone should have loved you, and I wish to hell it'd been your parents."

"She loved me," Jake whispered. "She just loved him… more. More than herself, Dal. That's what made everything so fucking sick is that it wasn't that she didn't love me. She didn't love herself enough to walk away. He killed her, long before he murdered her. He'd killed everything good in my mother, strangling her… poisoning her… until the only thing living in her was him. I'm worried he killed a little bit of me."

"Babe, you're fine. I'm fine. We're fine." He cocked his head to one side, then wrinkled his nose. "Okay, we're not fine because my parents have moved into my place and all I want to do is live in yours, but I can't because… my parents are living in my damned apartment. You're going to survive what your father did to you. And we are going to have a great fucking time together."

A piqued Dallas was… cute. There was no other word Jake had to describe the slightly crazed tightness around his mouth or the frustrated growls he made while searching for words he could say without offending his mom and dad. Jake'd heard a lot of those growls, usually when Dallas opened the front door of his apartment to let Jake in.

"Your parents are great."

"They're getting a rental car and driving back home on Monday. Chant that with me. Monday," Dallas griped. "It'll be our mantra. Of course, they're going to turn around and come right back for the grand opening, but fuck it, we'll have at least three weeks before that."

"We could go on that date we never went on. Maybe tomorrow night?" As suggestions went, apparently Jake hit the jackpot, because Dallas's face lit up. "Really go somewhere. Not just... I promise, we'll go somewhere."

"Hey, last time... everything happening on that day was important." Another kiss, and this time Jake leaned into the light to take it. Dallas sighed contentedly. "Besides, it ended up perfect... right up until the moment someone tried to kill my mother. Okay, Evancho wants to go over some of the billing. I think he's undercharging me."

"What does he think?" Jake suppressed a grin. His boss was known to squeeze a penny into copper thread, and the mere whisper of him cutting Dallas a break on artisan pieces was laughable. "Or has he told you?"

"He tells me it's fine, but judging on what we originally contracted to do, the complicated stuff we added on doesn't add up. I called him a liar, and he threatened to send someone else over to do the work instead of you."

"Evancho... Peter... would never do that." A reedy tickle of pride cut through Jake, bolstered by the nearly ten-minute bragging rant he'd gone on when they'd introduced him to Dallas's father, Brandon. "He likes you too much."

"Yeah, I'm not the one he calls son. Keep my dad company, will you?" Dallas hooked his finger into one of Jake's belt loops, preventing him from moving. "Kiss me good luck. I'd ask you to tie a favor to my arm before I go in to do battle, but well, that'd be like asking you to choose between me and Evancho."

"I don't want to have sex with Evancho," Jake growled through Dallas's brief peck on his mouth. "What am I going to talk to your dad about? I'm crappy with parents."

"My mom loves you. Go. Find something." A brief melancholy ghosted across Dallas's handsome face. "Just make sure he's okay? For me? Sometimes he can get lost in the shuffle, and I think he could use a friend. Let me go duke it out with your boss-slash-uncle person, and then we can lock up for the night. And if we're very lucky, I can convince Celeste to keep my parents busy so we can go out."

"If you put it that way, she's going to want something," Jake pointed out. "That's how you ended up paying for her nose job, remember?"

"That was Austin's fault. Get her to tell you the whole story." He got in a pinch to Jake's ass, then let go of Jake's waistband. "Love you, Moore. Go talk to my dad about metal thingies and how awesome I am. He needs to know these things."

"Surprised you didn't need someone to widen the doors for that ego of yours," he muttered, watching Dallas stalk off.

The hallway wasn't as long as it seemed, but it stretched out in front of Jake, ending in a gladiator pit filled with alligators and piranha. If gators and steely-teethed death fish looked like a quiet, unassuming dark-haired middle-aged man with gentle eyes.

"Hello?" A woman stood silhouetted in the front door's frame, the sun casting her into a dark shape against a corona of milky yellow. "Yates?"

"Yes?" Brandon glanced at Jake, an unspoken worried question clearly stamped in the wrinkles between his eyebrows. "Can I help you?"

The woman stepped into the building, and Jake recognized her as the cop who'd taken his father's gun. Her expression flirted with a brief confusion. Then she spotted Jake standing next to Brandon and she became all cop. Nodding, she crossed the floor, her eyes flicking about the space, no doubt catching every detail.

"Moore, good to see you. Detective O'Byrne. Don't know if you remember me." Her handshake was a quick, firm grasp, and then she nodded at Brandon. "Sir."

"I remember you. Good to see you." Jake did a quick introduction. "Are you looking for Dallas?"

"Actually, probably both of you," she said softly. "It's about the man you found in the storeroom upstairs. We know who he is, and it's definitely something I want to talk to the two of you about."

BOMBSHELLS' OFFICE served mostly as a storeroom since his mom'd been stabbed. They'd needed someplace to stash all the sound system equipment and the first few shipments of glasses that appeared on the doorstep about a month too early. So as a meeting room, it left a lot to be desired, but O'Byrne didn't look like the kind of woman who cared about the niceties of matching chairs and plush carpets. She actually didn't seem to care about chairs at all, preferring to pace about the room as if readying for a duel come the next foggy dawn.

"Your dad and Evancho are going to grab some coffee. Said they'd bring some back for us later." Jake edged in around O'Byrne. "Are you sure you don't want some, ma'am?"

"Ma'am." She shot Dallas a look, one weighted with a touch of disbelief.

"He's not mocking you." He tried giving her a small smile, hoping to draw one out to lessen the tension in her shoulders, but the woman wasn't having any of it. Jake, however, dimpled, warming Dallas's belly. "He just has better manners. Jake, sit."

The chairs were uncomfortable, mismatched metal pieces pocked with bits of rust and padded in an awful green tweed Dallas hated with a passion. The pieces he'd gotten for the office were pushed up against one wall and draped with heavy sheets to protect their wood finishes while the workmen finished up the outer areas. Once the rest of his office furniture arrived and he got the office the way he wanted, he planned to hold a bonfire on the back parking lot and sacrifice the damned chairs to whatever god took bad life decisions as tribute. For the time being, he was going to have to be happy with shifting about on the unforgiving foam and hope he didn't put his hip out.

"You know if this is about my mom, my father should be here." The thought of O'Byrne or the other detective catching who'd stabbed his mother finally occurred to him, and Dallas frowned, wondering if he could get ahold of his mother and get her to Bombshells before O'Byrne had to leave.

"No, I actually came by to talk to you about the man you found upstairs. We know who he is." She finally sat, and by the sudden grimace she gave when her butt hit the seat, she'd found the worst chair in the bunch. "Okay, Yates, get new furniture."

"I've got new stuff. We're just doing more work in here." He leaned forward, impatient. "The guy from upstairs?"

The unknown man weighed on him, echoing around his thoughts at random bursts. After they'd found the man, through Jake's trials and the murmuring confessions he'd heard from his lover in the middle of the night when they'd fallen onto the bed and spoke of the everythings and nothings of the world, Dallas feared for the man they'd found. The thought of dying alone, forgotten, and buried under the debris of someone else's life grew into Dallas's greatest horror, especially after Jake spent hours sitting beside the toxic waste he had for a father, determined not to let the man slide off into death unremarked and unseen. He reached for Jake's hand, held on tight, and waited for O'Byrne to speak.

"Come to find out the people you bought this place from, lovely people, very caring, knew exactly who he was." The detective's sarcasm was thick and unyielding. "They knew since the moment I asked about him and didn't fess up until one of them had an epiphany."

"Then why didn't they say something?" Jake asked, echoing the surprised tumble of words caught in Dallas's mind. "Who could do that to a man? Just leave him without a name?"

"They didn't want to be involved, but one of them, the youngest daughter, had an attack of conscience. She came in yesterday morning, against the wishes of the rest of the family to ID him. Once she gave us a name, everything fell into place," O'Byrne answered. "He was Mike Dontano, and he used to work here back when the place was a bar, probably around thirty years ago."

"But they knew him? Mike, I mean." Dallas worked out the timeline in his head. The people he'd met over signed papers were in their midforties. "I mean, they couldn't have been old enough to drink back then. Or just barely."

"They didn't know him personally but were aware he was connected to their father, who owned this place before. Guy by the name of Charles Johnson. Ran cheap liquor through here, and according to some of the older police reports, provided a bit of company for lonely guys looking for a good time," she explained. "There's four kids total. Their old man— Charles—divorced their mom, and they were raised by their stepfather. Apparently their parents got divorced because he couldn't keep his pants on and really liked to drop them for pretty boys. His children didn't even know he was in the state, much less running a bar in the city."

"Back then, even over here, that would be a good way to get the shit kicked out of you," Dallas mused. "So what does this have to do with… Mike?"

"That upstairs room was used by men to hook up with other men. Cash-only business. According to what they found out from their aunt, Dontano used to be really popular, especially with Charles. One day they got into it, it went ugly, and Mike walked away. A couple of weeks later, Charles is missing and Mike is nowhere to be found. The uncle— Charles's brother, Barry—wanted to have Mike charged with murder, but he slipped away. After a few years, they had Charles declared dead, and Barry turned this place over for commercial use." She stood up, bending slightly to stretch her legs. "They found Charles a few months ago. His car went off a cliff and was lost in some heavy brush in a ravine. Some hikers found the car and, well, what was left of him. They buried him, shared some stories, and that's how Charles's kids heard about Dontano."

"Can't even imagine being accused of murder. Shit." Dallas glanced up to the ceiling, figuring out they were just under the upstairs room. A man'd died above where they sat, alone but cleared of murdering a lover. "Did he know everyone found out he was innocent? Did the family tell him?"

"Family wasn't going to go near Dontano, not after he was cleared for lack of evidence. Barry went after Dontano as he was coming out of a bathhouse and beat him almost to death. Dontano refused to press charges, and well, the cops back then weren't exactly sympathetic. But Barry practically crippled him. Dontano spent a lot of time in and out of hospitals after that and on a hell of a lot of painkillers." She pursed her mouth and nodded when Jake hissed in displeasure. "When we came around asking questions, the aunt recognized Dontano. That's when she told the kids about everything that happened. The family was afraid he'd succumbed to those old injuries, and since Barry was already dead, they figured it didn't matter."

"Didn't matter?" Dallas pressed. "Jesus, we found a dead man, one they recognized, and they just let him be… no one? Who the hell does that? Do we even know what he died from?"

"Coroner suspects he probably died of natural causes, but we don't know for sure yet. Might never know. From what we found out after asking around, he couldn't find work after the beating. I got hooked into one of his caseworkers before I came over to see you. He'd been told Charles's body was found, and according to the woman I spoke to, he was pretty broken up about it. Man didn't have a family, or if he did, they'd tossed him out because he was gay." This time O'Byrne let a bit of sorrow bleed into her expression. "I can't find anyone he's related to, and I know you wanted to do right by him. It doesn't sit right with me Charles's family didn't do jack to help us. They'll have a bit of time in front of a judge if I have anything to say about it, but before I kicked that off, I wanted to let you know about him. We can arrange to have him turned over to you for burial if you want."

"Yeah, he's ours. We'll take care of him." Dallas glanced over at Jake. His lover's knuckles were white, tense from the bone-breaking grip he had on Dallas's hand, but he was staring off into the distance, lost in some thought. Patting Jake's arm startled him out of where he'd gone, and he relaxed his grip, murmuring an apology. "We owe him that."

"Someone should have been there for him," Jake agreed. "It should be us. We found him. We should give him peace."

"It'll be a couple of weeks, but we'll make it happen." O'Byrne's phone chirped, and she dug it out to glance at the screen. "Okay. I'll have someone get ahold of you, but let me know when you're going to do the service. I'd like to be there."

They said a round of quick good-byes, walking her out to the front of the building. O'Byrne asked about the grate work Jake'd done, and he lost both of them to a discussion on art styles and architecture. Jake warmed as he spoke, his gestures opening wide, and a dimple appeared next to a flash of white teeth, and he ducked his head a bit when O'Byrne complimented him on something. He'd grown so much, healed so much since the day they'd gone up to the room above the bar, and Dallas basked in the light sparkling in Jake's soul.

"Shit, I love you." His words were unheard, falling into the golden-edged shadows of the main room, but something must have resonated through Jake because he looked up as O'Byrne chattered, meeting Dallas's gaze.

The smile Jake gave him touched every nerve in Dallas's body, filling his soul, and his heart sang in his chest, a stupid, silly reaction to a man he'd only met a few months before. O'Byrne said something, drawing Jake's attention back to her, but the swell of emotion in Dallas remained, lingering in the edges of his sadness over the man they'd found, a soul beaten down, then abandoned by the world around him.

"That's never going to be you, babe. I promise." Dallas leaned on the bar, drinking in the sight of his lover laughing with a stern-faced cop. "I've got to make things right between us too. I'm just going to need a little bit of time to do it."

NINETEEN

DALLAS KNEW it was officially fall when the coffee shop across the street put up a sign announcing the arrival of pumpkin spice everything. It didn't need to be in everything he ate and drank, but it seemed to contaminate even the starkest of coffee orders, a lingering presence of nutmeg and burnt cinnamon in every sip he took. His afternoon latte reeked of spices, probably simply from being around the syrup or possibly a figment of his overworked mind, but there it was, stinging the tip of his tongue and clogging his senses.

"Hell, for all I know, Jake loves these damned things and I'm going to be smelling pumpkin spice crap every fall for the rest of my...." His thoughts trailed off, flaking beneath the weight of possibilities. "Shit, don't get ahead of yourself, Yates. It could all go to shit before you know it."

There was a thread of grumpy in his mood. Dallas knew it. He could feel its bitter, sharp strop whetting the edge of his anxieties. The time he'd shared with Jake thinned out over the past couple of weeks as the renovation took up more of his time. Then the staffing and talent calls for Bombshells' grand opening sucked up the rest of it. Jake'd been busy working on the club's foyer piece, and it was maddening to know while they worked into the night, only four lanes of busy, sticky asphalt separated them.

It might as well have been an impassable sea of black tar for all he saw Jake.

Being fully immersed in the construction ground Dallas down, but everywhere he looked, there was a bit of Jake to keep him going. His lover'd left a discernible imprint on the nearly finished building, every piece of metalwork bent, polished, and laid into place crafted by his hands and artistry. The effect was subtle but rich, bouquets of stylized tulips and ivy welded into fields of waves and sunbursts. With the grates covering the exterior windows, Jake suggested a pebbled clear glass instead of the opaque yellow they'd removed from the frames.

The new windows sparkled, allowing the light to shine in or out without compromising security or privacy, and Dallas had to admit, they made the place look damned good.

Bombshells gleamed. In the two months since the attack on his mother, the building went from bare bones to a golden oasis of metal, wood, and stained glass. Salvaged wood panels and tables were cleaned up and stained a rich cherry, then installed around the interior walls. With hanging pendant lights and the oak bar with its elaborate back piece in place, stepping into the club was more of a journey back to clandestine dances under star-drenched skies.

Liquor bottles gleamed from their spots behind the bar, the shelves lined with amber and pale gold, with spots of neon green and electric blue. The stage was ready to go, a half circle low platform with a shallow backstage, its space more for dressing the set than hiding the performers, but a newly built short hall to the left led to the performers' waiting room, its vanity lights blocked out by a sea of blackout curtains and a sliding bamboo screen. There was only a bit of wiring left to do, and the sound system's remaining speakers sat in boxes near the wall the main floor shared with the office, but nearly everything was already in place.

Except for a large empty wide riser installed next to the reception pedestal, a squat cherrywood square lacquered to a high sheen and waiting for the piece Jake'd been working on since he'd finished the building's grates.

Or the formerly naked dais, because there was definitely something enormous and metallic throwing up a bright sheen under the afternoon sun.

It was a life-sized woman, or rather the shape of a woman flowing around a bronze-hued circle set at an angle off the pedestal's flat surface. And she took Dallas's breath away.

Her beaten matte-silver shape dominated the space, tucked into a corner they'd designed for the piece. He'd worried the brushed nickel sculpture would be lost against the rich wood and ornate lighting, but there was no missing her fluid form against the cherry-stained panels. Naked to the waist, she was caught in middance, her face turned up toward the lights and her stylized hair tumbling down to her shoulders. A long skirt hung low from her hips, its pattern mimicking the tulips and lotus flowers in the grates Jake restored, a delicate bronze fabric cascading down and between her graceful bent legs. Her arms wove into the copper circle she held up, a fringe of bronze spangles strung up across its front, and her features were a beatific hint across her heart-shaped face, her lips parted in a swell of ecstasy.

She was beautiful, stunning Dallas into silence, and it took him a moment before he recognized the tightness in his chest as his lungs screaming for air.

"Don't touch her yet," Jake cautioned as he came out of the back rooms. "I've got to get her settled in properly. Evancho and I got her locked in, but I've got to go underneath and tighten the rest of her anchors so she won't move." There was a skip of a heartbeat, and then he said in a very quiet voice, "I hope you like her."

"She's damned gorgeous." He caught himself whispering, grinning around the silly happiness pouring up out of his soul. "So different from what I've seen you do. It's... wow."

"Evancho helped a lot. We poured a few pieces, then hammered them into place. She's fitted around a frame so she can take a beating if she has to."

"No one's going near her," Dallas argued, shaking his head. "I'll kill anyone who even breathes on her wrong."

"Well, once the other part of the wraparound is put in front of her and the underlights are in place, it'll be hard to get in around her. I came in from behind by taking the panel off. Right now it's just leaning there, but I'll screw it back into place once I'm finished bolting her down."

Jake stood in the light, bathed in the golden stream coming through the pebbled-glass jalousies he'd helped choose. His rich brown hair was a bit of a mess around his sweetly handsome face. The tiny spare freckles on his nose were being kept company by a smear of black dust, a streak of dark over his right cheekbone. Dallas knew that face, loved that face, and wanted to see it age, softening a bit or deepening his dimples with a bit of weight. He longed to see Jake's hazel eyes sparkle from every sunrise-painted sky or grow heavy and hooded after sex on a warm summer night. He wanted to feel Jake's spark-scarred hands on his body, their roughness an erotic burr on the tender skin of his thighs and back.

169

He needed to taste Jake's kiss with his coffee, sweetening his mornings before the day stretched out long and hard in front of them.

"I'm glad you bought the club, Dal." Jake slung his arm around Dallas's hips. Pressing his mouth to Dallas's jaw, he murmured, "Love this place. It turned out great."

The club was a blend of their lives, their laughter, and their love. The walls held their conversations and tiny quibbles over types of panes for the windows and the horror they shared over finding a man's life ended in the loft's cold, dark silence. Dallas heard the echoes of their relationship whenever he walked through the doors and felt a bit of sadness knowing other voices would soon overwhelm the time they'd spent there, building the bridge between their hearts.

Jake warmed him. Warmed him in places Dallas hadn't even known were cold or neglected. The sadness in his amber-flecked eyes faded, leaving only a flicker or two of melancholy when the world got a little too tight around him. Jake fit into him, into his life, a quiet, sweet, and creative soul he hadn't been looking for but was damned glad he'd found.

"You're looking at me funny." Jake's eyebrow lifted, and he studied Dallas carefully. He was still sometimes unsure of how to read people, but he was getting better, and the trust in Jake's face when he looked at Dallas humbled him.

"I was thinking we should head home. Well, to your place." Dallas gave his lover a smile. "I've got a little surprise for you."

THE BRICK-WALLED studio was a brighter place now, and Dallas was the sun he'd brought into the dark to lighten it. There were odds and bits of their time together scattered about the long space: a framed poster and ticket stubs of a concert they'd gone to, the tiny pink plush elephant they'd won at a farmers' market raffle, a muted rainbow quilt Dallas bought at a swap meet and flung over their bed.

Their bed.

At some point in their time, Jake no longer thought of the space as his but theirs. Dallas was everywhere, in his life, in his home… in his heart. The penguin salt and pepper shakers were now joined by a blown-glass sugar bowl so ugly it should have had a cozy to protect innocent eyes, but the wonky, lopsided piece felt so right to Jake. Dallas bought it and gave it to him one morning after they'd woken up tangled around each other and wrapped up tight in love-scented sheets.

They'd had silly, tiny adventures and long walks through the canyons, sometimes stopping to watch the sunset over the ocean, then stumbling back to the car in the fading remains of the day. They had favorite taco trucks and run-down diners, knew where to find bacon-stuffed waffles in Millbrae, and racked up countless hours sitting on the sofa with their noses buried deep into a couple of books.

He'd sculpted to the sound of Dallas's voice cajoling construction crews to build a little bit faster and sometimes discovered a hot pastrami sandwich on his workbench after a few hours of welding and swearing at a piece that refused creation.

Dallas was everywhere, poured into the wrinkles of his soul, taking up space where only emptiness existed before, and when Jake inhaled, the feel of Dallas's love inside of him stretched, filling every bit of him.

Still, the old-fashioned picnic basket Dallas dragged in from the car gave Jake pause.

He'd come out of the shower to find the lights turned down, leaving only the glow from the strands of faerie lights strung up around the wrought-iron chandelier he'd gotten at a garage sale and hung over the kitchen table. The coffee table was clear of everything but a thin cloth, a blue linen spangled with gold stars and swirls of white glitter. A few feet away, the basket sat open in front of the couch with Dallas crouched over it, digging through its contents.

"Shit, I'd wanted to get this all out before you were done." Dallas straightened up, his hands full of something pink wrapped in clear plastic. After tossing the bag on the coffee table, Dallas sauntered across the floor to Jake, raking a long, sensual glance over the length of Jake's body. "Nice jeans, by the way."

The teasing was nice, unexpected in the beginning but comfortable now, soft words wrapped with a bit of spice. The jeans were almost indecent but worn down enough to hug his body without being stiff. Dallas playfully mocked them, saying they were held together with little more than a thread and a promise, but his pale blue eyes always glittered when Jake tugged them on.

"Stop. They're all I had that were clean." He tried to make sense out of the bundle on the table, but Dallas got in the way, blocking his view. "So what if they're old?"

"I'm not complaining. Best pair of jeans ever," Dallas murmured, sliding his index finger through one of the holes along Jake's right thigh. "Now how long do they need to stay on for you to say you got dressed after your shower?"

The music playing on the stereo was a mournful, soft sigh of love and regret, a song they'd first heard while parked in the Tesla, watching the sun sink down past the horizon at the Santa Monica Pier. Dallas's hands skimmed up over Jake's hips, drawing him in, and he stepped into the spaces left empty by Jake's body.

"Dance with me, Moore," Dallas whispered into Jake's ear.

"I don't dance, Yates," Jake reminded him, resting his hands on Dallas's hips.

"You can sway." His lover bit his lobe, rolling it between his teeth in a light, sharp caress. "You just hold on. I'll do all the dancing."

"Didn't you say that the first time we did this?" He let himself be pulled into the steps, his bare feet tapping Dallas's when they turned.

Dallas cocked his head, the faerie lights running blue through his hair. "Probably, but you also said you didn't dance back then too, and look at us now. We dance at least once every week."

They made a circuit around the room, saying nothing but letting the music speak for them. Dallas's hands grew bolder, encouraged by Jake's stuttering moan when his thigh brushed up against Jake's cock. Their rhythm was off, or at least not in time with the song being played, but it didn't matter. The song playing between them was older than the ballad slithering from the speakers mounted to the wall. Jake's cock liked the feel of Dallas on his body, straining to reach the other man through their jeans, ripe for a bit of heat from Dallas's wet mouth.

"God, I want you to make love to me, J," Dallas sighed through one of their kisses. "I brought cotton candy to feed you, and some chocolate, but honestly, I just want to feel you in me. Can't we just put the rest of the world on a shelf and forget about it all until tomorrow morning?"

"We can forget about it forever if you want, Dal." Jake laughed at Dallas's wicked smirk. "Going to be hard to pay the bills."

"That's what I love about you, babe. Always practical." Dallas leaned in, leaving Jake with a fierce kiss, one hard enough to knock him off his feet, then tugged him toward the bed. "Come on. I'll get you sugared up after I wring you dry."

The taste in his mouth was pure Dallas. His world was no longer spiced with gun oil and acrid powder. He didn't wake up to the steep of death on his tongue in the morning. Now Jake liked ending his night with laughter and joy chasing him into his dreams, and his day began with a pretty-faced, blue-eyed sunrise of a man and a kiss deep enough to wake his soul. Life was still taut at times, stretched nearly to the point of splitting when his thoughts sank back down into the mire he'd wallowed in for years, but Dallas was there now, his hand reaching out, ready to support Jake's weight.

Bright, glittery moments grew more frequent with each passing day as Jake stepped farther and farther away from the black metal death he'd shoved into his mouth and prayed to take him.

Their clothes hit the floor in dribbles and slithers, tiny mounds of fabric kicked aside by impatient feet and a brief yelp from Dallas when he struck the bed frame with his big toe. The mattress creaked when Jake flopped onto it, landing on his back, and then again when Dallas leaped on him, narrowly avoiding elbowing Jake in the nose with a twist to the side at the last second. The bed took the extra weight with a loud complaining groan, and for a moment, they both held their breaths, waiting for something to give, but other than the rocking of the mattress when Jake moved to give Dallas room, the bed grudgingly held up.

"Do you want crude or romantic?" Dallas asked, his chin poking a bruise into Jake's chest. "Because I've got two options I'd like to show you."

Dallas's cock was hard, his velvety head already sticky with a drop of arousal at its slit, and his nipples were pearled in tight, nearly begging Jake to taste them. He turned onto his side, bending his head to capture one with his lips, but Dallas popped a hand across Jake's mouth, stopping him. Jake looked up, mouth clamped shut with his lover's fingers, and concern rushed into him when he saw the worry in Dallas's face.

Freeing his mouth, he sat up a bit and asked, "What?"

"I just wanted you to know that I love you, Jake Moore." Dallas cupped his face. "I think I've always loved you. I just hadn't found you yet. And now that I have, I never want to let you go."

Jake pushed Dallas back onto the bed, spreading his lover out underneath him. He knew Dallas's body more intimately than he knew his own. From the tiny rasp of scar on Dallas's right knee from the time his older brother pushed him off a bike onto gravel to knowing the exact spot near Dallas's collarbone where he could bite and send shivers through Dallas's entire body, Jake knew the landscape stretched out on the bed. And he knew exactly where he wanted to start.

Dallas's lips were soft on his, a silken glide of skin, one wet with promise. He kept Dallas's mouth busy while he explored with a surer touch than the first time they'd made love. Now he knew where to stroke, how to take his time in stretching Dallas's body to take him in. They'd tussled and played, satisfying any desire they might find along the way, but tonight, something was different. Dallas needed Jake in a way he hadn't before, as if somehow the unveiling of the sculpture brought out a neediness in Dallas only Jake could satisfy.

"God, I love you." Dallas suckled at one of Jake's nipples, drawing a tingle up from his balls and pulling it up over his belly. "Can't get enough of you."

"Stay still for a bit," Jake grumbled, grinning when the lube bottle eluded him, dropping under one of the pillows and nearly out of reach. "Ah, here we go."

He loved sliding his fingers into Dallas. Loved the heat of the man on his skin, loved the slick feel of his inner flesh on the coarse catch of his fingertips, and most of all, loved the little gasp Dallas made when Jake breached him. They didn't take long. Within seconds of Jake sliding an oiled finger into his lover's core, Dallas was ready, writhing around Jake's touch. Pushing in deeper, Jake stroked at the tender spot he knew lay inside of his lover, and Dallas jerked around him.

"Swear to God, Jake...." Dallas gasped again. "Come on."

When he slathered lube on his own cock, Jake's balls lifted at the chill. Condoms weren't a necessity between them now, but he did half miss the slight protection one gave from the icy tingle of the straight-from-the-bottle lube Dallas liked.

"We're going to get the warming gel," Jake threatened, more than a little ruffled at Dallas's mocking laugh. "I mean it. This stuff's cold."

"This is warm, babe. And if it needs more warming up, I know where you can put it." Dallas reached down and groped at Jake's cock, heating the oil at Jake's tip with a twist of his palm. "That was my sexy porn proposition. I've also got awkward geek. I used to have smooth operator, but I don't think the upgrade worked."

"Stop, I'm going to miss," Jake growled, pressing Dallas into the mattress and sliding slowly into his heat. Dallas's smirk faded, his teeth biting into his lower lip, and a soft, contented sigh escaped him. "Ah, there you are. Hold on to me, Dal."

Dallas's hands dug into his shoulders, his grip bruising and tight. Sliding into Dallas took time. He was wider than Dallas could take easily, but if he went slowly, pushing past Dallas's ring, he could seat himself into his lover's warmth. And from the sounds coming from Dallas's mouth, slow and steady was the way to go.

There was something sublime about gliding into someone he loved, a near perfect join Jake never thought he'd ever have. Everything about Dallas fit in him, around him, and after a few long strokes, Jake knew he could die happy right at the moment, before he even reached his peak, simply because he had Dallas wrapped around him.

Then his body took over, a primal, visceral need riding him, scooping him up into a river of senseless pleasure, and Jake let himself fall. His hips moved, seemingly of their own accord, pushing his cock deep into Dallas, yanking huffs of breaths and murmured encouragements out of the man he plunged into. He rode Dallas, rocking into his body and lifting him up with each slap of his hips. His balls were low, swaying in time to his thrusts, and every once in a while, he moved in such a minute way the bed linens tickled the soft sac.

His cock ached to release, throbbing and sensitive, growing more so with every stroke. Dallas tightened on him, clenching and pulling while exhorting Jake to go faster and deeper, a bead of sweat running down the crease of his chest to trickle down his ribs, dampening Jake's hand where it lay on the bed.

The storm hit Dallas first, and he jerked, throwing Jake off rhythm. Another tight clench followed, and Jake quickened his pace, maddened by the rush of desire flooding him. His release struck him, slapping his face with its rush of blood, and his cock felt like it was screaming, begging Jake to find the single moment where his body finally gave in to the mounting tenderness across his shaft.

Reaching down between them, Jake closed his hand over Dallas's shaft and began to stroke him, working Dallas's cock in time with every roll of his hips. He knew Dallas was close. His fingernails digging out scallops of Jake's skin was enough of a hint, but it took the sharp ache of teeth sinking into his shoulder to drive Jake over the edge.

He let the fire consume him and took Dallas along for the ride.

Jake rode the sensations of his soul being broken apart and stitched back together. He loved this... loved Dallas... longed for an eternity where he didn't have to wake up alone. He was so tired of being by himself, exhausted to the point of his heart breaking under the weight of the world, but then Dallas came along, and suddenly his life exploded with color and light.

He let go, and his body arched, shoving his cock deep into Dallas's heat while sliding one arm under his lover's body to hold him close. The rush of his seed, hot and quick, flooded the recesses of Dallas's body, and Dallas gasped, finally losing control, and his orgasm gushed over Jake's clenched hand, stinging both of them with the powerful punch of emotion in the wake of their release.

Dallas quivered. Strung out and worn from their joining, he held on to Jake, refusing to let go until his body could no longer hold Jake's softening dick to him. Rolling to the side, he made room for Jake to collapse beside him, and they lay on the bed, panting and sweaty, with the musky scent of their sex lingering in the air.

Jake pulled Dallas in, their limbs as sweat-damp and limp as their hair, but the contact felt good. He wasn't quite ready to be without his lover on him, around him, and when a soft, slightly chilled breeze ghosted over them, Jake felt he could lay there forever and a day, so long as Dallas was at his side.

"Jake baby?" Dallas said, panting slightly. "Can I ask you something?"

"Sure." He smiled when Dallas's elbow, once again, nearly took out his nose when the other man struggled to sit up. "Hey, watch that arm of yours. You're going to kill me with it." Jake waited until Dallas was situated, sitting up on the mattress. "What's up?"

"I was going to do this whole seduction thing tonight, sugar, but one look at you in those jeans, under that light, and I knew nothing between us needed embellishments or ribbons. I'm as romantic as the next guy—even without you being the next guy—but sometimes, I need more than romance. I need... a promise. I need to know you'll be here forever. Right here. In my bed. Okay, in your bed, but no matter what or where, I want to reach out and know you'll always be there to take my hand.

"So, Jake Moore...." Dallas took a small breath and whispered words Jake thought he'd never hear from another man's mouth. "I love you very much, and I want you to know, I will treasure you to your last dying day, if you just promise to marry me."

EPILOGUE

A DRAGONFLY skimmed over the pond, its jewel-toned body carried by a set of whirring golden wings, its flight a singing crescendo whispering toward the shore. The wind carried a slight sweet hint from the bank of orange-yellow flowers peppering the gentle hillock behind Jake. A few hundred feet away, Dallas stood shoulder to shoulder with his brother and father, their fishing rods casting long shadows over the rippling water. Their soft chatter was indistinct, nearly as inaudible as the insect swooping past them, and their low, rumbling laughter rolled and dipped, a comfortable quiet murmur adding to the peaceful morning.

The sun smeared a wet lemon hue over the lush powder blue and fading dove gray remaining from the final hour of dusk, a stretch of popcorn clouds blushing pink and gold reflected in the pond's slightly choppy surface. A fish jumped, its scales a sharp silvery rainbow in the light as it twisted to snap at a passing bug, then fell back into the pond with a less than delicate splash.

They'd dragged him out before it was time to milk the cows or the llamas, Jake wasn't sure which. It didn't much matter, so long as they got off the ranch proper before the lolling began, or so Austin muttered when he started up the truck and told Jake to get in. It'd been an ugly scramble from the house as the Yates men tumbled off the porch, half-dressed and juggling tumblers full of coffee and a shopping bag filled with biscuits they'd stolen from the cooling racks on the kitchen counter. A second after Dallas slammed the truck's door behind him, shoving past Jake in the front seat to get to the back of the cab, Victoria stomped out onto the verandah, her mockingly furious shout lost under the roar of the truck's engine as Austin raced past the house with a smug smile plastered on his face.

The others left Jake the one phone they'd brought with them after they got their fishing rods ready and spread out a thick cover of unzipped sleeping bags to sit on. He'd fallen asleep. He was almost certain of it, because the sun was barely a hint on the horizon, and when he had a slow blink, it'd risen enough to burn the mist off of the pond's surface.

Dallas caught Jake's eye, winking at him from his perch on the edge of the water. Austin elbowed the middle of his brother's back, nearly pushing him in, and a few flails of Dallas's arms were followed by a soft admonishment from their gentle father to not scare the fish. Slapping at Austin's shoulder, Dallas shoved his pole into a length of PVC set into the bank, then slogged up the shallow rise to where Jake sat.

"Hello, husband." Dallas leaned over to kiss Jake and nearly lost his balance. Plopping down on the sleeping bag, he chuckled, then said, "Let's try that again."

Dallas tasted of coffee and nectar, a bit of honeyed green pulled up from a purplish bloom they'd showed Jake how to suckle for a bit of sweet. The kiss lingered, warming Jake more than the rising sun and firing up an arousal he didn't think he had left in him after they'd spent most of the night in a languid exploration of each other's bodies. He ached in places, muscles stretched to a comfortable throb, and his back smarted where Dallas bit him a little too fiercely when he'd found his release in Jake's body.

"You're making me hard," Jake muttered through the kiss. "Bad enough I'm worried your parents are going to hear us—"

"No one can hear us in the bungalow," Dallas promised, then grimaced. "Okay, maybe the chickens, but who the hell are they going to tell? Move over a bit and hand me the bag."

Moving brought another reminder of how they'd spent the night, and the heat across Jake's cheeks promised he'd flushed pink under his freckles. The bag was heavy, its ends tied tightly into a bow, and Dallas grabbed it out of Jake's hand when he began to undo its loops.

"Nope. No peeking." Dallas tsked. "Give me a second. Look over there at that tree."

It was a very uninteresting tree, but Jake obeyed, keeping his attention pinned to the fluff of green waving in the slight breeze. Whatever Dallas was doing seemed to take forever, but he didn't mind. They had a lifetime ahead of them, and the slight weight of the gold ring Dallas put on his finger a few days ago promised an eternity beyond even that.

It'd been nice to glance back at the pews of the small church they'd found for their ceremony and see the joy in their loved ones' faces. He'd walked down the aisle with Dallas, their hands joined together in anticipation for the lives they were merging that morning, and Evancho winked at Jake when they passed. It'd taken them seven months to get to that day, weeks filled with Bombshells' opening, a stray, disgruntled gray cat named Belimai, and Jake's first exhibit at an art gallery in West Hollywood.

Still, the tree wasn't growing any more interesting, and if anything, Dallas's curses were getting hotter and hotter with every crinkle of the plastic bag.

"Finally. Shit," Dallas grumbled. "Last time I ask Tick to help me wrap something up. Okay. Turn around."

Jake twisted back around and found himself enveloped in the scent of fresh, hot bread when the wind shifted to blow over his face. Dallas sat with his hands out, a small wicker basket of pale, aromatic slices peeking out of one of the blue napkins they'd used for their wedding dinner. A short open thermos of nearly white butter sat on the sleeping bags, a blunt knife resting on another blue square next to it. The silvery insulated bag next to Dallas's knee steamed in the crisp air, the discarded sleeve holding down the plastic bag he'd fought to get open. Dallas's habitual quirky smile was gone, replaced by a shy, sweet hint of a grin, and he carefully placed the basket down in front of Jake, scooting up across the slick fabric and bunching a bit of it up around the butter.

"I made the dough yesterday when you guys went to the antique market with my mom. Okay, well, my dad helped, but still, I did everything but put it in the sleeve this morning. I had to sneak out early to get it in the oven, and then Tick watched over it while it baked. It's why we had breakfast in the bungalow this morning. Because I wanted it to be a surprise." Dallas took a breath as if to steady himself, then exhaled. "I… wanted your mom to be here for our wedding, to see how happy you are right now, and well, I got to thinking about how I could somehow bring her here… for you, and this is what I came up with.

"See, babe, I love you. I am so forever gone for you I can't believe I get to wake up next to you every morning, so in a way, this bread is from me too." Dallas cupped Jake's face, rubbing his thumb over Jake's cheek. "Oh, honey, don't cry. I didn't mean to make you—"

"I'm never going to apologize for my tears, Dal. Not anymore," Jake whispered into Dallas's palm.

Sliding the bread aside, he pulled his husband into his arms and held on tight, reveling in the beat of Dallas's heart against his chest. The thump was steady, pounding a pulse through him, and Jake pressed his face into the crook of his husband's neck, filling his senses with the man he'd come to love.

"You peeled away the dark I lived in, and if I cry, it's because I'm happy... so damned happy, Dal." He felt a bit of wet on his shoulder, and Dallas's arms tightened, locking around him. "I wouldn't be here if you hadn't come into my life. I know that. I wouldn't be the me I am now without you. Even if you say you only walked beside me as I made my way out of the dark, I wouldn't have found my way without you. I am never ever going to let a day go by without you knowing that, because you never let me spend a minute without knowing you love me. You are my starlight, my moon, and my bread, Dallas. And I can't wait to spend my life loving you."

RHYS FORD is an award-winning author with several long-running LGBT+ mystery, thriller, paranormal, and urban fantasy series and was a 2016 LAMBDA finalist with her novel, Murder and Mayhem. She is published by Dreamspinner Press and DSP Publications.

She's also quite skeptical about bios without a dash of something personal, and really, who doesn't mention their cats, dog, and cars in a bio? She shares the house with Yoshi, a grumpy tuxedo cat, and Tam, a diabetic black pygmy panther, as well as a ginger cairn terrorist named Gus. Rhys is also enslaved to the upkeep a 1979 Pontiac Firebird and enjoys murdering make-believe people.

Rhys can be found at the following locations:
Blog: www.rhysford.com
Facebook: www.facebook.com/rhys.ford.author
Twitter: @Rhys_Ford

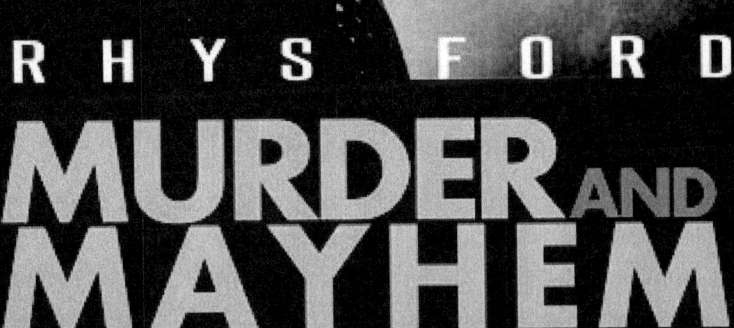

RHYS FORD

MURDER AND MAYHEM

Dead women tell no tales.

Former cat burglar Rook Stevens stole many a priceless thing in the past, but he's never been accused of taking a life—until now. It was one thing to find a former associate inside Potter's Field, his pop culture memorabilia shop, but quite another to stumble across her dead body.

Detective Dante Montoya thought he'd never see Rook Stevens again—not after his former partner falsified evidence to entrap the jewelry thief and Stevens walked off scot-free. So when he tackled a fleeing murder suspect, Dante was shocked to discover the blood-covered man was none other than the thief he'd fought to put in prison and who still makes his blood sing.

Rook is determined to shake loose the murder charge against him, even if it means putting distance between him and the rugged Cuban-Mexican detective who brought him down. If one dead con artist wasn't bad enough, others soon follow, and as the bodies pile up around Rook's feet, he's forced to reach out to the last man he'd expect to believe in his innocence—and the only man who's ever gotten under Rook's skin.

www.dreamspinnerpress.com

A HALF MOON BAY MYSTERY

FISH STICK FRIDAYS

RHYS FORD

Half Moon Bay: Book One

Deacon Reid was born bad to the bone with no intention of changing. A lifetime of law-bending and living on the edge suits him just fine—until his baby sister dies and he finds himself raising her little girl.

Staring down a family history of bad decisions and reaped consequences, Deacon cashes in everything he owns, purchases an auto shop in Half Moon Bay, and takes his niece, Zig, far away from the drug dens and murderous streets they grew up on. Zig deserves a better life than what he had, and Deacon is determined to give it to her.

Lang Harris is stunned when Zig, a little girl in combat boots and a purple tutu, blows into his bookstore, and then he's left speechless when her uncle, Deacon Reid, walks in hot on her heels. Lang always played it safe, but Deacon tempts him to step over the line… just a little bit.

More than a little bit. And Lang is willing to be tempted.

Unfortunately, Zig isn't the only bit of chaos dropped into Half Moon Bay. Violence and death strike, leaving Deacon scrambling to fight off a killer before he loses not only Zig but Lang too.

www.dreamspinnerpress.com

A HALF MOON BAY MYSTERY

HANGING
THE STARS

RHYS FORD

Half Moon Bay: Book Two

Angel Daniels grew up hard, one step ahead of the law and always looking over his shoulder. A grifter's son, he'd learned every con and trick in the book but ached for a normal life. Once out on his own, Angel returns to Half Moon Bay where he once found… and then lost… love.

Now, Angel's life is a frantic mess of schedules and chaos. Between running his bakery and raising his troubled eleven-year-old half brother, Roman, Angel has a hectic but happy life. Then West Harris returns to Half Moon Bay and threatens to break Angel all over again by taking away the only home he and Rome ever had.

When they were young, Angel taught West how to love and laugh, but when Angel moved on, West locked his heart up and threw away the key. Older and hardened, West returns to Half Moon Bay and finds himself face-to-face with the man he'd lost. Now West is torn between killing Angel or holding him tight.

But rekindling their passionate relationship is jeopardized as someone wants one or both of them dead, and as the terrifying danger mounts, neither man knows if the menace will bring them together or forever tear them apart.

www.dreamspinnerpress.com

CPSIA information can be obtained
at www.ICGtesting.com
Printed in the USA
LVOW01s1615240317
528386LV00007B/746/P

9 781635 334982